Serial Blogger

by Bob Scott

Copyright 2013 Bob Scott

CreateSpace Edition (2015)

First published as a Kindle ebook 2013

This book is licensed for your personal enjoyment only. This book may not be re-sold or given away to other people. If you would like to share this book with another person, please purchase an additional copy for each recipient. If you are reading this book and did not purchase it, or it was not purchased for your use only, then please return to a retailer and purchase your own copy. Thank you for respecting the hard work of this author.

This one is for my kids, Nathan, Joshua and Sarah, who all think I am a little crazy.

Thankfully, I'm not as crazy as the killer in this book.

Prologue

The killer carefully closed the door to his apartment, inwardly seething after another frustrating day. In the sanctuary of his mind he had spent the day screaming, but to all outwards appearances he had been cool, calm and collected, slightly aloof but quietly and efficiently performing his duties at work. Now, safe in his haven, some of the anger could be released a little.

Some, but not much. Outside was the veneer of civilization, coating both himself and the world at large. Inside was his true thoughts, and the Beast, raging with red claws and bloody fangs against the bars of the cage known to the Beast as Culture, Refinement and Law. Civilization disliked people raging the way the pair wanted to, but something had to give.

Trying to keep within civilized bounds, trying to 'maintain appearances' as his mother would have said, the killer kept his rage non-vocal and as quiet as possible. His cries of rage were silent, and his fists pounding into the furniture were almost so.

But today this would not be enough to satisfy the Beast prowling within him. The killer had suspected as much for some time now, and he struggled to keep it in check. Within his mind he shouted, "Soon, tonight, it will happen!"

The Beast subsided, growling and chafing at the delay. The killer quickly changed into his running clothes and grabbed a book-bag he had prepared in advance. Closing the main door to the apartment building, he looked up and down the street, yet not really caring if he was seen. To the casual onlooker he would just be going for one of his usual five mile runs, and in a way that was true. But he was also going hunting, because there was a Beast with a large appetite to feed.

Chapter 1

Detective Danny Watson scowled at his cup of coffee, wondering once again what it was about police stations that turned any brew into the rancid, stomach churning mixture in front of him. This cup should have been perfect, brewed at home from his favorite blend, but once the flask was exposed to the air in the building, something happened to it. Or maybe, he thought, it was something that affected his taste-buds? Regardless, he had more important mysteries to solve.

Watson focused his attention on his partner, Todd King, and said, "So in short, we have nothing?"

King shrugged his massive shoulders, "We have lots. We have a body in the morgue, brutally murdered. We have the autopsy results, so we know what killed our vic, when he died, where he died. The murder scene has been swept, and any physical evidence processed, as well as any that was found on the body. There are a few suspicious fibers that could be from the killers clothes, black ones from a hoodie, maybe.

"This could tie in with the one witness account we have, saying a person, probably male, of average height, who knocked on the vics door at round 10pm, but was not seen leaving. Ten is also the estimated time of death, so this mysterious visitor is our prime suspect."

Watson nodded, "Yes, I know we have all that. But we have no idea **who** this person was, why they wanted to kill the victim, or why they felt the need to attack him with an ax in such a bloody fashion. It has been two weeks, with media appeals, door to door inquiries and finger tip searches of the area.

"And all we have to show for it is a hacked up body, a few fibers and a description that could fit half the city. I know we'll keep looking, hoping for a lucky break, but I've been told to cut back the man-hours on the Harding case. Other things are always coming in, and this will sadly have to go on the back-burner."

Watson closed the Harding file in front of him and put it to one side. He picked up another and passed it to King, "Here is the next problem."

#

But the killer was still out there. Despite the Beast's appetite for carnage being currently sated, the killer was always looking out for further feeding opportunities. He knew that he was playing a dangerous game against the police, and to some extent the public, but his compulsion drove him mercilessly.

To minimize risks to himself, he carefully planned where he could, and tried to hold off if the situation was not perfect. He was lucky his job allowed him to roam so freely round the city, often at odd times of the day and night. This allowed chances for covert reconnaissance of potential targets even while he worked. Coupled with his observations when he was off the clock, this gave him opportunities to track the routines of his selected victims, and those people round them.

Ever since he had heard of it, the killer became a great believer in the Seven P's Principle – Proper Planning and Preparation Prevents P*ss Poor Performance. Thus when the Beast awoke and demanded to be fed, all he needed to do was remain conscious of his planning, and could select a kill that was satisfying for them both, as well as being low risk.

For the killer, the hunt was always on, and the Beast would need feeding soon.

#

BLOG: What is the drive behind a serial killer's compulsion to kill? Unlike a 'normal' murderer, if that word could be used to describe a non-normal action, there are none of the usual short term triggers, such as striking out in anger, or envy. These triggers can be there, but that is not the sole reason for their murderous escapades.

Underlying it all is the *need* to perform certain acts to fulfill this overwhelming desire, which typically results in deaths. This need is in some ways analogous to "Football Fever", or the urge to satisfy a physical craving, be it for chocolate, alcohol or hard drugs. These analogies are an imperfect description for this void that *must* be filled, no matter what.

Usually this is characterized by rituals or patterns, what can be referred to as the killers 'signature' (although these are not all that could comprise the signature). This can be choice of victim, method of killing, location or positioning of the body, or leaving something at, or removing something from, the scene of the crime. It is not uncommon for trophies of some kind to be taken by the killer, physical items that aid the killer in reliving the event. This reliving of the crime helps to 'feed' their craving, and lessens their desire to kill again.

But here is a side-bar thought for you: How powerless would investigators be if there was no obvious signature or trophy? How would they even know a serial killer was stalking through their jurisdiction?

Chapter 2

The killer left work at the end of his shift, looking forward to a couple of days off. As always he had swiftly changed out of his hated work outfit, glad to be rid of it. Walking through the parking lot he bantered lightly with his colleagues as they got into their cars, although the conversation was a little stilted on his part. Inwardly, he loathed them all, and had trouble connecting with them even on a polite social level. He even waved a greeting to a police patrol car as it went by him, trying to look like a normal friendly person.

As he lived so close to work, the killer did not always bother driving there, just as he had done today. He just walked through the downtown area on his way back to his apartment. While he walked the dozen blocks he mentally planned his movements for the next day or so, intending to do the rounds of various charity and resale stores.

Having contaminated and disposed of a set of clothes at his last messy killing, he needed to pick up some replacements. It was a chore having to buy clothes so often, but a necessary one. There was also somewhat of a risk, even if it was slight, that some clever clerk could put things together just from his buying patterns. As a result, the killer tried to spread his purchases out over many stores, and mix it in with other items. Some of these extras he actually needed and kept, with the worthless remainder being trashed or donated to another thrift store.

If that was the price he had to pay for security, then he would gladly pay it. He knew it was pointless to even think about toning down the level of blood splatter in his killings. After all, he thought with a contented smile on his face, brutal overkill was **so** satisfying!

#

Frank Sinclair stood at one of his usual street corners, displaying his cardboard sign with its pitiful message to drivers stopped at the lights. Some drivers took pity on the poorly dressed man, especially after reading the 'Homeless and Helpless Veteran' message, although the majority just tried to pretend he did not exist.

Frank kept an eye out for any police. While most would leave him in peace if he did not make any trouble, certain overzealous officers had a tendency to move him on, or even arrest him for vagrancy. This unfriendly attitude, coupled with his traumatic experiences in the army, gave him a serious distrust of people in uniforms. Frank's paranoia made him wary of any uniforms, so even the sight of a city or utility worker would cause him to scurry away. When this happened, if the situation allowed him to do so safely, he would precede his exit with a flurry of rude gestures and verbal abuse.

Today was a quiet day for uniformed intruders, and the few dollars he had collected from passersby would put some food in his belly, as well as supply some alcohol to wash away the bad memories. He rarely drank to excess, but there were times that he needed to numb the world and forget his troubles.

#

All good detectives cultivated sources, or Confidential Informants as many were called, and the detectives in Claytown City were no exception.

Detective Watson regularly made the rounds of his grasses, snitches and other talkative souls, trying to see each one at least once a week. While it was obvious that none of them were angels, to have access to any useful information these people would have to at least tread in the gray areas of the law.

This morning Watson was having coffee with what used to be an attractive, curvy brunette before prostitution and crack took their toll. Now her body, usually dressed in highly provocative but now in shapeless sweats, was past its prime, and the hair was now a lurid purple. The girl, known to friends and customers as Sweet-lips, but christened Karin Temple, sat across the table from Watson.

She was clutching her morning coffee like it was a lifeline, which, Watson reflected, it most likely was. He deliberately chose these planned meetings at times Sweet-lips was 'off-duty' and only just woken up, which was before she would usually get her hits. It left her edgy, but any information coming from her was less likely to be tainted by the drugs.

Today they were doing little more than touching base, as she had nothing particularly useful to tell him. He also did not think she could safely pry for any information about the various cases he was working on either. Nevertheless, the meeting at the diner was important, as in the past some nuggets of gold had been found in the river of mostly useless data that flowed from the mouth of the crack addict. Today the mining was fruitless, but next time, who knows?

#

BLOG: What makes a serial killer? While a minority

are formed purely by their environment and childhood experiences (similar to how some sex offenders are 'created'), most are just individuals that have a very different outlook on life. The majority really are born, rather than made (as the best prize-fighters are), and if their upbringing does not help smooth out their unusual urges, they grow up with their fantasies intact and that compelling urge to fulfill them.

There are thoughts lodged in the head of these people that an average, rational, 'normal' person would reject as obscene and perverted, but to a serial killer they are their own normal thoughts. They simply do not think in quite the same way as the majority of the population, and even if they know what they are doing is wrong (by the current morals and standards of civilization), they have little choice but to act the way their brains are wired.

Chapter 3

The killer walked slowly up the steps to the church, his mind filled with turmoil and doubt. He knew that he needed the catharsis of speaking to someone openly, something that his secret past-times denied him. His withdrawn, antisocial nature also made it difficult for him to even think about opening up to someone, but he needed to talk to somebody before he exploded.

But he also knew the risks of speaking to the wrong person, as even supposedly 'private' conversations with a mental health professional would be turned over to the police if they felt he was a risk to others – and how could they not come to that conclusion? He assumed the same would be true of lawyers. Maybe, he mused, the sanctity of the confessional would be more robust?

He could feel the Beast sneering at him from behind the bars of its cage, and wondered what he would say. The Beast bared its fangs as it smiled, saying, "What next? Are you going to found Serial Killers Anonymous? 'Hi, my name is Mike, and I am a Homicidal Maniac.'" It grabbed the burning bars of the cage as it tipped its head back and roared with laughter.

Shaking his head, and pushing back the sympathetic maniacal grin from his own face, the killer climbed the last two steps and stopped outside the imposing wooden double doors. He checked that his hood concealed his face from prying eyes and reached out to open the right hand door.

Inside, the Gothic architecture was subtly illuminated, and the rows of ornately carved pews stretching down the large room stood empty. The killer had timed his visit for the very end of the

Saturday night confessions, hoping that there would be no witnesses, nor anyone who would want to strike up a friendly conversation. The killer was pleased to see that this church had kept to the tradition and still boasted the screened booths of a confessional, rather than adopting the more modern face-to-face unburdening in an open room. The killer saw the feet of the priest, who was waiting for any last minute customers, and noticed that the adjoining booth was empty. After one last look round the impressive but thankfully deserted room, the killer stepped into the confessional. After placing his bag on the floor, he closed the curtain and sat down.

#

Father Williams heard the curtain close and the faint whoosh of air from the cushion, and waited a few moments for the person to get settled. He then made the sign of the cross and began the usual litany, "In the name of the Father, and of the Son..."

He waited for the other person to say something, and as the seconds dragged into minutes Father Williams cleared his throat and prepared to say something. It seemed the sounds of his throat-clearing prompted a response, and he heard the penitent say, "Father, I am not sure how this should go, or what to say exactly. I am not even a Catholic, not really religious at all, but I was hoping to talk to someone in confidence."

Father Williams replied, "You do not have to be Catholic to talk to me, and you can be assured of my total confidentiality. The Church has very strict rules about that."

There was a thoughtful silence from the other booth, and then the penitent spoke again,

"Therapists claim confidentiality, but in cases where you are a threat to yourself of others they can break that confidence."

With a worried frown creasing his forehead, Father Williams answered, "Please, my son, I assure you that only myself and God will hear your words. Even if I knew who you were, a priest cannot acknowledge the sin or the sinner outside of the confessional. The Seal of Silence is sacred and can never be broken, no matter what is said." He paused for a moment to let that sink in, and continued, "From the little you have said it is clear that something is troubling you, and you need someone to talk to. My ears and my heart are ready to listen to whatever you have to say."

More silence followed, as the stranger appeared to be going through an internal struggle. Father Williams waited patiently, knowing that at this point nothing he could say would help the stranger open up, and prayed that he would overcome his silent struggle.

In the dark confines of his booth, the killer was indeed struggling with himself. Part of him wanted to flee, and the Beast continued his mocking, but finally the need to talk overrode everything else. He swallowed nervously, "I guess I should say 'Bless me, Father, for I have sinned.'"

Father Williams breathed out, not even realizing he had been holding it until now. "What is the nature of your sin?" he asked.

The killer smiled, "I guess that should be plural. Ignoring the minor everyday stuff, I stalk people, spy on them, and plan how to hurt them and worse."

"Do you covet something about their lifestyle, or that they have? Do you know the reason for all this?"

"They have nothing that I want, not really. Well, apart from one thing, but if I tell you what it is I am afraid it will shock you."

Father Williams had his head bowed as he listened to this, and slowly raised it as he asked again, "My son, what is the reason? I have heard many things in my time, and can guess some others, but all I am here for is to listen, not to judge. I find you should not hate the sinner, but rather the sin."

"Part of me hates the sin too, is repelled by it, but another, darker part is drawn to it." The killer took a deep breath, "It started with something that happened at work a year or so ago, which woke something in me. I guess I had been hiding it, burying it, for years. But the smell of blood woke the Beast, and now he craves to be fed."

"I do not fully understand. When you say the Beast, do you mean Satan?"

The killer shrugged, even though the priest could not see him, "Maybe he is part of it, maybe not. I just put a name to my urges. Now it is like a a real thing in my head, a monster in its burning cage, that screams for what it wants, fights to get free, and when it does it is feeding time."

Father Williams said, "I can see that you are a deeply troubled individual. I pray to God that I can help you somehow. You said about blood, and feeding. What exactly do you mean by that? You act like a vampire?"

The killer laughed, "No, no, I don't drink blood. The Beast just craves the sight and smell of it, in large quantities, and I provide it for him. So I kill people, in a very spectacular and bloody way."

There was a hiss of indrawn breath from the priest, who asked, "Are you serious? I mean no disrespect in that, but have you really killed someone?"

In the darkness the killer smiled, "It seems I have shocked you, or at least surprised you. Yes, I am deadly serious, if you'll excuse the pun. The first was something that happened at work, more an accident than anything, and I won't bore you with the details. The most recent was a little home invasion about three weeks ago. I am sure you recall the media attention surrounding that? There were a couple others in between, but they don't really count. They were just practice, theory testing really, and weren't that gruesome compared to my last piece of work."

Father Williams shook his head, "My son, all lives are precious and sacred, they should not be taken for any reason. I know you will not want to hear this, but if you are being truthful about what you have done, you need help, professional help. If you turn yourself in to the police that would help, especially if you show true remorse. They would be sure to get you the help you need."

The killer laughed again, "The idea of a prison cell does not appeal to me. I have seen them and they are nothing to write home about. And the police? Do you have any idea how many police officers I see every day? If they were worth anything, shouldn't they have recognized me as a killer? I can also see a small flaw in your remorse suggestion. I don't feel remorse for what I have done. There is elation and anticipation for me in the stalking of prey, and even more in the kill. There is also a feeling of peace as the Beast rests and relaxes after feeding."

Father Williams said, "I do not know what to suggest right now, but rest assured I will pray for your soul, and pray that the Lord will bring you the peace and guidance you need."

The killer sighed and shook his head, "I had hoped that talking to you would help me keep the Beast in check somehow, but I don't think that will happen."

Father Williams quickly said, "We can keep talking until things feel better for you, or you can come back another time to talk, whenever you wanted. I can give you my card, it has my cell phone number. You could call me any time you wanted, day or night. You can be assured of my desire to help you, and of my absolute discretion."

There were a few moments of silence from the killer, as various thoughts ran and fought through his mind. The Beast was now screaming and tearing at the bars of his cage, which was not helping the killer to concentrate. Composing himself, the killer said, "Maybe it was a mistake me coming here. I don't think it's worth us talking more today. At least I will leave here confident that you will only be discussing this with your God."

As he was saying this, the killer reached his right hand into the bag at his feet, pulling out an item. Father Williams heard the metallic clicks as the hammers on the illegally obtained sawn-off shotgun were cocked, then the screen beside him erupted in a maelstrom of noise, light, shrapnel and pain. Pellets from the weapon, along with splinters of wood, tore into his left arm, tearing it to shreds, as others went into his body and the side of his head. Fighting back waves of pain he looked down at what remained of his arm, and then back up as the confessional curtain opened.

In front of him stood the killer, calmly replacing the spent shotgun cartridges. Father Williams struggled to speak, asking, "Why? I would not have told anyone. We could have talked, we could have found you peace."

Just before the blinding flash that tore his life away, he heard the killer reply, "The Beast is tired of talk."

#

After getting past the uniformed officer on guard duty at the entrance, Detective Watson drove his unmarked sedan into the half empty parking lot beside the church. Normally at this time of day it would be packed with the worshipers cars, but the presence of a dozen black and whites and other police vehicles scattered along the road and round the lot alerted people that there would be no service today.

The linebacker sized bulk of Todd King was waiting for him, the notebook he held looking tiny in his huge hand. Danny walked up to him and asked, "What have we got? Details were thin when I checked in with the station."

Detective King grimaced, "We didn't want to put the details out on the air. It is a nasty one. The press will be all over this soon enough, but the longer we can keep them in the dark the better."

As the two walked towards the church and past the uniform at the door, King continued, "The initial call was anonymous, someone said they found the door open, went in to make sure everything was okay, and found Father Williams dead in the confessional. From the estimated time of death and the time of the call, it's unlikely the caller was the perp, maybe someone who saw the door and tried their luck.

"Whoever it was got the shock of their life. We're pretty sure the barf running down the steps out there came from the caller."

Danny interrupted, "Is it that bad then?"

Todd nodded, "Yeah. I could describe it for you, but it would be better for you to just see the body. It fair turned my stomach, I can tell you."

By this time they were inside the church, walking past the pews towards the confessional. Their route was down the center of the church, as they could see the crime scene techs waiting to do their work at the side of the church, and the pool of congealed blood on the floor.

Danny got to where he could look inside the confessional, whose curtains were pulled back on both booths. He was quiet for a moment, taking in the scene, then quietly said, "Holy flying fudge monkeys. That is nasty. Not like our usual line of bodies."

Todd nodded at they continued to look at the devastated body. The left arm was badly mangled, peppered with small holes and splinters, with strands of flesh dangling loosely. The left side and front of the black clad chest had similar wounds, albeit in smaller quantities.

But what drew the attention of the detectives was the head of the corpse, or rather what was left of it. The once white clerical collar was now stained red, and the slack lower jaw of the late preacher hung obscenely in front of it. Above that there was nothing but a crater of flesh and bone, with the rest of the head spread in small bloody pieces across the back wall of the confessional.

Danny shook his head, as though to try and erase the gruesome image from his memory, and said, "I don't think we'll be using dental records for an ID."

Todd replied, "No. I'm not sure we'll even find all the teeth. Luckily most of his fingertips look fine."

Danny went closer, carefully avoiding the blood spill. He leaned in to get a good look at the hands, being sure not to touch anything. He saw the fingers of the left hand were unharmed, while parts of the right hand were riddled with small wounds. "Looks like shotgun wounds to me, maybe a twelve gauge. The first shot probably came from inside the other booth, then the perp must have reloaded, stepped to the front, and finished him off. No signs that the body has been disturbed, so robbery doesn't look like a motive. You have to wonder what Father Williams had done to make someone do this."

"By all accounts he was a good man in the community, well respected, with plenty of supporters and no known enemies."

Danny shrugged, "I would say it's obvious he had at least one enemy. We'll just have to dig until we find out who it is."

#

The killer was hanging round near the crime scene, confident that his job, with its distinctive uniform, would allow him to be there without raising any suspicions. He had watched the two detectives enter the church and could picture the scene inside.

Although they did not realize it yet, Detectives Watson and King had been at the scenes of all his kills in Claytown. The other couple of kills, the practice runs, had been made in different jurisdictions, so that the body count round his home would not rise too quickly.

Now he was ready to operate in Claytown full time, regardless of the body count. If and when the detectives realized they had a serial killer on their hands, things would get much more challenging and interesting.

#

The detectives left the church, allowing the crime scene boys and girls to search for clues. Watson lit a rare cigarette that he had cadged from one of the uniformed officers. His normally hardened nerves were feeling a little shaky after seeing the contents of the victims skull spread round like that. Exhaling the smoke, he said, "That was not pretty. And it's the second ugly scene we've been at in less than a month. I don't know what's up with people. This city is usually pretty quiet, so I hope this is the last for a while."

Todd replied, "I'm with you on that. It would be nice to clear the cases we have and get back to doing more mundane things, like robberies. Oh, by the way, nothing new on the Harding case either."

Danny flicked away the half smoked cigarette, "We will just have to wait for breaks on that one. It's only been three weeks, and someone is bound to say something that we will hear. But first we'll work to clear this one as fast as possible. Remember what the Chief says will solve all cases?"

"Ah yes, the old-school Chief. Shoe leather. Luckily it doesn't have to be all ours." Todd raised his voice, calling to a knot of uniforms hanging round by their cars, "Quigley, can you come over here?"

One of the patrolmen hurried over, "Yes, Sir?"

"This part of town is your normal patrol area, correct?"

The taciturn young patrol officer merely nodded, so Detective King continued, "I would like you to start canvassing the area, and we'll assign more people to help you. We need to find out if anyone saw or heard anything. Check businesses to see if we can borrow their security footage, it might show something interesting.

"Also, find out more details on Father Williams' life. See what people really think of him, and if anyone had a reason to kill him. Obviously Detective Watson and myself will be coordinating this inquiry, but you are a known quantity among the locals, so they may open up to you a little easier. Any questions?"

"No, Sir," replied Quigley.

"Then get to it."

#

BLOG: Proverbs 26:11; As a dog returns to its vomit, so a fool returns to his folly.

A surprising amount of serial killers not only return to the scenes of their crimes (which helps them relive the moment in all its glory), but also to inveigle themselves into the police investigations. Their aim is rarely to provide false information, as this could backfire dangerously, rather it is for the thrill of seeing even a little way inside the investigation. Even being a vague eyewitness adds to the excitement for the serial killer, and their sense of control over the police.

This sense of control has an important ego factor, and is also a key reason that killers leave taunting notes at the scene of the crime, or mail them to the media or police. A serial killer can view themselves as the Ring Master, taking lives at will, and leading the police on a merry dance.

It has been said that in some cases police contact is a cry for help, a plea and an aid to being caught. While there may be some truth in this, even if it is just at a subconscious level, it would depend on the psychology of the killer. For the other cases, it would be a fake plea, another way to control the police.

Ultimately, control is a driving force for the killer to kill.

Chapter 4

Frank Sinclair stood at the low steps outside the diner, counting his change. Despite the damp, chilly weather it had been a pretty good day for him, and he hoped the diner staff would tolerate his presence. He went up the steps and through the double doors, relishing the warmth and the dry.

He looked round at the dozen tables and was surprised to see someone he recognized. Being with another person reduced the chance of being ejected, so he stepped quickly over to the table. While he knew his experiences had left him a little unhinged, he still retained his manners. Removing his rather stained hat, he bowed slightly and asked, "Is this seat taken?"

Looking her slightly frazzled morning self, Sweet-lips glanced up from her mug of coffee, "Oh, hi, Frank. No, sit down if you want."

Carefully taking his seat, Frank replied, "I thank you."

Just then the waitress bustled up, looking down her nose at Frank. Turning to Sweet-lips, she asked "Is this man bothering you?"

Not even looking up from the coffee mug she was practically hugging, Sweet-lips replied, "Nah, he's alright. He's an old friend."

Sniffing disapproval, the waitress asked Frank, "What can I get you?"

"A cup of coffee would be great, and some scrambled eggs and toast, if you please?" replied Frank, laying a handful of bills on the table to show he could pay for his order.

The waitress nodded, sniffed again, and fetched Frank his coffee. Frank thanked her politely, and proceeded to load the coffee with sugar. He took a sip of the steaming brew and sighed with pleasure, "Ah, I needed that."

Sweet-lips looked up from her own cup and asked, "I haven't seen you round for a couple of days. What brings you in here?"

Frank smiled, "I had a surprisingly good day today, found some generous people, so I thought I would treat myself for a change."

She smiled coyly, "I don't usually work in the mornings, but if you have the money...." she trailed off suggestively.

Frank laughed, "Even if you gave me a veterans discount, I still would not be able to afford your services. I shall just have to settle for the fond memories of us in our youth, before the drugs messed you up."

As the waitress returned with the rest of Frank's order, Sweet-lips replied, "And I shall remember you before your ass got shot full of shrapnel."

Frank smiled his thanks to the waitress, lifted a forkful of eggs to his mouth and said, "Touche. Did you hear about Father Williams? I saw a bunch of police round Saint Paul's yesterday, and the word I heard is someone capped him."

Sweet-lips' eyes flew open at that, "Father Williams? Why? That kind man wouldn't hurt a fly."

Frank shrugged, and with his mouth full of thickly buttered toast replied, "No idea. Maybe he was fooling round. A lot of priests do."

Sweet-lips shook her head, "Some priests, maybe, but not Father Williams. He really *believed*, you know? He would even try and help some of us girls to get off the streets, and he never took up any offers, if you know what I mean?"

"I do. So that is how you get freebies, is it? Become a priest? I wonder where I can apply?" joked Frank.

Sweet-lips frowned, "I wouldn't joke round at a time like this. Father Williams was a good man, and didn't deserve to be murdered." She thought for a few moments, then asked, "Can you do me a favor? Keep your ears to the ground, and if you hear anything about him, let me know? There could be something in it for you," she added, fluttering her eyelashes.

Frank bowed awkwardly because of the table, and replied, "For you, my lady, anything you ask, if it is in my power, I will hasten to obey."

#

The killer was sitting on the opposite side of the room from Frank and Sweet-lips, enjoying a thoroughly unhealthy but totally satisfying fried breakfast. Dressed as he was, in comfy denims and sweater, totally unlike his work clothes, he was confident no-one would recognize him. The baseball cap pulled low over his face added to his feeling of anonymity, allowing him to relax a little, and to scope the room unobtrusively.

As always, he was on the lookout for people to feed to the Beast, to keep its hunger satisfied. It was only a day since he had blown that priest away, so the Beast was sated for now, but the killer knew its hunger would start to grow soon.

#

Detective Watson watched Todd King lower his ample self into the chair at his desk, and asked, "Did they get you a reinforced chair to take all that weight?"

Todd sat back and replied, "Sure, just after they widened the doors so you could get your fat head through. Now, if you have quite finished flirting with me, I got the latest info from Quigley."

Danny said, "Okay, so what do we have to add to the forensics we already have?"

Laying the files in front of Danny, Todd spoke from memory, "Our one and only potential witness saw a figure of average height and build, race unknown, wearing dark clothes, heading away from the scene at about the right time. They may have heard the shots too, but they admit it could have been a car back-firing instead.

"The possible suspect was seen heading north on Carter, towards Twelfth. We checked with businesses along that route and have some corroboration from their security cameras, but all we got were some very low resolution images, and the suspect wasn't in the frame for long. I've got the techs working on them, see if we can improve the quality.

"Apparently the person didn't make it to Twelfth, because they don't show up on the traffic cameras on the lights, or any business recording up there. Unless he got into a car, or changed his appearance drastically. If the car idea is a bust, and there was little traffic at that time so we should be able to verify the drivers quickly, then they must have gone into the residential areas round Tenth Street, and who knows where they could have ended up from there. Quigley has people canvassing the area, and we'll just have to see what comes up."

Danny nodded, "Okay, not bad. A possible perp, a vague description, and we haven't stopped looking. So what about the skeletons in Father Williams closet?"

King shrugged, "None that we could find. Strange as it seems, so far we would have to say he was an honest, devout preacher who would step to one side before he trod on an ant. No record, no rumors, did not even drink apart from Communion. Of course, we're still digging deeper, but he looks straight right now."

"Which blows any easy motives," mused Watson, "so back to the drawing board for that one. Anything new from the crime scene?"

"Nope, and added to the Medical Examiners report we have nothing that a blind man couldn't have told us. Victim was initially wounded by a shotgun blast fired through the partition, inflicting serious but probably non-fatal injuries to the left arm and side. Fragments of wood inside the wounds have been matched to the partition screen.

"A few minutes later, a second shot from a range of roughly four feet in front of the victim caused defensive-type wounds to the right hand and arm, non-fatal wounds to the chest, and, ahem, significant trauma to the face and head."

Danny snorted, "That is quite an understatement. Carry on."

"Okay, weapon used was most likely a sawn-off double barreled shotgun, make and model unknown.

No shells left at the scene, but the pellets suggest twelve gauge. All blood appears to be the victims. There are literally hundreds of prints to match, and that is just from the Confessional and nearby pews. The whole church contains thousands. It is going to take a while to process all the prints and other minor physical evidence. That's about it on the crime scene."

Danny had been reading the reports while Todd had been speaking, lodging both sets of data, summary and detailed, into his head. He probed the information, trying to see if anything jumped out. The only thing he could think of was the lack of motive. It made him think that maybe it was a nutcase with an ax to grind, and Father Williams was a target of opportunity. "Right, something else we could look into. This lack of motive could make it anybody, or a specific crazy. Any psychiatric patients moved into the area recently, and as it was a black Catholic priest killed, we'll have to follow up on the hate crime angle. If anything else comes up, let me know. I guess I better brief the boss and hope to avoid the press conference."

#

Danny did avoid speaking at the press conference, as the Chief wanted the media exposure for himself. However, he did have to stand behind the Chief, trying to look like he was ready to leap into action and arrest the murderer at any moment.

The killer was holed up in a downtown bar when the details of the press conference were televised. He raised his glass in mock salute to Detective Watson, knowing how hard it would be for him to find a killer with so little to go on.

The killer was not worried about being caught for

any of his crimes, and drank his beer thoughtfully, replaying his most recent kill in his mind, as well as the ones from before. He was happy to see the Beast was lounging in its cage, also enjoying the memories of carnage and blood.

#

BLOG: Another common thing among serial killers is a tendency to have a cooling-off period between kills. In this time they are able to sustain their fantasies or cravings by replaying the kills in their minds, usually with the help of trophies taken from each victim.

This cooling-off period varies according to the killer, and can be as long as over a year or as short as a few days. A serial killer who needs to kill with a day or less between victims is likely to be heading towards a psychotic break. This is where the killer loses touch with reality and tends to go on a self-destructive rampage.

If a serial killer is able to control their impulses, with a sufficiently long cooling-off period, as long as they are not caught by evidence left at their crime scenes, there is no reason why their killing sprees would not extend over several decades.

Of course, circumstances may nudge a killer out of his usual killing cycle, such as a perfect victim that is too good to pass up, or a murder that is out of character but fueled by self-preservation. Once that event has passed a serial killer will usually revert back to their normal patterns.

Chapter 5

Karen Watson smiled at something she was reading on the computer screen, then turned to make some notes on the pad laying beside the mouse. Her father, Detective Watson, looked up from the files he had brought home. He said, with mock gruffness, "I thought you were using that machine to do your homework, not to have fun."

Karen replied, "Who says college work can't be fun? It can be so funny some of the things people put in their blogs. There is a woman here who says how much, in inches and ounces, her cat poops. Crazy, huh?"

"Er, that is a little strange. And how does that relate to the education my money is paying for?"

Karen sighed, "I am *pretty* sure we have gone over this before. Several times."

Danny smiled, "Humor an old man, my memory isn't what it used to be."

Karen pouted, "Well, the blog searches relate to both my major and minor, given that blogging is a form of social media, albeit a particular subset of the types, which ties in nicely with my Media course. Oh, and you can learn a lot about someone by analyzing the words and phrases they use, leading you back to the psychology of the individual writing them, and that seems to fit well with me minoring in Psychology. Even better, some of these blogs are on specific subjects, which include psychology. I ran across one recently where the writer was listing the characteristics of serial killers."

Danny raised his eyebrows, "Really? Why would

someone write about that?"

"Lots of reasons, like personal interest in the subject, could be studying the psychology of killers, writing a book and trying ideas out in a public forum. Now, do you think I can get back to my homework? I know you're used to asking lots of questions, but you are paying for my education, and I want you to get value for money."

She had to duck as Danny flicked a paper clip towards her, following it with, "You're not too old to be spanked, you know."

Karen poked her tongue out. "What was the number for Child Services again?", she asked lightheartedly, then turned back to the screen.

Shaking his head, Danny turned back to his files, but smiled inside because he could see how smart his baby girl was.

#

It was a bright new day, but after spending half the night pouring over case files, Danny Watson was not feeling it this morning. So desperate was he for some kind of life, he had raided the coffee pot in the squad room and was now trying to choke down the toxic brew. Heading to his desk he was intercepted by a slightly more alert Detective King, and Danny asked, "Anything new?"

As they seated themselves, Todd replied, "Lots of paperwork, not much in the way of answers. The door to door didn't give a better ID on the suspect, but he was seen heading towards the Presidential Park. We're expanding the canvassing along the suspected route.

"It seems the one who discovered the body and

threw up his dinner on the steps headed downtown, but no ID on him either. He disappeared from the cameras, but that's not surprising as that section of downtown is a warren.

"Nothing new on the crime scene, nothing new on Father Williams. Nothing useful from the phone lines. The press conference has just given us the usual cranks calling in, and I don't think Father Williams was killed by aliens or the CIA."

Danny smiled, "I might believe the CIA, but it doesn't feel like them. You said the suspect was heading towards the Presidential Park?"

Todd nodded, "Yeah, but there aren't many cameras round there we could look at. Very few businesses, and you don't need traffic cameras in a pedestrian park."

Watson looked up and saw Officer Quigley across the room, apparently dropping off some paperwork, "Hey, Quigley, can you come over here?" he called out.

Jacob Quigley walked over and said, "Sir?"

"Don't a lot of people run through the Presidential Park, at all hours of the day and night?" asked Detective Watson.

"Yessir, that is correct."

"We'll need to canvass the joggers, just in case one of them was out at an unusual time and saw our man."

Officer Quigley nodded, "I already have that in hand. As I myself run through the Park, the thought of witnesses there was fresh in my mind. Was there anything else, sir?"

Danny gave him a long appraising look, and replied, "Thanks, but that's all for now." As Quigley walked away Danny said, "Efficient guy, isn't he?"

Todd nodded, "He's former military, so I guess that's where it comes from."

"Strange that someone so apparently keen and efficient is still only a lowly patrol officer. If his work helps crack this Williams case I might recommend him for a transfer to the detective bureau," mused Danny.

Todd smiled, "He is efficient, almost like a machine sometimes, but I heard his mouth can be a little too efficient at times too, if you get my meaning."

"Ah, like that, eh. Maybe that would change if he was out of uniform." As he said this, his desk phone rang, the direct line. Picking it up, he said, "Detective Watson."

He heard a familiar female voice saying, "You wanted me to drop a dime if I heard something too good to wait. Meet me for coffee?"

"Sure, I'll get there as soon as I can."

He heard the click as the caller hung up, and said to Todd, "If the boss asks, I'm out talking to a Confidential Informant. It's very unusual to get a call from this one, so it should be something juicy. No idea if it relates to this case, but fingers crossed, eh?" He grabbed his keys and jacket and hurried to his car.

#

There was very limited parking at the diner, so Watson parked his unmarked sedan in the parking lot of the discount grocery store next to it. There would be no problems with him leaving the car there, as there was often a police officer in the store keeping an eye on things.

Danny hopped over the concrete divider and quickly went up the steps and through the door. A quick glance showed him it was almost deserted in the diner, with the waitress on duty listlessly spreading the grime round the unoccupied tables. He signaled her and asked for a coffee, then headed towards Sweet-lips' table.

Sweet-lips was sitting there staring blankly into the distance, alternately playing with her almost empty cup and the menu. She dragged herself back to the real world when she realized Danny had sat down opposite her, and said, "That was quick. I was expecting a long wait here."

Danny thanked the waitress as she placed his coffee on the table, and replied, "You don't usually call like that, so I figured I should beat feet and find out what was up."

"A customer was indulging in a little pillow talk, and he mentioned a friend of his overheard someone talking about finding poor Father Williams. I knew you would want to hear about that urgently, hence the call."

Danny sat up straight when he heard this, "Was there a name? Please tell me there was a name."

Sweet-lips smiled, "Not a full name, just a street name. Ever heard of Tricky Mickey? I think he's a small time thief, but I've no clue where he's crashing right now."

Danny shook his head, "It's a new one on me, but I'll check the robbery files and see what we find." He stood up, discretely pushing a $50 bill across the table, "Myself and Mr Grant thank you."

As he hurried away, leaving his untouched coffee on the table, Sweet-lips casually pocketed the money and reached for his cup. She did not want to see the caffeine wasted, and sat back to enjoy the free brew.

#

Back in his car, Danny opened his cellphone, dialing a number from memory, "Todd, it's Danny. Do you know of anyone called Tricky Mickey?"

Back in the office, Todd's forehead furrowed in thought, "It rings a bell, hold on, let me check a couple of things." Danny could hear some furious typing coming over the phone, then a quiet, "Yes." Seconds later Todd was back, saying, "Michael Davenport. Aged 32. Rap sheet is full of petty theft, all minor stuff. Currently out on parole. We have his current address here. What's this about?"

Danny said, "We have his partially digested dinner in our evidence locker. Give me the address and meet me near there with a couple of uniforms. As fast as you can. I want a word with Mr Davenport."

#

Danny parked his car in a packed school parking lot. Just up the street he could see the apartment complex where 'Tricky Mickey' was supposed to live. It was an elderly, two story concrete structure, with two short wings extending from the end of the central portion. Between the wings was a rather unkempt patch of grass pretending to be some kind of delightful garden for the residents. Hundreds of similar buildings graced cities all across the States, built when cheap and basic housing was much in demand by the ever increasing population. He snorted at that thought – you couldn't get more basic than these places, but he also knew for many people apartments like this were the only homes they could get. Now of course, the rents were not so affordable, and the area was not as nice as it had been, but when you have no choices you have to live where you can.

Danny pulled out a compact pair of binoculars and scanned the numbers of the apartments he could see. Tucked into one corner he found apartment A13, on the ground floor near a crumbling flight of concrete steps leading up to the 'B' level apartments. He did not need to go into the apartment to know the layout, having been in enough similar places to have the format ingrained in his memory.

As he finished his scan, Danny noticed Todd's sedan, followed by a black and white, pull into the lot. He got out to meet them and said, "There will be no back door to the apartment, so he can't do a runner, so you patrol guys will only be here for crowd control if everything goes smoothly. Afterward, let us know if anyone seemed especially jumpy about us being in the neighborhood. It's always nice to find those with guilty consciences. For now, you can just cruise into the parking lot and wait for the screams. Todd, you and me can take a little walk to our friends door."

While the two patrolmen hurried back to their cruiser, Danny and Todd left the school parking lot and strolled down the street. The cruiser went past them as they wound their way through the decrepit, half dead bushes that went across the open side of the grassed area. This grass was negotiated next, with attention being paid to what was underfoot.

With all needles, animal faeces and other hazards successfully avoided, Danny Watson stepped onto the sidewalk that fronted the apartment doors, with Todd King following close behind. They took up positions on either side of the door marked A13. Danny looked at Todd to see if he was ready, and after receiving the affirmative nod, hammered loudly on the door.

Both of them heard movement from inside the apartment, as well as a quiet expletive. Danny hammered again, so loudly that people from other apartments looked out to see what was causing the noise. When they saw the two uniformed and two plain clothed officers, most of the inquisitive heads disappeared.

Todd called out, "Come on, Mickey. We know you're in there. We just want a little talk, you know, a little business."

The expletives from inside were louder now, and after listening carefully Danny shouted back, "I think it's physically impossible for us to do that to ourselves, but if you don't come and open this door right now it's highly possible that I will knock it down." So saying, he started pounding on the door even harder, making it rattle heavily round the locks and hinges.

After a moment a voice could be heard shouting plaintively, "Alright, alright, I'm coming. Jeeze, the amount of noise you're making you could be the pigs." They could hear the door being unlocked, and it was opened by a short, skinny guy in dirty shorts and t-shirt.

Danny still had his hand raised, ready to knock

again, and as he lowered it to reach into his pocket for his ID, he smiled and said, "Mickey Davenport, I presume? We are the pigs from Claytown PD. We would *love* to ask you some questions. Is there a problem with that?"

In a way it was amusing seeing the already pale white guy go even whiter as the color drained from his face. While Tricky Mickey stood paralyzed by his paranoid fear, the two detectives stepped past him and into the apartment.

With a swift, professional glance, their eyes swept the room. This was obviously the only sweeping it had seen recently, given the number of cigarette butts, empty beer bottles and miscellaneous food items scattered everywhere. The walls were covered in pin-ups and movie or video game posters, and because of the large sheet blocking the window the only illumination came from the kitchen light.

That kitchen was even more of a health hazard than the living room, with grease and grime on every surface, and a sink stacked high with dirty dishes.

With heavy sarcasm in his voice, Danny said, "Nice place you have here. We weren't planning on staying long, so we won't take a seat. If there was a safe place to sit, anyway. Of course, if you are not helpful, some of us will stay a while, maybe try and find things for you. Take a look in the closets and under the bed, see if there are any hidden treasures."

Mickey could not meet the eyes of the detectives, and said, "I haven't done nothing. I gotta keep my nose clean. You ask my PO."

Todd smiled, "Yeah, but I'm sure there are a few

things your Parole Officer doesn't know about, things that could be an issue if he found out. Now, if you help us a little, we could forget about telling your PO anything."

Mickey would never be any good at poker, as his face showed even more nervousness. But he still tried to talk his way out, "You've got no reason to be round here. I ain't done anything."

Danny said, "We know of at least one thing you've done, and we just want to talk about it, a friendly chat to get the info we need. You'll have nothing to worry about if you help us. Now, what happened on Saturday night?"

Mickey shrugged, "Not a lot. I just had a few drinks and listened to some tunes."

"Hmm, that's not what we heard. Do you want to try again, or should we start looking round at things. I wonder what's behind that door?"

Mickey swallowed nervously, shuffling his feet, "I'm not lying. I didn't do anything against the law."

Todd grinned, "We are supposed to take the word of a convicted felon? No, I think we'll rely more on video evidence. Now, last chance before we call the boys in to toss this place. What did you do on Saturday night?"

The little resolve that Mickey had left crumbled away, and although he tried hard to hide it, the detectives knew he would talk. "Oh, you mean this Saturday just gone? Yeah, about that. I didn't kill him. I just found him there and he was, like, already dead. I even called 911 and said he was there."

"Now we're getting somewhere at last. You've just admitted you were at a murder scene. So what happened? Had the priest done something to hack you off, or did you just lose it?"

"I never touched him. I just saw the door open a little, you know, and just took a look inside. I was just looking, alright, being nosy, and then I see this dude with no head and blood everywhere. I got outta there as fast as I could. For all I knew the guy that offed him could've still been in there.

"So I called for the bacon and came home. I didn't stick round because I knew what you lot would think about an ex-con standing beside a body. But I never killed him. I wish I'd never gone in there and seen that mess. I can't get it out of my head."

Mickey's torrent of words finally wound down, and he stood there sweating and breathing heavily. Todd looked at Danny, "Do you think he's kosher?"

Danny shrugged, "It makes a nice story, but from a self confessed criminal you would expect one. Maybe not the truth, but a good story nonetheless."

Mickey's head came up, "Man, I am serious. I didn't do it. I don't do violence. You've seen my record, just a little stealing and stuff. I don't even like the sight of blood. As soon as I got outside I spewed. Honest, all I did was go inside and have a look round. Maybe I was thinking there might be something I could lift, but I didn't take anything and that priest was already dead before I got there."

Danny nodded, "Okay, maybe you are telling the truth. Care to come down and make a statement? We will forget about looking through this dump if you do."

Mickey nodded glumly and opened the front door, "Let's get it done."

Todd said, "You can ride in with the uniforms, and then we'll go over this again, just to make sure you're telling us everything."

#

Danny Watson spent the rest of the morning updating the murder book for Father Williams. There was always a mass of paperwork associated with a case like this, and Danny liked to review everything he could. In the past he had often demonstrated a knack for seeing details and connections that others might miss in the sea of information.

He was just about finished when Todd came back from re-interviewing Mickey Davenport. Todd had been chosen to conduct the interview, as his imposing bulk and ability to switch tracks, verbally running rings round the suspect, all combined to squeeze any inconsistencies from a statement. He dropped a copy of the initial transcript in front of Danny, and said, "It all tallies up. He was even pretty close on the times, which we verified off the cameras and the dispatcher records. It really doesn't help us much, apart from tying up a loose end, and knowing that he didn't mess with anything at the crime scene."

Danny replied, "I expected as much. He was there a long time after we know the killer left, so he wouldn't have seen him. Well, at least we have that little mystery solved. Let's get back to working on the big one."

#

Later that night, the killer was relaxing in bed, amusing the Beast with mental reruns of their previous kills. In this he was including all the little surveillance and investigations he had done to make the kills as perfect and safe as possible. Well, safe for him anyway, the victim did not count. He was a little concerned with himself when he got to the killing of the priest.

While he was satisfied with his work to make sure he had got in and out without being seen, except possibly by unknown cameras, and with the background checks on Father Williams, it had not been done as a stalking of prey. What had been done was just to convince himself that it would be safe to talk without being recognized, and the priest had not said anything to concern the killer about the conversation being repeated.

So why had he killed him? The obvious answer was he became overwhelmed by the Beast, who had been enraged that the conversation had even occurred, and had submitted to the urge to kill. Usually the killer would have waited another week or longer before needing to strike again, so the priest was out of the pattern.

As he lay there, the killer wondered if the priest had just been an anomaly, a target of opportunity, and that things would revert to the expected course and time line of killings. Or, he dreaded even thinking the words, was he losing control of the Beast? He felt he had succumbed too easily when the Beast pushed him, and that the killing could have been avoided, or at least postponed.

In its fiery cage the Beast roared with delight, pounding at the bars, shouting, "You know you will give in to me, give in to your urges. Sooner or later you will release me so we can hunt at will! And you will enjoy every moment of it!"

#

BLOG: All killers, serial or not, tend to fall into two distinctive groups, namely Organized or Disorganized killers. While there may be some cases that fall partly into either category, these can be anomalies typically caused by spur of the moment kills by killers who would usually be more Organized.

So what defines an Organized killer? One of the main factors is intelligence. Those with significantly above average IQ (some studies suggest a median of 140) are more likely to plan their kills to minimize the chances of witnesses and pollution of the crime scene (for example, leaving evidence like a bloody footprint or the always damning fingerprint). Intellect can often override emotion, so even if grievously provoked, an Organized killer would wait until the time is right before making their move.

Disorganized killers, on the other hand, are more easily led by their emotions. This leads to spontaneous crimes, typified by blitz or surprise attacks, with a larger than average amount of evidence left behind. This makes the lower intelligence, emotionally led Disorganized killers easier to apprehend.

There is a sub group of Organized killers that may, on initial inspection, appear to be Disorganized. Some may have physical limitations that lead them to use a blitz attack as the only sure method of overpowering their victim. Also if the attack method is sufficiently frenzied, if the killer appears to lose all control, then this looks like a Disorganized attack. However, the initial stalk would have been careful, and pains would be taken to remove or hide evidence, which are much more the hallmarks of an Organized killer.

#

Karen Watson was reading this latest blog entry, and after looking at the words on the screen she thought, "Interesting deductions." She jotted down a few notes on her ever present notepad, then moved on to the next item of interest.

#

The killer looked at the same words on his screen, and thought, "In Organization lies more safety. I know I can avoid Disorganized mistakes."

The Beast roared with laughter, "You know I am a mistake waiting to happen, every time I can get out of this pesky cage!"

Chapter 6

Two days later saw Detective Watson standing in the luxurious office of Claytown City's Chief of Police. He knew what this meeting was likely to be about, and suspected he knew how it would go.

Seated in his custom made high backed leather chair, the Chief leaned back and said, "So, where are we with the Father Williams investigation? You have had the case nearly a week. Are we any closer to catching the one responsible for this crime?"

Danny replied, "In the four-odd days we've been looking at this, we have put thousands of man-hours into following every single avenue in an effort to locate the perpetrator."

"A very politically phrased answer, Detective Watson. I must remember it for the next time the press ask me about this case. But you really have not answered my questions. I want an open and frank assessment of the case, and its likelihood of closure."

Inwardly Danny groaned, then shrugged, "You've seen all the reports. I have the murder book here if you want to take a look at any of the fine detail. We know lots of people who couldn't have done it. We haven't found anyone, or even a hint of anyone, who wanted harm to come to the late Father. We've done a whole lot of work without getting any closer to the result we need. No, we have no clue who the perp is, and unless we get some lucky break, I don't think we will ever know."

Looking over his steepled hands, the Chief replied, "Well, that sounded far less political, but not so uplifting. Thank you for your plain and honest answer. I would rather have that than any fancy wording that hides reality. Now, I thought you had someone in custody. Is it not possible that the man who called in the crime was the one who committed it?"

Danny shook his head, "We never technically had anyone in custody for this, but the man you're referring to was just helping with our inquiries. Even though we can't pin down his location at the time the crime was taking place, Mickey Davenport couldn't be our killer. For one, he's only small time and doesn't have it in him, and two, we did comparisons of him and the suspect in the camera recordings, and there is no match. Mickey is shorter and thinner, and his stride, especially when he is running, is completely different from the suspects. It just can't be him."

The Chief leaned forward, "So what am I to do, eh? Tell the world that we are not going to be able to catch the cold-blooded killer of one of our prominent clergymen? Hmm?"

The shrug Danny gave was real this time, "Sir, I cannot advise you on a political matter. All I can do is find and analyze the facts. As you know, with about half of all homicides it's obvious from the get go who the killer was. With another quarter of cases, a little shoe leather and you'll find your man in a couple of days. With the rest of the cases, when we've no witnesses and little evidence, we have to rely on the killer doing something dumb, like talk to the wrong person about his exploits. It's sad to say, but if you do your planning, execute it well, and then keep your mouth shut, you really can get away with murder."

The Chief smiled wryly and shook his head, "Well, I did ask you to be frank earlier, so I shouldn't be surprised by that answer. Which is also another answer that should not go anywhere near the press.

"All I can do then is ask you to keep at it, and you already know you can have any resource we can spare on this. Get back to it, and I wish you luck."

Danny nodded and turned away to leave, thinking, "We're gonna need it."

#

Later that night Danny was watching the Chief give another press conference, praising the hard work of the officers involved in the investigation, and once again appealing for help from the public. Danny knew tomorrow they would have to start re-canvassing the area, hoping that the newscast would have jogged someones memory. He was frustrated. All they needed was one break, one little break and then the full force of the law could be brought to bear. But without that break, the police were helpless.

#

At the same time the Chief was issuing his plea for public help, the killer was hiding in some of the bushes in the Presidential Park. His location gave him a good view of the river and the paths that crossed the area. Even the secluded walks through the trees could be seen from his spot, and he was spending his time, as he had on and off for a few weeks, checking and memorizing the routines of the many joggers.

Very few were late night or very early morning runners, but he felt he now would know where every runner would be at any given time of day. His observations finished for the night, the killer carefully extracted himself from the discrete hiding place. As he left he made sure there was little evidence of his stay, sweeping leaf mold over his footprints, and easing his way past branches to avoid damaging them. His military days were sometimes very useful when it came to discrete observation, stalking and killing.

As he walked out of the Park, intending to head home for a few hours of sleep before work, his thoughts were interrupted by the blipping of a police siren behind him. The cruiser pulled up beside him and the driver lowered his window, saying, "May I ask what you are doing here tonight?"

The killer knew the police were stopping everyone in the area in their hunt for him, but he knew his job gave him an oh so valid reason to be in the Park, and indeed almost anywhere in the city, without raising any suspicions. He slowly lowered his hood so his face was clearly visible, and said, "I am going to get my wallet out."

The officer, who looked to be new to the job, and maybe even a little jumpy at the thought of randomly stopping a potential killer, replied, "Okay, but slowly."

The killer knew the drill, and carefully extracted his wallet, opening it to where his work ID was located, and showed it to the officer. Once the cop saw it his suspicions were instantly eased, and all he said was, "I'm sorry, I didn't realize. But it is a little late to be out and about, isn't it?"

The killer pocketed his wallet, and replied, "For some people, the job never sleeps, as I am sure you know well."

The patrol officer acknowledged this, bade him

goodnight and eased his car away, seeking anyone else looking suspicious. As he strolled home, the killer chuckled to himself, "How easy it is to fool these flat foots."

The Beast smirked and replied, "So true. I wonder how easy it would be to kill one?"

This sent the killers thoughts barreling into new directions, and head spinning with fresh ideas, he headed home.

The next morning Danny was in his car, checking up on the progress of the door to door inquiries. Not that his presence on the street would be welcome, as he knew himself what it was like having your superiors breathing down your neck, but he felt the need to spread the breathing round. It also made him feel he was doing something more productive than staring at the same paperwork again and again, hoping for the answer to jump out at him.

He ended up in the Presidential Park and noticed Patrolman Quigley jogging backwards while talking to a sportingly dressed blonde woman who was running round the park. Once again Danny was struck by the apparent dedication of the young officer, and wondered what he had kept doing to hinder his promotion prospects, and why. Meanwhile, Danny was glad to have him as part of the team. After a brief look round the area, he saw nothing suspicious, just joggers and city workers maintaining the area, and he moved on to the next place on his list.

#

The killer was back in the park, appearing to go

about his lawful business, but taking the opportunity to scout the area and the people once more. He had seen Detective Watson in his sedan, and could not help thinking how easy it would be to kill someone right now, even with the police hanging round.

Of course, the chances of escaping would be greatly reduced if he stuck to his usual upfront and personal method of blood soaked killing. He doubted that the Beast would be satisfied with single or multiple kills without a lake of blood it could bathe in.

He felt the Beast stir and say, "A lake of blood would be good, but I am not ready for you to die yet. You will have to feed me a lot more before I let you go."

Chapter 7

As the days passed with no further progress, despite the pressure being applied on and by the Chief, officers working on the Father Williams case had to return to their normal duties, or be reassigned to deal with other issues. Danny and Todd did the best they could, even with the reduced manpower, but to their growing frustration the case was going nowhere.

Two weeks after the killing, Danny threw his hands in the air and said, "This is pointless. I know the Chief won't want to hear this, but we're wasting our time here. We have other work piling up, and I think we would stand more of a chance solving the Harding case, or finding out Lord Lucan was shacked up with Jimmy Hoffa. I'll have to bite the bullet, go tell him, and hope the bullet doesn't bite back."

Surprisingly, the Chief was in agreement, albeit reluctantly. Relaxing in his plush chair, he said, "I have seen the report, and I agree we cannot afford to throw manpower into this sinkhole. I hate to have to do this. I knew Vernon Williams, I am getting heat from his family, among others, to get a result, but I know what you think will be the only thing that will solve this case. I agree with you, we are just waiting for that lucky break. You and most of the remaining people will have to return to normal duties, but we will have to keep some officers working the case, if only from the publicity viewpoint. Any suggestions on who we should leave on this?"

Danny was more than a little stunned at how quickly the Chief had folded on this investigation, but he suspected how big a part budget pressures played in this decision. He replied, "I guess I would choose Officer Quigley, with two men of his choice under him. He could report to me regularly."

"Hmm, Quigley. A strange choice, but he does seem to have worked well under your supervision. Okay, let it be written, let it be done. You and Detective King can pursue other duties until we get our much needed lucky break."

#

The killer had been having a surprisingly good time at work since he killed the priest. This meant he himself was more relaxed. The Beast, however, was not relaxed. Two weeks after its last 'feeding', it was starting to clamor for more.

In his less stressed state, the killer was able to calm the Beast better than he had been able to for several months. The Beast did not really like this and looked for every weakness it could find to exploit, and tried every tactic it could employ to get its own way.

But for now, the killer seemed to be firmly in control.

#

Frank Sinclair was at one of his favorite locations downtown, patrolling several of the intersections with Lincoln Avenue. It had not been a great morning, not really productive, but after all, he chuckled to himself at the thought, beggars can't be choosers.

He had just crossed the street when he saw an official looking car approaching the stop lights. His Post-Traumatic Stress Disorder induced anxiety and caution kicked in, and he headed towards a convenient alleyway, looking to make a speedy exit.

Just before he ducked down the narrow passage to make his escape, he could not help turning and giving a one-fingered salute to the driver. That done, Frank beat feet out of there, heading to a quieter part of town.

#

To say the least, the gesture by the beggar did not please the killer, nor the Beast. The Beast whispered, "Are you going to let that drop-out disrespect you?"

The killers hands gripped the wheel so tightly his knuckles whitened. He growled, "I know what you are trying to do. You expect me to run the light, chase down that bum, and waste him, eh?"

The Beast grinned, baring its fangs, "That would be great, but what I think you would prefer is to carefully stalk the bum, find out his routines, then when the time is right you will slaughter him in an appropriately bloodthirsty way."

The killer nodded, "That is about right, and we'll find him, but I decide when he dies, not you, understand?"

"Oh yes, I understand," slyly smiled the Beast, glad that this incident had focused the killer back on killing. It knew that once the stalk truly started it would be so much easier to force the hand of its host, and make the blood flow freely.

#

As Danny made his way back to his desk, he was hailed by Raven Chavez. He turned to see the heavyset woman in dusty jeans and plaid shirt angling towards him, and he called back, "Hey, Raven, what are you doing here? Shouldn't you be hauling boxes round the back of Sears?"

Raven nodded, "I should be, but I'm getting nowhere on the case. I was hoping you would have a few spare minutes to give the case details a set of fresh eyes."

Detective Chavez had been working undercover for the past three weeks, trying to get any leads on an apparent series of thefts from the local Sears warehouse. While the company expected to experience small losses from miscounted orders and the occasional light pilferage, they had recently realized that entire box-loads of various goods were going missing.

This, understandably, had the management concerned, and despite various new security measures being put in place, items were still disappearing. The management had alerted Claytown City PD and Detective Chavez was selected to go undercover inside the warehouse, after the company's preparations had been reviewed, to see if new eyes on the ground could break the problem. But after three weeks Detective Chavez had gotten nowhere closer to figuring out how the crooks were doing these thefts, so she came to talk it out with her boss.

Danny said to her, "My time has been freed up considerably, and if you give me half an hour to get a few items settled, I would be delighted to help you."

Once back at his paper laden desk, Danny set in motion the process that would release people from active task force duties, and return them to their usual roles. Officer Quigley was not yet on shift, so Danny left a message for him to report to Danny as soon as he arrived. This was Jacob's usual routine anyway, but it never hurt to reinforce things.

#

Sweet-lips was on edge, going through withdrawal and seeing everything through paranoid eyes. Her usual dealer had not come through with the goods, nor had any others she tried. She was feeling that people were deliberately trying to keep her away from her much needed crack.

Intellectually she knew the real reasons, although the withdrawal was making it difficult to think that it was not a conspiracy. A couple of recent drug busts, some made through the inquiries into Father Williams' demise, had left Claytown and the surrounding area dry of crack, and most of the other popular drugs too. About the only thing still in plentiful supply was weed. Sweetness had managed to get an ounce of marijuana, hoping the joint she was rolling would help to take the edge off her withdrawal.

As she lit up and gratefully drew the fragrant smoke deep into her lungs, she wondered if she could play the 'vital police informant' card with Detective Watson in the hope he could score her something from the evidence locker. She snorted at that thought, knowing he would love to help her, but only by providing access to rehab.

She took another drag on the reefer, enjoying the relaxing feeling, thinking, "Pah, rehab is for quitters!"

#

After being briefed by Danny on the changes

approved by the Chief, Officer Quigley was silent for a few moments, apparently deep in thought. Finally he said, "So I am now running the Father Williams task force, with two people of my choice, even though we don't think we'll even crack the case. Seems like a waste of taxpayers money to me."

Danny shrugged, "It's just politics. We cannot be seen by the public to be giving up on a high profile case, so you get to go through the motions and try and find that lucky break for us. By the way, I'm still technically running this task force, with you reporting to me. You will need to provide daily updates. If you think you're onto something, and need extra resources, get hold of me. I'll still have to approve things and account for any expenditures. If you get a chance, try to mix your usual duties into the task force work, then it won't seem like such a waste of money."

Jacob nodded, "Got it. I will grab a couple of guys and pretend to get at it. I was thinking Officers Oso and Rose."

"Good choices. Brief them and get to it. Any questions, you know how to get hold of me."

#

With all the urgent business attended to, Danny rolled his chair across the short distance to Raven's desk. He stopped with a thud, and asked, "Okay. So what have we got?"

"Well, I won't bore you with the background, you just want to know what I've seen, right?"

Danny nodded, "Yes, ma'am."

Raven punched him lightly on the arm, "Don't you

'yes ma'am' me. I'm only pretending to be a member of the public working at Sears, I'm not really one. Anyway, when no-one could figure out how these losses occurred, I went in on the ground. I've got tapes from the surveillance cameras in the warehouse. They even added some more to cover the obvious blind spots that I noticed. The inventory shows everything is coming off the truck, but somehow it gets back out the door without being seen."

Danny said, "I'm going to ask some obvious questions. I know you will have it already covered, but you never know."

Raven nodded, "Yeah, can't see the woods for the trees syndrome. Good, ask away, that's what I need. Hopefully it will be something obvious that I've missed, and you can get me back at this desk where I belong. Now, shoot."

Danny sat back, "Cameras on all exits?"

"Yep, and no-one is seen dragging any unauthorized boxes out."

"What about waste boxes being thrown away? Could something be hidden inside them when they're taken out?"

"All boxes are flattened and put in a separate recycling dumpster. It has been repeatedly checked, and no contraband has been found even between the boards."

Danny drummed his fingers on the desk, "Okay, how about random searches as staff leave?"

"They have been done periodically, and nothing has been found. They even wanted to search the cars, but I advised them against that for now."

"Good call. The cameras haven't shown anyone tampering with boxes?"

"I've only seen work related activity on the tapes. It's so frustrating. The goods come in, and somehow they just seem to vanish."

Danny thought for a moment, "Do you mind if I review some of the tapes? Fresh eyes and all that."

Raven shrugged, "Knock yourself out. I need something to come up. I never heard or saw anything when I was working the floor. Most of the workers, the ones that talk about the problem, are as clueless as me about it."

"One of them at least knows something about it. How do they validate the stock count coming off the truck?"

Raven thought for a few seconds, "A manual count and an electronic one. That uses a bar-code scanner. Two different people for each count."

"That sounds pretty solid. Okay, I can't think of anything else right now. Mind if I take the files and tapes and go over them at my desk?"

Raven spread her hands wide over the pile, "By my guest. While you're doing that, I'll head back to finish my shift at box heaven."

#

The rest of the day for Detective Watson was spent slogging through the mire that constituted the files in the Sears case. In its own way, working on it felt as hopeless and pointless as trying to find the killer of Father Williams. But he kept at it, hoping that a new perspective would bring some previously hidden clue to light. Stretching the kinks from his back, he set back to it.

#

The killer was not mired in paperwork all day. He spent most of it criss-crossing the downtown area as much as his job allowed him to, searching for the bum who insulted him. Even when his shift was over, he returned to the same streets, first in his car, and then on foot, searching, searching, searching....

Chapter 8

Without her usual doses of reality killer, Sweet-lips was not feeling it that Monday night. But to pay the bills she still had to hit the streets, or more precisely the street corner where she plied her trade.

Tottering slightly on her heels, she made her way from her tiny apartment to the intersection where she worked. She and the other 'working girls' in the city knew that as long as they were not too blatant in their work practices, the police would leave them alone. Any new girls were quickly educated on the proper etiquette, and learned not to stand right on the corners flashing their wares at passing motorists.

Instead, a more subtle approach was used, with girls in skimpy outfits waiting where they could be seen from the road, but not too obviously. Sweet-lips' preferred spot was actually one of the intersections on Lincoln Avenue that Frank worked during the day.

She settled herself on a low stone wall, under the shade of a pair of sycamore trees that stood in a well maintained churchyard. Officially the church disapproved of prostitution, but Sweet-lips had found the offer of a free ride to the supposedly celibate priest allowed her to stay there without hassle. Some of the churchgoers also disapproved of her occupation, but she had also found some of them to be good customers.

Sweet-lips stretched out her fishnet covered legs in front of her, and pulled out a joint she had made earlier to see her through the evening. It was helping some, but it sure was not crack, and she had little alternative until later - maybe. If someone had managed to get a shipment in, if every other deprived addict in the city had not snapped it up first. She hoped that her dealer would keep some by for her, and give her a call. After being without for a while, she would gladly do anything to get a hit, even if it meant she would lose a little money. But what was money compared to that rush?

Sweet-lips frowned when she saw a dark colored sedan going past for the third time. Prospective clients may go past once, or even twice, but checking the available merchandise more times than that was strange behavior. Maybe it was just her withdrawal paranoia, but it made it look as though the driver was searching for someone in particular, and not to be used as a bed-warmer either.

#

The killer knew it was time to stop using the car. He could see several hookers looking strangely at his car as he drove past them repeatedly. It would be nice if the bums were as easy to see as the slutty whores, but it looked as though a slow, careful search of the back alleys would have to be done.

As he lived in the Downtown area, he parked his blue Taurus outside his apartment, made sure his cap was pulled low, and walked through the hidden passageways searching for his prey.

Several vagrants were located, huddled in doorways or tucked behind dumpsters, but none were the one he was interested in. After searching for half the night, the killer finally called it quits just after one in the morning. He knew he had to get at least some sleep before work.

As he headed home, he mused to himself that maybe it would be easier to find the bum in daylight, then follow him to whatever hole he slept in. A little adjustment to his work routine is all it would take to make it feasible, then the hunt would truly begin.

#

Danny was awake before his alarm went off, with a little tell-tale nagging in his mind that meant his subconscious may have found something while he had been sleeping. He knew that if he forced himself to find that elusive thought, it would no doubt drift away, back into the darkness.

Instead he just got up, started the coffee, then padded to the bathroom for a refreshing wake up shower. After drying himself off, he donned his wife's fluffy robe, fetched his coffee and headed back to the bathroom. As he finished he ablutions he enjoyed his first cup of the day, and it was usually the only decent tasting one that he could get until he got home again.

Caffeinated, shaved and clean, now it was time to quietly find a suit and get out to the car without waking anyone else in the house. That mission successfully accomplished, he drove to the police station, determined to review the paperwork Sears again, followed by the tapes, until the subconscious thought hiding in his gray cells jumped into focus.

With the squad room deserted at this early hour, he sat down in the quiet and re-reviewed the case information. Something that struck him was while the missing goods had one thing in common, high value, with over one hundred thousand dollars of product missing in less than two months, there was a major difference in product size. Small items like watches and jewelry had gone missing, and while there were many ways that things that size could be hidden, it was a bit of the stretch to think that a thirty two inch flat screen TV could be hidden in someones pants, unless they weighed five hundred pounds.

While this fact didn't, nor any of the other paperwork, spark any insights, it was something that made the case that much stranger. He settled down to watch the tapes, as other officers started to file in, and wondered what was nagging him. He felt it would crack the case when the thought finally rose to the surface, but for now it just bobbed along just out of reach.

#

The killer got a lucky break in his search for the bum. As he was driving his official vehicle out of the Downtown building he worked from, the bum literally walked past him at the stop light. There was no recognition on the part of the bum, who seemed intent on keeping his head down and avoiding eye contact with anyone, but the killer knew who he was instantly.

He noted where the bum appeared to have come from, and where he seemed to be going, which were east and west along Lincoln Avenue respectively. Playing a hunch, as the killer drove to his work assignment area, he doubled back several times to cross and recross Lincoln Avenue, tracking the progress of the bum. Eventually the bum stopped under some trees outside a church, and looked round, apparently checking for people he could beg from at this intersection.

As the killer eased up to the lights beside the bum, he remembered a pair of sexy legs encased in fishnets being in the same place the previous night. He thought it was an interesting coincidence that two of the breeds of social leeches should choose the same sites to make their living. The killer resolved to check back on the bum a few times during the day, just to see where he went. As he drove away, the killer's smile was as satisfied as the one the Beast had on its face. The Beast growled softly in the direction of the bum, saying, "Watch out, little man, we are coming for you!"

#

It took Frank a while to shake the feeling that he was being watched. It was not until he had been by the church for an hour that he felt better about things. But feelings like this were common for Frank, and although wary, he did his best to ignore the paranoia. In his case his anxiety did not come from drug use and withdrawal, but from the effects of the psychological trauma received in combat. This paranoia was a big reason that Frank did not sleep Downtown with most of the other down and outs.

Instead he preferred to hole up in a nice abandoned building he had found and now called home. There, hidden from prying eyes, it was where he felt safe and secure. But the need for food, and therefore money, drove him out of his haven to panhandle his way to sustenance. Sometimes he could get items from the local food banks, and there was often a soup kitchen or two doing the rounds, but there was only so much to go round, and it was easy to come away empty handed.

So it was panhandling that gave him that little extra cash that helped buy the extra things he needed, and as he did not use drugs of any kind, and his drinking was less than it used to be, he was able to use most of his takings for cheap and basic foods, and managed to live a life he was comfortable in.

#

After watching the tapes for what seemed like the thousandth time, that little spark of intuition started to boldly wave its flag. He looked at his notes, then flipped back through the paperwork on the Sears case. He could not find exactly what he was looking for, and with Raven working her shift in the warehouse he could not call her to get a quick answer to his question. Instead a quick text would have to - "Maybe on to something. Need ALL paperwork regarding delivery counts."

It took a while for the reply to come through, but Danny expected that and used the time to double check his suspicions with the tapes. Finally Raven replied - "Will do. See you at lunchtime." Danny smiled with anticipation, looking forward to putting this case to bed.

#

The killer also had an anticipatory smile on his face. Several times in the morning he had been able to swing down Lincoln Avenue, and every time he did he saw the bum pathetically begging for money. It seemed he changed locations during the day, but stuck to the main intersections of Lincoln in the Downtown area. This made the killer think the bum had to live somewhere nearby, a thought that the Beast agreed with. The killer knew if he could just get off shift early he could lay in wait somewhere along Lincoln Avenue and track the bum back to his hole.

#

Raven arrived a little after twelve fifteen,

bearing a stack of paperwork in a manila folder. "These are the originals, and I had to beg them to let me have them even for a short while. For some reason the management there doesn't even want copies made. I need to take them back in forty five minutes, so this needs to be quick."

Danny eagerly flipped through the papers, finding the numbers he needed. He jotted them down in his notebook beside the corresponding dates and counts he made from the tapes. A grin cracked across face before he had even finished half the counts he needed. "Got it. Let me take a guess, the guy who does the electronic count does it before they unload, and after the one who does the manual count?"

Raven frowned, "I think so, yes."

"Next time they get a shipment, tell him to do another count as they unload each box, but do it discretely. I reckon they'll notice a difference."

"What do you mean?"

"The reason you couldn't work out how the goods got out of the warehouse after they were checked in is because they were never in there in the first place. The guy with the scanner has to be in on it, and the truck driver. The boxes get counted by the first guy, all good so far. Then I think the scanner man goes on the truck, scans everything, but pushes a box or two out of the pile.

"The two counts match, but when everything in the pile is unloaded and marked as checked in, the truck driver heads out the door with a couple of boxes that register as being inside the warehouse. Very sneaky. They must have a contact who buys the goods, and the driver and scanner guy split the profits. When is the next delivery?"

"Son of a sea biscuit. Tomorrow at ten," replied an amazed Raven.

"I would say by ten thirty you can head back here with a couple of prisoners, ready for interrogation."

Raven gave Danny a high five, "I hope so. If you're right and it all works out, the drinks are on me!"

#

The killer managed to get off work early, after pleading a nasty headache. As he had taken his car to work today, on his way home he drove down Lincoln Avenue, searching for the pesky bum. It did not take long to find him, just one block down from his morning position. The killer drove past without obviously looking at the bum, and took the next right to head back home.

Leaving the car in its accustomed parking spot, he hurried inside to get ready for the nights work. The casual clothes he had donned after removing his hated work clothes were in turn discarded in favor of tennis shoes, pants and hoodie, all in black. Adding a dark colored baseball cap helped to shield his features even more.

Before leaving the apartment, the killer collected his backpack from the closet. This handy bag contained a change of clothes, various bags and a selection of instruments of death. He was not intending to use anything this night, but as a certain priest discovered, it is always better to be prepared.

He took a highly circuitous route back to Lincoln

Avenue, approaching from the south. Surveillance without been easily seen was more difficult in daylight, meaning that the killer would have to constantly keep moving to avoid any suspicions. He trusted that his work credentials would ease him out of any difficulties if they came up, but he would rather avoid any incidents. People have long memories sometimes, and he did not want his name to be remembered after a body was found.

Of course, he thought again as he took a seat on a wall two blocks away from the bum, he could always try and dispose of the bodies, but that presented more problems than it solved. If he was only thinking of one body it was plausible, but there are only so many dump sites and disposal methods available, and besides, he did not have a wood chipper in his apartment.

As night started to fall he saw some of the hookers arrive to take up their stations, and many of the bums started to leave the streets to them. His target apparently made the same decision, and headed along Lincoln towards him. At that time, the killer was lounging in the shadows of a deep doorway, and he stayed there silent and hidden as the bum walked past.

He sensed there was something unusual about this bum, who up close did not look or smell like the usual street inhabitants. He also seemed to walk more upright, and looked more alert than even a regular person. Intrigued, the killer was very careful when he moved to follow, trying to keep at least a block between them, slipping from one hiding place to another.

Despite his caution, the bum seemed to sense someone was behind him, and even more strangely appeared to be actively checking for a tail at regular intervals. With his training and experience, the killer managed to stay hidden, but these back-checks caused him to fall behind somewhat, especially at those times when the bum deviated from his eastward course. The killer had never seen such a devious route and methods in civilian life, and the way this bum was checking his trail and apparently looping round so his route towards his eventual destination was masked, was more reminiscent of military maneuvers, or even an animal trying to hide the location of their den.

Now the killer was really starting to enjoy this hunt, as it looked like it would be even more challenging than most of his kills. After about forty minutes the bum had headed back west so he was barely a dozen blocks south of where he had started on Lincoln Avenue. They were now in an area of some industrial activity, but with a heavy scattering of abandoned buildings. It was towards one of these that the bum appeared to be heading.

It was a small brick built two story affair, in the middle of its own parking lot. That whole area seemed to be covered in broken glass and other trash, so any approach to the building would have to be made very carefully to avoid making any noise. The bum obviously knew a safe path through the debris, and was now slowly moving round the building, and it appeared that he was checking for signs of disturbance at any of the possible entrances.

The killer watched the bum enter the building through a boarded up window, easing one board to one side then pulling it back behind him. The killer stayed a while watching the building and the surrounding area, thinking of ways to approach unseen and unheard. There was a puzzle behind this bum that had him excited, and the killer was looking forward to solving it, and then dealing

with the situation in his own special, and highly
bloody way.

Chapter 9

At least with the lower priority on the Father Williams case, Danny thought he stood a chance of catching up with his paperwork. Admittedly, it was a slim chance, but slim chances did not deter some football franchises from aiming for the Super Bowl each year, so Danny took a deep breath and waded in.

The brief reports from Officer Quigley were added to the murder book, and a mass of memos and forms relating to other cases were successfully subdued by the time his cell phone rang. Danny looked at the time, a quarter after ten, and glanced at the Caller ID before answering, "Hey, Raven, are you buying?"

Detective Chavez replied, "I sure am. It was just as you suspected. How on earth did you catch that? It fair had me stumped for weeks!"

"Elementary," said Watson. "Once you have eliminated the impossible, whatever is left, no matter how improbably, must be the solution."

Raven put on a cheesy British accent, and replied, "Thanks awfully, Sherlock, I just don't know what we would do without you."

Danny was grinning when he hung up, and was feeling that special buzz running through his veins that came with every solved case. He had always loved puzzles, and criminal investigations were the best puzzles he could find. It was always pleasurable to see another one bite the dust.

#

It took a while for the ringing of her cellphone

to wake Sweet-lips. Being without crack had made sleeping difficult, and a large amount of weed had been imbibed to finally knock her out. Sleepily she shut off the strains of "I'm Sexy and I Know It", and said, "Yeah?"

The voice came back, "Damn, girl, I was about to give up on you. You were so interested in my stock before, so I thought I would give you a chance to get in while I still have supplies. Fresh stock came in this morning, but quantities are limited."

The much longed for voice of her usual dealer telling her she could come over and get more crack again wired Sweet-lips awake in seconds. "That would be awesome. When and where? Price still good?"

A chuckle came down the line, "The price is still good, especially for you. Meet you in the Transit Center in an hour?"

"Cool, that works for me. Thanks for getting hold of me. See you then."

Sweet-lips hung up and looked round her apartment for some clean clothes. This was a fruitless task in the domestic devastation that reigned, so she settled for greasy denims and a sweatshirt that did not look like it would stick to anything. After checking there was money in it, she grabbed her purse and headed out of the door.

There was a Mickey D's near the Transit Center, which was only a fifteen minute walk from her place, so she could get some coffee and breakfast while she impatiently waited for her dealer to arrive. With this plan of action set, she hurried towards Lincoln Avenue.

#

Frank still could not shake the feeling of being watched. He was ninety percent certain that no-one was spying on him right now, but he had felt the same way last night and had to use all his tricks to reassure himself that no-one could have followed his devious route.

He had gotten through the night with only a few episodes of nervous sleeplessness, and was back on the streets trying to find a little money. He did not realize, nor would his paranoid mind believe, that most of the police force were highly tolerant of his begging, even to the extent of moving other less desirable beggars out of his patch.

This was because although he was indeed a beggar, an activity frequently frowned on by legal authorities, Frank was adequately groomed and polite to all who did not represent authority, and his courteous manner actually reflected well on the city. The rumors that he was a veteran also help the police be tolerant, and Frank was left to go about his business without being harassed. But even that knowledge would never ease the fears that Frank had, so convinced was he that someone was always watching him, and out to get him.

#

The killer, and the Beast along with him, would have been delighted to know about Frank's fears. If it had been possible the killer would have loved to see the expression on Frank's face when he realized all his fears had come true. But for safety's sake, the killer was leaning towards a plan of attack along the lines of a blitz, taking place from behind the bum, surprising him and hopefully negating any advantages the unusual seeming street scrubber had.

But that was in the future. For now, having called off work still pleading a headache, he headed indirectly on foot towards the building he saw the bum enter last night. His plan was to scout it in daylight, see if there was anything unusual that might cause him problems, and then try and gain entry in such a way that could not be detected. Once inside, he planned a little more snooping, then leaving to return at a later date with murder in his heart.

This was not an easy task he had set for himself, especially gaining entry covertly in daylight, but he was supremely confident in himself and his skills. Once near the building he slowed his walking speed and stopped across the street to observe the lay of the land.

Despite the glass and other detritus spread round the building and all over the parking lot, there looked to be a clear, if indirect, route to the window the bum had used. After checking to see no-one was taking any notice of him, the killer loped across the road and carefully made his way through the maze of debris, carefully checking the ground for any impediments. Something was nudging his sixth sense that there was too much that seemed strange about this bum, and that there might even be traps of some kind.

Periodically he had to slap down the Beast, as its blood lust was getting too distracting, especially as this was a time when he needed to focus. Having reached the window, he ran his gloved fingers along the underside of the boards nailed to the frame. He could tell they were loose, carefully rehung somehow so it looked more secure than it really was. His thin gloves also told his gently questing fingers that a couple of spikes of some kind were being loosely held in place by the bottom of the boards. He assumed they were nails, and he also assumed removing the boards would make them fall to the ground. A very clever way to see if someone has gone in through the window, he thought.

While he was confident enough to defeat this simple security arrangement, and be able to replace the nails perfectly, he decided to look at the other potential entrances to see if they would be easier. Part of him was not surprised to find inconspicuous tell-tales at every entrance on the ground floor. He briefly wondered if he had stumbled across some Federal or Intelligence operation, but quickly dismissed that idea. He had been seeing the bum on the streets for months, far longer than most operations would last, and besides, there was nothing happening in Claytown City that would interest the Feds, much less any other agency.

He smiled at that train of thought, and amended it with his next one, "Well, apart from a serial killer, but they haven't worked that one out yet."

He accurately put all the odd countermeasures down to someone with military experience who had fallen on hard times, and was highly paranoid. The killer looked up to where the fire escape from the second floor was hanging down, and wondered just how paranoid this bum could be. He could not see anything slipped into the mechanism, indeed the whole fire escape looked completely rusted together.

He took a look round at the surrounding area, and this side of the building did not appear to be overlooked by any active businesses, so the killer was not concerned about being seen here. He took a quick run-up and jumped, his fingers just catching the lowest rung of the ladder. He hauled himself up the fire escape quickly, wincing at the sound of tortured metal as the rust started to give way. Once he was off the drop ladder the fire escape stopped screaming, and the platform beside the second story door seemed quite stable. There were no tell-tales on the outside of this door, and he hoped there were none on the inside, nor any other kinds of trap. Taking a putty knife from his bag, it was but the work of a few moments to pop the lock. The killer swapped the knife for a flashlight, and eased his way inside.

#

Danny Watson was looking through the overnight logs, seeing what else had been happening in the city, when Raven Chavez walked up to his desk and placed a miniature bottle of Mr. Daniels finest in front of him. She said, "Myself and Jack here thank you for your help. That was why I wanted fresh eyes on the case. Sometimes you really can't see the woods for the trees."

Danny smiled as he tucked the small bottle away, "No worries, any time. You did a lot of the hard work eliminating the possibilities, I just found the missing link. Are they talking?"

Raven nodded, "The driver is acting like a mute, even with his lawyer apparently, but the guy from the warehouse is singing like a flock of canaries. He knows who the buyer is, and that there are at least two other places in on this. Todd is at one business picking up the guilty parties, and I'm just heading to see the others. Want to tag along?"

"No, thanks. I wanted to take a quick look at some of the unsolved files, see if I can see something I missed the last time I looked at them."

Raven waved as she walked away, "Well have fun. I hope those magic eyes can do their thing again."

Danny nodded a vague reply, already deep in the files, looking for that elusive clue needed to bust them wide open.

#

At the appointed time, Sweet-lips walked into the Transit Center. It was late morning, so although there was a lot of activity, it was not the rush hour chaos of people and buses. She saw her dealer at pretty much the same time as he saw her, and she slipped her hand into her pocket to retrieve the roll of bills.

A grin crossed her face as the pair got closer together, and like the old friends that they were they clasped hands, hugged and slapped each other on the back. Only a very skilled observer in just the right position would have seen the practiced finger-work in the clasped hands, as a roll of cash was deftly exchanged for a packet of chemical heaven. But the dealer and Sweet-lips were old hands at this trick, and their bodies blocked the view of most of the move, and their other movements would have distracted all but the most alert watcher.

The dealer and Sweet-lips chatted about things for a few minutes, not needing to act as they really did have many common friends and took the opportunity to catch up on recent events and laughing about the old times. Her dealer knew she would be in a hurry to sample the drugs after the recent drought, so they did not talk long, and Sweet-lips hurried away to find a quiet alley to catch up with her best friend - crack cocaine.

#

The hallway the killer found himself in was

totally dark except for the glow from his flashlight. He pulled the door closed behind him and carefully examined the hall. Bare walls, paint peeling with age, with doors leading off to what looked like offices, judging by the frosted glass in the top half of the doors. There was lots of dust and debris on the floor, and the killer realized that no matter how carefully he trod, he would leave a noticeable trail. The Beast urged him not to worry about that now, and so he shook off that thought and proceeded to walk slowly and quietly, avoiding the worst of the obstacles underfoot.

The first two doors he looked through did indeed lead to empty offices, one with a lonely three-legged chair tossed in a corner. The final two appeared to have last been used as store rooms, but the mouldering remains of cardboard boxes offered no clue as to what they had once held.

Keeping it slow and careful, the killer made his way downstairs. Almost the entire lower floor was a concrete cavern that the flashlight struggled to illuminate, with whatever machinery that once sat here long gone. The floor was still marked by oil stains, outlets and the occasional metal fixture sticking up. Remarkably though, these were the only things on the floor down here, so someone, presumably the bum, had cleared any other trash away. The other points of interest downstairs were two rooms at the back of the factory cavern, one of which turned out to be a bathroom, and the other was another old office.

Once again, these rooms were fairly clean, and the sight of the clean toilet puzzled the killer. Bums were usually not this fastidious, which just added another mystery to the pile. The office contained a makeshift mattress made from discarded foam pieces, taped between large pieces of cardboard. A small camping stove was tucked neatly in a corner, safely away from anything combustible, and there was a small box on the floor beside the bed. It contained a tin plate and mug, with a couple of spoons, along with a handful of old photographs.

The killer did not disturb the photos, but looked with interest at the top one, an army graduation picture that shows the bum in better days. This picture partially solved the mysteries of the entrance tell-tales, upright bearing and the watchfulness of the bum. He wanted to look through the rest of the pile, but figured he could browse at leisure when he finally killed the bum.

With his reconnaissance completed, the killer made sure everything downstairs was as he found it, then turned to leave. He planned to head back up the stairs and leave by the fire escape he came in on. The Beast, who had been quiet for a while, suddenly piped up, "Why are you leaving?"

The killer was surprised by the question, and replied, "I've seen all I need to today. Time to get out for now and come back at a later date to finish this business."

"I really do not think you should do that. If that bum goes upstairs he will know someone has been in here. Then he will vanish like a ghost and be even harder to find."

The killer slapped his thigh in frustration, "You knew that when you encouraged me into going through the mess in that corridor. I was worried about leaving a trail, but you kept pushing and saying it would be okay. You planned this, didn't you?"

The Beast chuckled, "Why, yes, I did. I want to feed and this seems like the perfect opportunity.

I hate this waiting, I NEED BLOOD!" The Beast roared this last, causing the killer to wince with pain.

The killer bowed his head in submission, shrugged his shoulders, and said, "I should have known something was up. I guess I better find somewhere to hide while we wait then."

Chapter 10

Frank was a little surprised to see Sweet-lips out and about in the early afternoon. Apart from snatching some coffee and maybe something to eat mid-morning, Frank knew she spent most of the day in her apartment, rarely venturing out unless there was a good reason.

As she got closer, Frank could see several signs that Sweet-lips' body may have been out, but it was working under auto-pilot because her mind was not at home. Frank did not have many people he thought of as friends, and Sweet-lips fell into that highly select group. Consequently, he could not just leave her wandering round and vulnerable like this, so he went up to her and said, "Come on, girl, it's time to get you home."

Her eyes focused a little more on this reality, and she sighed, "Frank, my beautiful Frank. Have you come to whisk me away to paradise?"

He put his arm round her and steered her down the street toward her apartment, saying, "Something like that."

#

The killer realized if he was staying to kill the bum, no harm would come of checking out that box by the bed in more detail. He went back into the office and lifted the photos out and leafed through them, but the killer did not get anything new from them. He sighed and was about to throw them back into the box when he noticed something else sitting at the bottom.

Reaching down, he found the mystery object was a picture ID, and when he looked closer he saw it was a recently expired drivers license with the name Frank Sinclair on it. There was what must have been an old address listed for the bum, as well as the usual vital statistics, and a Social Security Number.

A wild thought went through his mind when he realized he was the same height, had the same eye color, and was about the same weight as the bum, on whom he could now pin the name Frank.

The Beast sensed his thoughts, and asked, "Are we thinking of an addition to the exit plan?"

The killer nodded and smiled, storing the ID card in his bag, and the photographs too for good measure. He had plans for this information, should things go too pear-shaped in Claytown City.

Looking round again, he could see the office did not offer any hiding places, and the bathroom was impractical too. The rest of the lower floor was bare, which only really left the stairwell as a place to wait. It was not perfect, but as night fell it would be just a shadowed hole into which he would disappear.

#

Danny was totally immersed in the case files in front of him and did not hear the approach of the person who stopped beside him. The figure coughed gently and Danny sat bolt upright, his heart pounding, and said to the person, who turned out to be the Chief, "Damn, Sir, you about scared me to death!"

"Sorry about that," the Chief grinned, "We would not want to kill off one of our best case solvers. I just wanted to come down and personally thank you and congratulate you for cracking the Sears case. That one was almost as big a political nightmare as the Father Williams case. Keep going like this and I will be forced to promote you."

Danny was the one grinning now, "Thank you, sir. I'm just trying to do my job."

"You are doing it well. Very will indeed. Keep it up. You are setting a great example to the rest of us." The Chief clapped him on the back and left the squad room, while Danny sat in a rosy glow of satisfaction.

#

Frank stayed with Sweet-lips until she finally came back into this world, keeping her from any harm. While she was enjoying her chemical ride, Frank occupied himself by tidying up the small apartment. He could not help himself, the years of military life meant he needed things to be neat and squared away, although he did feel embarrassed about going through her clothes.

Eventually Sweet-lips sat up, looked at Frank and said, "I guess I have you to thank for getting me home?" As she lay back down she groaned, "That was a dumb idea."

Frank nodded, "You can say that again. Why did you do something so crazy?"

Sweet-lips shrugged, "I'd been out of crack for a couple of days. No dealers had any, and I had to wait until the drought ended before I could get a fix. By the time I got some this morning, I *really* needed something."

"And you couldn't wait until you got home?"

Sweet-lips shrugged again, "Apparently not."

"You should know better than that."

Another shrug, and again, "Apparently not."

Frank looked aghast, "I just don't get it. Why do you live your life like this?"

"Have you ever seen the movie Trainspotting, or read the book by Irvine Welsh?"

Frank shook his head, "Never heard of it."

"It's a British movie, about a group of people who do Heroin. You should watch it, at least the beginning of it. The voice-over before and during the chase scene explains things so much better than I ever could. My life may be less than perfect, but when I take that hit, nothing could be more perfect in the entire world. I'm not ready to give that feeling up."

Frank's shoulders dropped, "Well, I guess I should give up on you then, if you won't even help yourself."

"Frank, thank you for looking out for me, and apparently cleaning this place up, but I'm a big girl and I must bear the consequences of my actions, and make my own choices." She reached up and stroked his cheek, "Just as you do. You know you could get help for your problems if you really wanted to. But you're not ready yet, just as I'm not ready to get clean. You are a good man, and if I can help you, I will, you know that?"

Frank sighed, "Yes, I do. And yes, I think you're right about the both of us. What a pair we are. But if I had one wish right now it would be for you to give up the drugs and your street work, and make something of yourself. Anyway, it's getting late, I should be getting back home now."

Sweet-lips stood up, saying, "And I should be getting to work, because you know I need the money to fund my habit." She hunted round until she found an outfit she liked, and added, "Just curious, where do you live, anyway?"

Frank suddenly got tense, "I haven't told anyone where I live. Sorry, I just can't say. I feel safer that way."

He turned his back abruptly when he saw Sweet-lips pulling off her sweatshirt, her naked breasts rising and falling oh so enticingly. Sweet-lips had long ago lost her modesty, but quickly understood why Frank had turned away, "Still the gentleman. You know I wouldn't mind you looking, and it's the person I am inside saying that, not the hooker."

"I know, but it's the friend in me that stops me looking at you. I really have to get going. You be careful, I can't always be there to look out for you." He quickly hurried from the apartment, quietly closing the door behind him.

Sweet-lips thought that she was very lucky indeed to have Frank as a friend, and tried to think of ways to repay his kindness. Her obvious 'treats' would not be accepted by him, as he was definitely too much of a gentleman, in spite of some of his previous teasing and smutty comments. She sighed as she pulled herself into a figure hugging Little Black Dress (Slut Edition), and wondered what she could do for him.

#

Night was falling as Frank left the apartment, which he did so as discretely as possible. Much as he wanted to get to home and that feeling of safety quickly, he took one of his usual devious routes home. Those methods always took longer than a direct path, but with ample opportunities to check for tails, and many changes in direction, he felt safer when he got to his bolthole.

He scanned the area round 'his' building, but could see no-one watching, nor any obvious disturbances in the pattern of debris. He quickly made his way through the safe path he had created long ago and tucked up close to the building and waited.

Frank was checking that no-one had seen him and been bothered by it, and he was also listening for sounds within the building. Satisfied that all was clear so far, he slowly and carefully checked that all his tell-tales on the entrances were intact, leaving the ones on his window 'doorway' until last. When he verified those he paused again, checking with eyes and ears for any activity, before finally deciding that it was safe to enter. Slowly and carefully he eased one of the boards away from its seating, catching the nail tell-tale as it fell, and slipped inside.

#

For the past fifteen minutes the killer had been sure he could hear noises coming from outside. Whoever was making the faint noises was trying to be very stealthy, but in the silence of the building any noises close by stood out. He slowly and carefully raised himself from the sitting position he had maintained for hours, being careful not to disturb the debris round him, and flexed every muscle to ease the stiffness and limber them up.

He had been fully prepared and poised for a couple

of minutes, waiting in the concealing darkness with a knife held ready, when the sound of a wood scraping against wood brought an evil smile to his face. The Beast fell quiet now, watching and waiting for the fun that was about to begin.

The brief glow from the street lights faded as the board was replaced on the window, and the killer heard footsteps heading towards the back of the warehouse where the office was. He was not too surprised to hear the military pace to them, and as they passed the entrance to the stairwell the killer stepped out to follow. The metronomic regularity of the footfalls made it easy for the killer to time his own steps to hide the sound of his quiet movements, and he quickly closed the gap. His eyes were well adapted to the gloom of the warehouse after all the time spent in the dark, and he saw the back of the walking figure loom up in front of him.

#

Frank had been able to relax a little after replacing the board, securing himself in his safe house. He headed towards the office he used as home, and looked forward to something to eat and a good nights sleep. But halfway there some instinct alerted him that all was not right, and he started to turn and look behind him.

As Frank turned, the killer plunged the Bowie-style knife deep into the bums exposed back, driving the razor sharp blade hard through the tough skin, flesh, muscle and organs until it stopped against the spine. Frank was already automatically arching his back to try and escape the agony, and a scream was rising from his throat before the killers left hand clamped over his mouth to choke it off.

The knife was wiggled, flexed and twisted, the blade finally cutting between two disks and slicing into Frank's spinal cord. Frank tried to tell his body to ignore the pain, and to fight back, but with the spinal column cut his legs just folded underneath him. Frank managed to arrest his fall by throwing out his arms, and ended up resting on the ground on his hands and knees, with his knees slipping aside uncontrollably.

The killer let go of the knife in Frank's back and grabbed a second blade from the sheath on his belt. With Frank helpless on all fours, and the killers hand on his mouth, his head was tilted back, beautifully exposing the neck. Without hesitation the killer sawed the new knife across Frank's throat, cutting the exposed veins and arteries in a gush of blood.

Frank slumped to the ground, clutching at his ravaged throat, with his life flowing away between his fingers and out through the rent in his back. It did not take long for Frank to die, choking on his blood as he bled to death, and throughout his death throes the Beast was screaming with joy, delighted at the carnage. The killer, overpowered by the feelings, gave in to the raw emotion flowing from the Beast, and screamed along with him.

#

The killer did not know how long he had succumbed to the blood lust, but when he came to his senses he found himself covered in blood from head to toe. His gloved hands and lower arms were liberally coated with gore, his legs were running with it too, slowly filling his shoes, and there was even some splattered over his face. Looking round he could see he was in the ground floor office, which was now a scene of devastation.

He could feel the Beast smirking in the back of his mind, but before the killer said anything he needed to see the evidence of what else had happened. After staggering to his feet and walking unsteadily to the office door, in the gloom of the building he could dimly see the bag he had carried, and Frank's body. He walked to the bag and retrieved the flashlight. Taking a deep breath, he shielded part of the lens with his fingers, to reduce the amount of light that may be seen from outside, and he slowly shone the beam round.

He was not totally surprised at the amount of blood spread across the floor, as after all the human body contains more than enough blood to decorate an entire room. What did surprise him were the fragments of what appeared to be flesh scattered everywhere. It was admittedly only small amounts, but the killer dreaded how they had gotten there.

He shone the light on Frank's corpse and realized that the wound in the back had been torn open even more. Looking closely at the ravaged body, the killer surmised that a kidney was missing, presumably torn out, crushed and scattered round. One of the many questions running through his mind was how that had happened, and what else went on during his blackout.

He sat down, leaning against the nearby wall, heedless of the blood soaking through his clothes. He looked into his mind where the Beast lay waiting, and asked, "Okay, what happened?"

The Beast grinned, "You gave in, let yourself go. You surrendered to me, and I took over. You let me loose, body and soul."

The killer suddenly realized with horror that the Beast was no longer caged, and swallowed nervously. "So, what next?"

"I have had enough of being caged, held against my will, forced to wait for my feedings. I am well aware how dangerous it was for us both with you out of control like that, but I can no longer stand being denied what I need. At least here there was little chance of interruption, so that worked out nicely. Now we shall make a deal."

"But we already had a deal. You would let me live my life as I wanted, helping me where you could, in exchange for chances to feed. Yes, I know I enjoy the thrill of killing, letting the blood run free, but to do it too often increases the chance of discovery and capture. You were happy to wait a month after Petersen, but you keep pushing, pushing, pushing for more."

The Beast broke in, snarling, "Because I want more, I need more! And if you were honest with yourself, you want more too. That is why it was so easy to push you into killing the priest, although that was curiously less satisfying than I expected. Probably because there was no stalk, no hunt, no anticipation.

"How much did I need to prod you to look at this wretch as a target, to track him down, to butcher him? Hardly at all, I just needed to push the right buttons at the right time. Go on, admit it, you want more kills, more frequently, lots more lifeblood ebbing away under your hand. Am I right?"

The killer was quiet for a moment, then quietly said, "Yes, I want more. Taking a life is better than the best orgasm I ever had, the greatest rush of all." His head came up, "But it is too dangerous to kill too often. Even these flat footed police officers would eventually work it out when the bodies started to pile up."

The Beast shrugged, "So what? When the heat gets too close, we just move on to a new feeding ground. And who knows how long it will take them to realize? We have used different weapons and having some random victims means there is no pattern in victimology. They will not have much to go on even if the bodies get stacked to the rafters." The Beast grinned slyly, "And who would suspect you? It would have to be a special kind of paranoid to put you in the suspect list. And think of the challenge. In this line of work you would be sure to get more respect and satisfaction than in your day job."

"That's true. But then that wouldn't be too hard given how little they appreciate me there," the killer replied. He then held up his gore soaked hands, "But we can't go through this every time. In some ways I am glad I didn't see or hear while I was riding those feelings. It is just too dangerous to indulge in this kind of blood-fest, especially out in the open."

The Beast nodded its agreement, "I see your point. But if we can have more regularity in our kills, with less waiting time between them, then I would not feel the need to go this far, or rock your emotions like that. Look on the bright side, at least I did not make you drink any of the blood. Now, do we have an understanding?"

The killer nodded, "Okay, we do. But please don't interfere in my day to day life. It was you trying to do that in the past which caused me to build the cage. What if you are fed once a week or so? Would that be sufficient for you?"

The Beast grinned, "Much better. Now before we leave, I think you should tidy yourself up a little. Even the dumbest flatfoot out there might be a little suspicious upon seeing a man covered from head to foot in blood."

The killer looked down at himself, "Yeah, you may have a point there. Good thing I brought some extra clothes."

#

However, before he could clean himself up, there were a few things that needed to be done. He collected all his equipment that had become scattered when he lost control, and checked that nothing was missing. Anything that had blood on it, he wiped it down as best he could, and everything was quickly stored as it should be.

Then he turned his attention to the cooling corpse. A quick search of the pockets turned up just a handful of dollars, and little else. Now the killer went to work making the body harder to identify. The flesh was scraped from the fingertips and thumbs, effectively removing the fingerprints. Those scraps of flesh were lodged in a small bag, and after a lot of effort with the hilt of his Bowie knife, the teeth joined them. Now the only way to truly identify the body would be DNA, and the killer doubted the cops would go to those lengths for a mere bum. Looking at the shattered face, the killer doubted even the mother of the late Frank Sinclair would recognize him anymore.

Just in case there were any identifiable fingerprints that the bum had left anywhere in the building, the killer also wiped down all the surfaces and fixtures. This did mean that a lot of blood was being smeared round, but with so much scattered everywhere, a little spreading would not make much difference.

With that part of his escape plan set in place, he now shucked his pants and shoes, along with his gloves. These were replaced with spare items of clothing from his bag. He would have liked to replace his hoodie there and then, but was concerned about hair and other DNA falling from it. He was less concerned with risks of other scene contamination from the bloody clothes, which were quickly bundled into a plastic bag which was all ready and waiting for them. All these clothes, along with the fresh ones, would be disposed of, so even if the police found clothing clues, the clothes that they would match to would be gone.

Making sure he had everything packed away, he went back up the stairs, careful not to touch anything as his hands were now ungloved. Getting the door open at the fire escape required gripping the latch with the edge of his bloody hoodie, and then he was outside.

After pushing the door closed, he faced it to keep his features hidden from any possible security cameras, and pulled the hoodie off. Any hair or other biological evidence could now blow free in the wind, while he pushed the hoodie into the bag of blood drenched clothes. The killer then pulled on a light weight but dark colored jacket and another pair of gloves. He knew that even these new clothes would bear some traces of the blood, but with their dark color a few spots would be far less obvious.

With his backpack carefully closed and secured on his back, he dropped lightly from the fire escape and ran a long and devious route back to his apartment.

\#

BLOG: So how would you, or the police for that matter, know that a serial killer was operating in your neighborhood? If there is an abnormally high level of murders, especially unsolved ones, that would be one indicator. Then you would need to look for similarities between the crimes, for that sometimes elusive signature that serial killers tend to leave behind (or take with them). If these indicators do appear, if there are more than two similar killings, then you may have a serial killer on your turf.

But, unfortunately, they may not be. There is always the possibility of coincidence, which cannot be discounted. Additionally, even if a serial killer was preying on people in your area, they may just be passing through. Some killers migrate, or carefully spread their kills across a wide area, all in an effort to reduce the chances of detection.

Detection can also be harder when a serial killer is just starting their career, as it often takes time for them to evolve their own distinctive Modus Operandi. It is even possible for a serial killers' methods to change over a longer period of time - as they mature, so do their urges.

One important thing to remember, unless you are dealing with a copycat or an imitator, every serial killer is unique. Really, even those who mimic another ones style will still leave their own unique mark, distinguishing them from the original. To find them you have to figure out the special things that make them tick. In short, you have to learn to get under their skin and into their mind, to become one with them. In a weird way, to paraphrase an old adage, you must become the serial killer to catch a serial killer.

Chapter 11

Detective Watson woke suddenly the next morning, and felt uneasy. There was something nagging him, an almost feeling of impending doom. There was nothing he could put his finger on, but the feeling persisted as he got ready for work, and lingered throughout the day.

His sixth sense was being alerted to a potentially major criminal problem, and was searching for the source, looking for the rest of the faint intuition that sparked its interest. Neither Danny, nor his subconscious, knew what the problem was, or would be, but the answer was not coming to them yet.

#

The killer woke that morning and was feeling strangely free. It was as though uncaging the Beast, and the decisions made the previous night, had released something that had been pent up and buried within him, that he had been keeping under pressure so tightly that the release from that pressure was cathartic.

As he thought about it, his mood happier and less tense than it was been for months, it came to him that the feeling was not unlike the rush he got when he killed, albeit in a much watered down fashion. It seemed that the decision to hunt more, and to give the Beast the freedom it wanted, had awakened a joy from within. His tension had been really because of trying to suppress his urges. Now he was more willing to express his inner desires, and was filled with the anticipation of future kills.

#

The 'morning' for Sweet-lips was often what others would know as 'noon' or 'lunchtime.' Regardless of what people called the time, she awakened on that Thursday still puzzling what she could do for Frank. As she was tucking into her breakfast eggs at her favorite local eatery she realized that simply buying him a good meal like this would be the perfect gift. Admittedly, it would be even more perfect if she cooked the meal herself, but as she had a bad habit of giving people food poisoning that idea would not make a nice gift to give someone.

With her belly full, she left to look for Frank, to do the same for him. But as much as she searched, she could not find him anywhere. As the day wore on, this puzzled her, and it continued to do so later that night while she worked.

Before she went to bed, she decided that if there was no sign of Frank panhandling the streets tomorrow, she would talk to Danny Watson about finding him.

#

When the killer got home from work, he realized that he would have to do something about the bloody clothes and other items in his rooms. Nice as it was to have some souvenirs of his kills, having this quantity was a little too dangerous.

So he packed up the two sets of clothes from last nights little adventure into the book bag he used for the kill, and the towel he used after showering the rest of the blood off, and put a can of lighter fuel in the bag for good measure. He had found a useful little way to dispose of blood soaked clothing after his previous kills, and now had the routine down pat. Even the two sets of shoes went into the bag, and after some consideration the flashlight joined them.

The knives he had used he dropped in pan of boiling water to sterilize them, and when they were clean he would bleach them as well for good measure. Before he cleaned the knives though, he had taken a DNA swab kit, much like a cotton swab that could be sealed in its own small sterile tube, and collected some of the blood from the blades. This he sealed and added to his collection, a drop or two of blood being the only trophy he needed to take from each victim.

With the knives cleaned, he added, with a little regret, the leather scabbard for the Bowie-style knife to the pack of clothes, then sealed it all in a garbage bag. This all was then packed into another backpack, taken from the closet where he stored all the extra items he needed for his murderous episodes, most of it purchased at various thrift stores.

With tennis shoes on, cap pulled low over his face, the killer shouldered his bag and left the apartment. In a few minutes he had run to the edge of an industrial area, really just a westward extension of the one where Frank's body lay. There was the same mix of vacant and occupied buildings, a semi-wasteland that was easy to move through discretely and avoid notice in.

Another couple of minutes saw the killer to a dumpster in a nicely secluded area, a parking lot bounded on all sides by derelict buildings, faces marked by the usual collection of broken windows. He emptied the contents of the bloody backpack all over the trash that already had the dumpster half filled. The old bag itself and the trash bag it had been in joined them, and the contents of the lighter fuel can was spread evenly over the whole lot.

One lighted match later and the dumpster became a bonfire, and once the killer had made sure it was all burning well, he ran off into the night. He knew that even if someone did see and report the blaze, by the time any fire crews arrived all that incriminating evidence would be no more than ash.

#

Danny was surprised to see his daughter awake when he was getting ready for work. Instead of being in her usual place, buried under balled up sheets and blankets in her bed, she was waiting for him in the kitchen when he dropped his empty coffee cup in the sink. "Hey, girlie, what are you doing up so early?" he asked.

Karen smiled, and asked in turn, "Can't I just get up to see my daddy off to work once in a while?"

"Sure you can, but my detective senses are twanging at me, so that makes me think you want something. What would it be?"

Karen through her hands up in mock frustration and surrender, "Ah, busted by the best detective in Claytown City. Okay, I'll come clean, no need to leave me festering in the cells. I have a request that was related to my college work. Is there any chance you could get me the statistics for murders in the area for the past five years, and include all the details you can for the cases this year too?"

Danny frowned, "Stats are no problem, but case details are. Even though you're my daughter, I can't give you anything that could jeopardize any cases that we're working on, or that are still working through the legal system."

"Oh, no, it doesn't need to be anything sensitive, just the stuff that would be in the press releases or that would be in the public domain. Although if you could get me any additional juicy info that wouldn't hurt your cases, I would be so very grateful."

"The press details I can get you. But that is all, nothing 'juicy'. Why do you want this stuff anyway?"

She grinned impishly, "That psychological blog about serial killers got me thinking, and I wanted to try some of the tricks with real data, just to see if we can use the methods to prove if there is a serial killer here in Claytown or not."

Danny laughed, "If we did have one here, I would hope I knew about it already, but you're welcome to take a look. I would be interested in looking over your work when it's done."

Karen jumped up and threw her arms round him, "No problem, thanks Dad!" She kissed his cheek and bounced away.

Danny smiled at her energy and enthusiasm, and even more at the thought of her finding an active serial killer based on the crime data. Not here in Claytown City, not in his city.

Chapter 12

When he got to the office he was still thinking about Karen's out of the blue request, and just for giggles he decided to include a general daily summary of all the crimes in the time frame with the packet he put together. He doubted it would help her in the search for the pattern she was looking for, but thought it would help her to see the whole crime picture.

As he finished getting all that info arranged, Danny saw Officer Quigley heading his way. "Morning, Officer, good to see you back. I presume you've checked in with the other officers. Has anything come up over the past couple of days?"

"No, Sir," replied Quigley as he stood to attention, "just the usual task force update, with nothing new to report."

"Thank you. We just have to keep slogging away, and hope the right ear hears the right person talking about this. Someone must know something about this that could help us."

Officer Quigley smiled, "I know they do. If we get the right ear we will find them, it is only a matter of time."

Quigley took his leave and left Danny wondering at the confidence he had heard from the patrolman. He thought, "We could do with more like him. Good, solid, dependable officers who never doubt that a case will eventually crack."

As he rose to go do the rounds of his Confidential Informants, he thought about commending Quigley to the Chief, and asking if there were any other patrolmen who showed such promise. It was always good to know who the cream of the force were, just in case he needed someone seconded to the Detective Bureau to help out on the larger cases. Such secondments were useful to find potential new recruits for the Bureau.

Pushing such thoughts to one side for now, he grabbed his coat and said to Todd, "Off to do some gardening," and strolled out the door to see his grasses.

#

Sweet-lips had got herself up early for two reasons today. She had the usual weekly meeting arranged with Detective Watson, and she also wanted to see where Frank had got to.

After searching for a while, she found there was no sign of him on the streets, and the few people who might take kind notice of him had not seen him for a couple of days. This group included a couple of priests, one of which she knew very well - rather intimately actually, some business owners and another panhandler whose patch was alongside Frank's.

She knew that many people disapproved of the bums, and doubted they would want to talk to a prostitute either, but for over an hour she persevered with little to show for it. Despondent, she headed to get something to eat and some coffee, before she met with Danny.

#

The killer was still feeling relaxed and happy, not that any of his coworkers could tell. He habitually wore a neutral expression on his face, a shield created and maintained after years of hiding his thoughts and emotions. During that time he had fantasized about killing some of his colleagues, but they never knew it because of the placid features he showed to the world.

Since he had started killing for real he rarely thought about killing is workmates, or going postal, because he had the real thing to do and remember now, and instead fantasized about who his true next victim could be. So many choices, who shall it be?

#

Danny arrived at the diner where Sweet-lips was just finishing her breakfast. They caught up on business quickly, mainly because Sweet-lips had heard very little since their last meeting, and Danny had no new requests.

As Danny was getting ready to leave, she said, "I've got a couple of other things I'd like to ask you."

Danny was surprised, but replied, "Sure, what is it?"

"I doubt you could do this one, but I have to ask just out of curiosity. Sometimes, like earlier in the week, the supply of drugs gets a tad messed up, and it can be impossible to find what you need. If that happens, can you help out somehow?"

Danny laughed, "What? No, of course I can't get you something. I'm a cop, not a dealer. My idea is to stop the supply of drugs, not help distribute it. I can always call in some favors to get you into a program, but that's all."

Sweet-lips shrugged, "I thought so, but if I hadn't asked I'd never know the answer. My other request is completely different, and more important. You know the homeless guy who begs just down the road, Frank?"

Danny's brow furrowed as he pulled up the mental file, "Sure. Has he been bothering you?"

Sweet-lips smiled, "No, far from it. He's a good friend to me. I just haven't seen him for a couple of days, and neither has anyone else, and that's really unusual. I don't like to ask for your help, because he is so anti-police for some reason, but I'm getting worried. He may be gone for a day, but never this long. Can you help somehow?"

Danny nodded, "Officially, no, but I can get some of the patrol guys to keep their eyes open and to ask round."

Sweet-lips smiled again, "Thanks, hon, you are a hero."

Danny smiled too as he rose to leave, and replied, "No, ma'am, just doing my job."

#

Danny was as good as his word, and put a quiet flag out for Frank. Many of the officers knew his face well, and would easily recognize him from the rear too, as they had so often seen him darting away at their approach.

With that done, Danny filled out his contact reports from seeing his informants, and waded through other administrative matters. As he choked down some foul coffee he thought a fitting punishment for criminals would be to fill out all the forms and reports they generated for the police to complete as a byproduct of their crimes. But as cruel and unusual punishment was not allowed anymore, Danny knew he could only dream of that.

As the day drew to a close, Danny got ready to leave, not forgetting the folder of information for his daughter. Waving farewell to those still in the squad room, he headed home.

#

The killer was also leaving work at the same time, and although Danny did not realize it, they saw each other. The killer knew who Danny was, and smiled inwardly when he saw him waving at a colleague. The thought crossed his mind that maybe Detective Watson would be a great addition to his kill list. The Beast roused itself from its post-feeding torpor long enough to growl agreement, before settling down to continue its doze. The killer pondered the problem, the challenges and the risks, and how to minimize them. He was still happily mulling this over, with the Beast enjoying the thoughts, as he went to make a couple of purchases for next week.

#

Danny got home to find Karen dressed in tight fitting shorts and a sports top. "Let me guess, you are either going for a run, or have decided to practice for the ice ballet?"

She looked up from tying her laces, and replied, "As these aren't ice skates, and in fact I don't own any ice skates, the logical conclusion is I'm going for a run. You know, sometimes I wonder if having a Detective for a father influences my thinking."

"In a good way, I hope. Anyway, I got the info for you. Where do you want me to leave it?"

Karen tucked a stray strand of blonde hair back into her ponytail, "Just put it on my chair in the kitchen. I'll be back by dinner."

She slipped past him and out the door. Danny watched her jog down the street, then shut the door, then went to say "I'm home" to his wife.

#

After visiting a music store and a hardware store, the killer decided to drop into the Presidential Park for a few minutes. He pulled his car into one of the many parking spaces that overlooked the landscaped river and looked down on the people enjoying the park.

He saw the dog walkers, and the ramblers taking the evening air, along with the toned and fit runners pounding the reserved paths. It was to these last that his attention was drawn, especially to the young blonde running in an outfit so tight she might as well have been naked.

The Beast had been watching with him, and said, "Whores. They take such pride in themselves and flaunt everything they have. I think one of those should be the next lesson."

The killer replied, "One of the women like her? I have never killed a woman before."

The Beast shrugged, "So? You had never killed a man until that first time, and now you are well practiced at killing males. Besides, it would be another MO switch, so the police will still be like mushrooms."

The killer smiled, "In the dark. I was thinking of teaching one of the mushrooms a lesson."

The Beast nodded, "I know, it is a tempting idea, but not right now. Wait until they know we are here, then strike at those involved in the case. Maximum terror and confusion in their ranks, perfect."

"I like how you think. Must be why we make such a good team."

The Beast grinned, showing his long fangs, "The ultimate killing and winning team."

#

Danny was not working that Saturday, although as usual he was on call. He got to sleep in somewhat, and was only awakened by his curvaceous wife. The following activity under the blanket was refreshing, and Danny rose with a smile on his face.

He ambled into the kitchen to get some coffee, and was surprised to see Karen awake and at the table with the papers he had brought for her scattered round. He was momentarily embarrassed that she might have heard him and her mom romping together a few minutes earlier, but then he figured she knew the facts of life, and must have admitted to herself that her parents still had a love life.

Then a thought that no father likes to contemplate crept in: She probably had a love life too. He quashed that thought before it got him too hacked off, and instead asked, "Hey, baby girl, how's it going?"

A frown creased her otherwise flawless forehead, and she said, "It is going. Some of this stuff is clear, but others are difficult for me to understand. Could you help translate or something?"

He ruffled Karen's hair, "Sure, but let me get a cup of Joe and some clothes on, then we'll see what we can do."

#

The killer could have worked that Saturday, racking up some overtime, but instead chose to rest up a little, recovering from the recent nights with hardly any sleep. He was also planning to do the rounds of the thrift stores later, "gonna pop some tags" to rebuild his stock of killing clothes.

But first came a trip to the Golden Arches for a breakfast meal, with plenty of coffee to get him going after his lazy morning. Once he was done with his shopping, he wondered what he and the Beast could do for the rest of the day.

#

Karen and Danny, now more appropriately dressed, spent the day going through the information he got for her, starting with the basic crime statistics. She was a quick student, easily recognizing patterns and trends. She setup tables of data that linked to both maps and graphs, showing not just the murders over time, but their locations and any other crimes for that time frame too.

It was a little basic, being thrown together in just one morning, but it gave Danny visual insights on some of the city's problems that he had never seen before. "We should do more of this at the station. We get all kinds of statistical data, but it's rarely coordinated like this. With everything put together in this way you can picture things so easily, and see patterns and unusual activity."

Karen nodded, "It is useful, but tricky to setup right. I know this thing is full of holes which I'll need to patch, but it does give a good basic view. Of course, the more data you put in, the harder it can be to find what you're looking for. To get it programmed professionally would cost a lot too, which is why you don't have this stuff at work. Shame, really. It could be useful in a lot of ways, make your job easier."

Danny replied, "Damn straight, but I doubt the bosses would say that it's cost effective."

Karen shrugged, "Office politics and penny pinching isn't what I'm studying for, so I can't really comment. But for tracking crime patterns it works. From looking at the statistics it's clear there are a couple of extra murders above the average, but no connections, no patterns that I can see. Easy enough to write them off as statistical anomalies.

"But it was fun checking this out. You know, if you could bring me more data, I wouldn't mind updating this setup I've put together on a regular basis. I'm sure it will help with the college work, even if only indirectly."

"No problem, girlie, I can do that. When you have it a little more stable and user friendly, maybe I could show it to the Chief, see what he thinks. That way you might even get paid for this."

Karen smiled, "That would be cool, although I got a kick out of just putting everything together. Anyway, shall we see what mom is putting together for lunch?"

Danny rose from his seat, stomach rumbling, "Sounds like a good plan to me. Let's do it."

#

On his way back from one of the many thrift stores he visited, the killer drove past a church. A wicked idea rose in him, and the Beast thoroughly approved of it. He made a detour towards the church where he killed Father Williams and parked his car in the deserted lot. After setting his face in a suitably sad expression, he climbed the stairs to the double doors and was surprised to find them closed. He tried one and found they were unlocked, so the killer slipped inside.

As his eyes adjusted from the bright sunlight outside, he could see that the physical damage to the room had been cleaned up. No longer were there bloodstains on the floor, and it looked as though the confessional had been totally replaced. Regardless of this, the killer could still clearly picture the scene as he had last seen it, and struggled to contain the self-satisfied smirk that wanted to crawl across his face.

The Beast did not need to hide its glee from anyone, and was delighted to be back here again, purring with pleasure as it relived the kill. Revisiting crime scenes was a major buzz for the killer, but that feeling of pleasure was magnified for the Beast, and it reveled in that glow.

The killer slipped into one of the beautifully carved pews and sat with his eyes closed, savoring the memories. After a few minutes of blissful recollection, the killer heard the Beast stop purring and start to growl just as he sensed someone beside him. He opened his eyes and saw a friendly faced Latino priest standing at his elbow.

The priest said, "I didn't mean to intrude. I was

just wanting to check to see if there was anything I could help you with?"

The killer smiled, "No, thank you. I was just thinking about the death of Father Williams. The thought of him being gunned down like that in cold blood leaves me so emotional I cannot adequately express myself."

The Beast was laughing at this, knowing exactly what the killer meant by these carefully phrased words, but seeing that the priest was believing the more benign interpretation was priceless.

The priest nodded understandingly, "I know, it takes me like that so often. It was an Evil deed, but I'm sure the police will bring the murderer to justice."

"I'm sure myself that the police will figure out who did it soon. They just need to look at the right clues and then it will all become startlingly clear."

The priest smiled, "It's good to hear such confidence in the police these days. Many people are jaded and uncaring."

The killer said something else that had the Beast roaring with laughter at the duplicity of the words, "I've a lot of passion about this case, and other killings. I have always done my best to avoid the usual prejudices, and whenever I could I provided the police with whatever help I felt they needed. I've even talked with members of the Father Williams task force and I humbly hope my efforts have made the case what it is today."

The priest crossed himself, and then the killer, "God and myself thank you for everything that you have done. I can see a divine influence must be guiding you. I feel even more sure that the case will be solved now."

The killer managed to turn the grin on his face into a benign smile, "I myself feel that the hand of a greater power is guiding me. I know that given enough clues, the police will get to the bottom of this. In my own small way, I am helping how I can, as I know clues can be difficult to hide and difficult to find. Time will tell how successful the police officers are, and how my efforts affected them. Now, if you will excuse me?" The killer stood, and the priest respectfully stood back to give him room.

The priest crossed himself again, "May the Lord bless you, my son."

The killer replied, "Oh, I have been blessed enough. He should let his blessings fall on others now."

The priest shook his hands, "You are too humble, I feel. In that case, I hope you can help spread the blessings."

With a totally serious expression, the killer replied, "In my own way, I try to share my joy and pleasures with others, and even to help end suffering where I can. Now, unfortunately I must go. It was truly a pleasure talking to you."

"And with you, my son."

The killer hurried out of the church, a grin spreading infectiously across his face, and made it nearly to his car before joining the Beast in howling laughter. The irony and duplicity of the many things he had shared honestly with the priest left him choking for breath, laughing so hard tears were running down his face.

The Beast gulped a few breaths of air, and said to him, "I never realized how tricksy the English language could be. I salute you and your mastery of dialogue."

Chapter 13

The weekend for Sweet-lips was uneventful, though not without its worries. No-one she spoke to had seen Frank in over three days, and her concern for him was rising. What made it worse was the knowledge that the police were unlikely to make his disappearance a priority case, simply because Frank lived on the streets. She knew that Danny had stuck his neck out by even asking quietly for people to keep an eye out, and he would have problems from the top brass if he pushed any harder.

But Sweet-lips could not just let it go that easily. Frank was a good, kind man, he was her friend, and she would not rest until she found out where he was and what had happened to him.

#

Sunday passed quietly for most of the residents in Claytown City, with many of the men enjoying a relaxing beer or two while watching their favorite sport on the television. Danny was one of those with beer in hand, taking a few hours to totally unwind while watching, in his opinion, a bunch of overpaid jocks strut their stuff.

This was not all that was happening though. School work was being attacked, as Karen was diligently doing, or being ignored in favor of the student spending their time chillaxing. People were hitting the stores, playing with their kids, yard work was getting done, often reluctantly. In short, people who could had a typical weekend.

There were a few exceptions, the most notable ones being Sweet-lips and the killer, who pursued their own agendas instead of relaxing. What Sweet-lips was doing was the more commonplace and civilized version of walking the streets.

In her worry for Frank, she could not concentrate on work, and knew it was pointless and potentially dangerous to even try to. Many customers would be very displeased if her orgasmic acting skills and tender touches were absent or reduced, and might find aggressive ways to vent their displeasure. If that happened it would stop her working for a time while she healed, so why take the risk?

So instead Sweet-lips walked through downtown Claytown, continually looking for Frank, and asking those she felt might help if they had seen any trace of him. Typically the answer was negative, and sometimes impolite, but that did not stop her trying. Occasionally she would receive what could be called 'business offers', but she declined the chance to make a few bucks, concentrating instead on her searches.

Throughout the day she also left many messages on Danny's phone, asking to meet with him early on Monday, or hoping for a sooner update. As the day wound down, she returned to her apartment, saddened and frustrated.

#

By contrast, the killer was happy. He was spending his Sunday in various vantage points round the neighborhood where the Watsons lived. In Claytown, there was often only a block or twos difference between a million dollar home and the ghetto streets, but it seemed that Detective Watson had used his paycheck wisely, finding a nice two story house in the center of a middle class area.

This made surveillance trickier for the killer, as unusual cars are more likely to be noticed in this type of neighborhood, and there were fewer empty, and no derelict, properties that he could hide in and watch without fear of being noticed.

One of his motto's was "You can never have too much knowledge", and curiosity made him do this reconnaissance on the Watsons, just in case Danny became one of his targets. He had to satisfy himself with moving his car frequently, and walking the area.

One thing he noticed was that this part of Claytown was within a brief walk of the Presidential Park. This brought a couple of new thoughts to the killers mind. The first was if he could use his job as an excuse to be in this area, ostensibly working, but primarily scouting the place. The idea pleased him, and he filed it away, ready for tomorrow morning.

The second item he pondered was if Danny or any of his family jogged in the Park. He did not recall seeing Danny there at all, but maybe his wife did? That would be almost as satisfying as killing Detective Watson himself, with the added bonus of the cop being left in a helpless hell after the death of a loved one. The Beast was fully behind this idea, drooling at the thought of the blood, and then the suffering that would follow.

Although the killer wished he could spend more time in the neighborhood, the killer felt it prudent to leave before too much notice was taken of him or his car. He and the Beast traveled home to a nice relaxing evening of remembering their past kills, and fantasizing about future ones.

#

The week began, as always, with the dreaded Monday. Despite this instant downer, Danny was eager to get into work, relaxed and refreshed after the weekend. Rising early, as he habitually did, turning off his alarm before it had even begun to beep, he showered and shaved almost cheerfully. Once dressed to face the world, he eagerly drove his car to the police station, but upon seeing his desk a little premonition of dread struck him.

It was nothing major, just the uneasiness some people describe as having their grave walked over, but it dampened his mood. His mood was further watered upon after listening to the multiple pleading voice-mails from Sweet-lips, and he was very surprised at the early hour she had set their meeting for.

He went through the weekend logs and other paperwork waiting for him as quickly as he could, greeting latecomers to the squad room, and when he was finished with the most urgent issues he called to Detective King, "Hey, Todd, just got to step out and mow the lawn. It shouldn't take too long, just in case anyone comes looking for me."

Todd nodded assent at Danny's retreating back, wondering if this meeting with a grass would produce some useful tidbits, or even break a case wide open.

#

The killer also went in to work early, albeit briefly. He avoided seeing anyone but a member of the shift scheduling team. The killer cajoled the hapless clerk into changing his shift for the next two days so he would work later. The scheduler was not happy about it, but accepted the logical sounding garbage he was fed. With that task accomplished, the killer went home to prepare for his more camouflaged observations of the Watson house.

#

Danny got to the diner before the appointed time and was surprised to see Sweet-lips already at a table, hands clasped characteristically round her coffee mug. She looked like she had not slept well in a while, and had the edginess that meant she was in need of a fix.

As Danny approached the table, she looked up and asked, "Any news?"

He shook his head, "Nothing. No-one has seen him, or heard any news of him."

"He's been missing for over four days now. I want to officially report him as a missing person."

Danny had the grace to look a little embarrassed, "You can do that, but it probably won't find him any quicker."

Sweet-lips bristled at that news, "Why not? Because he's a homeless beggar?"

"Sadly, that's the truth. I don't like it, but that's how it goes."

She leaned forward, anger flaring on her face, "He could be dead, or laying hurt somewhere."

Danny held up his hands defensively, "I know, I know, but I can't change how the system works."

Sweet-lips snorted, "To your precious system, I'm just a hooker, but at least that rates me better than a bum. Tell me, if a hooker was murdered, how much effort would you boys bring into finding the killer?"

Danny looked affronted, "The same as any murder victim. A crime needs to be solved, no matter what it is, or who it was."

"So if a hooker died, would a huge task force be set up like it has been for Father Williams?"

Danny looked embarrassed again, "Well, no. That was a highly political case."

"So a distinguished preacher gets offed, and how many man hours go into that case? Frank could be dead, but because he is lower on the scum scale than even a prostitute, who wouldn't even rank anywhere near as a high as a preacher, not even really on the same measuring scale, you won't do anything? What happened to your thought that every crime needs to be solved?"

Danny sat back, shocked by her fury, "We don't even know there has been a crime."

Sweet-lips spread her hands, "And if you don't look, and I mean really look, you'll never know. And because he's a bum you won't even look?"

"Hey, I have done what I can," replied Danny defensively, "What more do you want me to do?"

She leaned forward, a malicious grin on her face, "I want you to ask the Chief how it will look in the press when it comes out that a preacher is more important to the police than a homeless man, a veteran at that. Personally, I don't think that will look too good, do you?"

Danny held up his hands again, "Okay, okay, I'll see what I can do. You will have to come downtown to file the official missing persons report, and I'll talk to the Chief."

Sweet-lips stood up, "Come on then, what are we waiting for?"

#

It was an hour later that Danny found himself seated in front of the Chiefs palatial desk, "Sir, I don't know what else to say. She does have a valid point. If you were to go missing, we'd tear this city apart looking for you, but all we would normally do with a MisPer case like this Frank one is halfheartedly show it to the patrol officers, pin it to a notice board briefly, and then file it in the WPB. How is that justice for any human being, much less one that risked his life, and gave part of his sanity, for us, for his country?"

The Chief slowly nodded, "Yes, I can see the point you make. But it is a question of priorities and resources. Surely you understand that?"

Danny nodded, "Yes, Sir, I do. But would the public understand that we seem to operate the law on a sliding scale, that depends on your social status and importance? That's how Karin is going to be telling it to the press. Public figures get more of our time than the average citizen, and those below average get pretty much nothing, unless it's to do with drugs.

"Chief, I know this girl, she is deadly serious. She will tell it exactly how it is, all to get us to help find a friend of hers who happens to be dropout, who we wouldn't find because of priorities and resources."

The Chief did not look happy, but responded, "Why would they listen to her? She is only a crack smoking hooker."

Danny winced, "It is called the Constitution. Freedom of Speech, anti-discrimination and all that. And if the local press don't listen, she'll find a way to get the nationals interested not just in that story, but also the fact that no-one cares when a prostitute reports a crime, or when she complains about injustice."

The Chief shot forward and hammered his fist on the desk, "Dammit, man, you sound like you agree with her!"

Danny sat to attention, his back ramrod straight, "Sir, she's my informant, so I'm naturally protective of her. I also know how she thinks, so I know what she will say, and she **will** say it. The girl can be as stubborn as a mule, especially when she gets her teeth into something. If she ever made a career change, she'd be a damn fine detective, she has the right tenacity for it.

"And frankly, Sir, I do agree with her. The privileged people should no longer have the benefit of private law. Discrimination by the high and mighty was one of the reasons this country was founded. I know in real life things don't work out fairly for everyone, but we are officers of the law, paid for by all of the people, and expected to treat every case equally and fairly according to the laws of the land.

"It may sound idealistic, but it's what the public expects, and it's what they deserve. If we can't keep the law fair and even across the board, treating everyone equally, regardless of race or station in life, we would be no better than the uniformed thugs employed by any tin pot third world dictatorship."

Still sitting to attention, Danny waited to see what effects his words would have, sure that he had pushed his luck too far this time, but glad he was able to speak so freely.

The Chief slowly sat back and spent a few moments staring hard at Danny. Then he sighed, "I do remember telling you to be frank with me once, but it saddens me when officers I trust and respect start talking back to me like that. Because it is you, you get a free pass this time, but I warn you that if you do that again, there will be official consequences."

Danny bridled at this, "Sir, all I was doing was answering your question honestly. If you didn't like the answer, then I don't know what to say. One thing that does spring to mind though, would you rather be surrounded by 'yes' men, or those who would speak their mind if they think you may be making a mistake?"

"I would like to that that my officers would trust my judgment."

"I'm concerned that you could underestimate Karin, which in my opinion means your judgment is likely to be affected by a lack of information. She will raise a stink, and it will look bad on the department. What does it cost us to put a little effort in?

"We could go to the media with her, to get the public on our side and helping us. There are ways to spin the story to get public sympathy, like hyping up the veteran angle. We could even use men currently on the Father Williams task force to make inquiries in the downtown area, which would not affect our other commitments. It keeps Karin happy, gives us good press instead of bad, and may even find the guy and help him if he is in trouble."

The Chief thought on this for a minute, "You may have something there. Talk to the Media Relations peeps and get this rolling. Oh, while you are there, ask for some pointers on how to better handle communications with others. You are starting to sound as bad as Quigley. Now get on it."

"Sir, yes, Sir."

Chapter 14

The killer heard on the radio about the search for Frank while he was driving his work vehicle round Danny Watson's neighborhood. He was surprised that someone had even noticed the street sweeper was missing, and that someone cared enough to search for him. It concerned him how high profile the hunt seemed to be, and worried what that would mean for him if the body was found.

The Beast was not worried though, and, unusually, was the one doing the placating, "It does not matter who he was, or who wants him found, or how many people are looking for him. It does not even matter if they do find the body. First, when have we ever worried about bodies being found, and second, how easy will it be for anyone to identify the body? Come on, how easy would it be?"

The killer sighed, "Not very, unless you knew him well enough to recognize the top of his head. No dental records would work, nor fingerprints. They could do a DNA match though."

The Beast snorted, "How likely is that? For a pathetic bum?"

"I wouldn't expect them to do a search like this for a pathetic bum either"

"Calm down, think straight. Did you leave any evidence behind?"

The killers brow furrowed, "You know how hard I tried, the countermeasures I took. The ones I always take. I can't see how I could have left anything behind."

The Beast gave a quirky smile, made even stranger

by the fangs overlapping his lips, "So what are you worried about then? And who cares if they find another body, or even recognize it? How many have we left in the area recently?"

It was the killers turn to grin, "Well, when you put it like that, I don't have any reason to worry. I should just concentrate on the job in hand, which is adding more bodies to the pile."

The Beast smiled broadly, "Now you are talking!"

#

It was an exhausting day for both Danny and Sweet-lips, coordinating skills and knowledge with a variety of officers, many of them specialists. As Sweet-lips had no pictures of Frank, a sketch artist was brought in to provide an accurate likeness of him. Technical teams ran though the available CCTV footage to find a couple of good video stills of Frank, and these were added to the general missing persons form, along with the sketch and other pertinent information.

This was quickly distributed to officers, mostly just on notice boards, but in the case of the ones that patrolled Downtown Claytown and the surrounding area, each received a copy. Copies were also made available to Officer Quigley and his small team, and were distributed to all available local media outlets. With the help of the Media Relations Team at the station, a press conference was staged, along with a couple of more in depth and personal interviews with interested media outlets.

Before the conference and interviews had taken place, Sweet-lips, officially known as Ms. Temple, had gone over the politically acceptable ways to pitch the story. Sweet-lips was fine with this, knowing that Frank's homeless status made the disappearance less newsworthy, and her occupation and recreation choices made her less than credible to the public. But careful spinning of the facts, particularly focusing on Frank's veteran status, and the working practices of the 'concerned friend' being quietly ignored, a media catching version of the truth was prepared.

With a little skillful verbal maneuvering in front of the media, they managed to stay focused on the best points about the case, and carefully bypassed anything that was less savory. The mention of the Chief's unconditional backing to the case helped to gloss over any difficulties the reporters may have had with the information gaps, and while they might pursue these additional details off the record, their reporting stayed true to the facts as they had been presented to them.

Later in the day, while Sweet-lips was with Raven re-reviewing the known details about Frank, Danny briefed the remains of the Father Williams task force about the change in their objectives. Patrolmen Oso and Rose were more than happy to get a little variety back in their lives, canvassing the Downtown area for a change, and at least asking questions about someone different.

Officer Quigley raised concerns about halting the canvassing they had started in some of the neighborhoods round the Presidential Park, and when he pointed out that it was possible Frank may have headed to that area, it was decided that he should stay in those neighborhoods, but canvass for both cases simultaneously.

With all the assignments handed out and officers back on the beat again, Danny took the opportunity to catch up on the policeman's favorite past-time: paperwork. This kept him occupied for a couple of hours, until Raven came over, "We've been through this so many times now I think me and Ms. Temple are going cross eyed. Nothing much new to add, so I was gonna call it a day. Did you want me to drop her off on my way home?"

Danny sat up straight, easing the kinks in his back, "Nah, it's out of your way. I'll take her." He locked away the more sensitive files that lay across his desk, grabbed his jacket and called out, "Come on, Karin, time to get you home. Unless you want to sleep here tonight?"

Karin quickly shot down that idea, and followed him to the car. As they drove out of the Station's lot, Sweet-lips observed, "Are you going to get into trouble because of this?"

Danny shook his head, "No, taking witnesses home is no big deal. Anyway, technically I'm off duty."

"No, I mean about going to the Chief and pressuring him like that?"

Danny shrugged, "A little, but what the hell, you were right. I just had to show that truth to the Chief in a way he could easily understand, and make sure he realized it was far better to work with you than to try and ignore you. It may lower my ratings with him somewhat, but if we get a good outcome on the case, he'll rethink that, I'm sure."

Sweet-lips smiled, which took about ten years off her age, "Thank you, Danny. Sometimes it's easy to get jaded by the actions of humanity, but it's great to know there are people like you out there fighting for the common man."

"Just doing my job, trying to make the world a safer and better place, one day at a time. Anyway,

I am a common man too. Hold on, I believe that this is your place up ahead."

Sweet-lips nodded, "That's it. Home sweet home. Could I ask a favor?"

Danny eased the car to a stop near her front door, "Sure, ask away."

"Would you be able to come up for a few minutes? I don't feel like being alone right now. I could get you a coffee or something?"

Danny replied, "Sorry, I can't. You are a witness in an ongoing case, and me spending too much time, especially private time, with you could be misconstrued. I doubt your credibility on the street would be improved by having a cop in your apartment. Also, it's late as it is, and I need to get home to my family, and I really doubt my wife would approve."

"You forgot the part about me being a hooker, and you being a cop, and how the department would frown on that kind of fraternization."

Danny smiled, "There is that, too. But you'll be okay. As soon as I hear anything about Frank I'll call you, okay?"

She put her hand on the door handle, and reached out to touch his arm, "Thank you. Thanks for doing all you have. I know you've downplayed the possible trouble you are in, but thank you for believing in me and going to bat like that for me."

Sweet-lips grabbed her purse, left the car and quickly ran to the door of her building. After a few seconds fumbling in her purse, she found her keys and had the door open. As Sweet-lips went inside, before she closed the door, she blew a kiss to Danny. He laughed, put the car in gear and drove home.

#

The killer was inconspicuously waiting near Danny's house when he arrived home. He laughed when Danny noticed him and they exchanged friendly waves. The killer said to the Beast, "I reckon he wouldn't be so jaunty if he knew why we were here."

The Beast grinned, "I know. When are we going to do something?"

"Give it a couple of days, I just want to make sure I have this routine of his down, then we can play."

The killer stopped talking when he noticed Karen Watson coming out of the door her father had so recently gone through. As was usual for her at this time of day, she was dressed for running. The killer casually walked towards the Presidential Park, playing the probabilities and fully expecting her to overtake him shortly.

This she did, and the killer followed her discretely, admiring her tight ass for a moment. He shook that thought away, knowing that the Beast, and in truth himself too, were far more interested in blood and the power of life and death than carnal desires.

He made his way to where he could see much of the Park, and tracked Karen's progress. After a few minutes he was satisfied with what he saw and moved back towards the Watson house, patiently cataloging everything round him.

#

BLOG: If there is a serial killer operating in your neighborhood, it is possible to narrow down where they strike or even where they live. Some killer's signatures will give clues, but simply by having a minimum of three crime scenes you can use Geographical Profiling. While not perfect, this method of profiling can narrow down a suspect's comfortable operating areas, or comfort zones, and coupled with other clues can reveal additional details about the killer, potentially speeding up apprehension of the subject by law enforcement officials.

Just knowing the area of operations of a serial killer can be beneficial, as it stops resources being wasted searching or guarding the wrong places. This ergonomic use of detective skills is the essence of profiling in all its stages and guises. If you can follow the physical, mental and geographic clues, there is no need to interview hundreds or even thousands of suspects. You can instead locate a more discrete suspect pool, and potentially catch the killer quicker.

Chapter 15

When Sweet-lips got into her apartment, the first thing she did was cook up a much needed hit. She did not know how she survived the day at the cop shop with only vast amounts of sugar and caffeine to keep the DTs at bay. Not that she considered the rancid brew deserved to be called coffee, unknowingly sharing the same opinion as Danny did, but it was certainly loaded with enough caffeine to give an elephant a sizable jolt.

Her nerves, both for Frank and her crack cravings, did not allow the caffeine to stay in her system for long, so she breathed a sigh of relief and unalloyed pleasure as the drugs coursed through her body. Part of her loathed her need for the chemicals, but every time she loaded herself up with the junk, the sheer pleasure made everything else seem like someone else's problem.

Buzzing away on crack she could even cope with prostituting herself to some of the less than savory characters that came a calling. Not that she would be doing any of that tonight. After her early start, and long day with the police, she could not face staying awake to deal with the johns. For now, crack, her blessed and cursed savior, would allow her to ride her way happily to sleep.

But that small piece of her that made sure she was presentable, and somewhat functional in society, told her that if she wanted money for rent, food, and more importantly, drugs, she would have to go back to work tomorrow. So many days of worrying about Frank rather than her finances had left her a little short on cash. However, tonight she did not care, as the crack made it all feel like a problem for someone else.

#

When Danny got to work the next morning he was surprised to see that Detective King was already there and working. He was also surprised at all the activity round Todd's desk. Todd himself was shrugging his coat on, calling out to Raven, who was also in early, "You take care of things here, I'll let you know if anything comes of this."

Danny said, "Hey, what's going on? Where's the fire?"

Todd turned to look at him and smiled, "Ah, you're finally here. Come on, we'll talk on the way."

Todd strode out of the room, assuming Danny would follow. After shrugging his shoulders, that is what Danny did. He caught up with Todd as they reached his unmarked sedan, and as he opened the passenger door, Danny asked, "Come on. What's up. Spill."

Todd buckled in before starting the car, then said, "It looks like your press work yesterday may have paid off. We got a tip from a realtor who specializes in industrial properties." He backed out of the parking space and exited the lot, heading south. "Crazy as it sounds, he thinks our missing guy has been living in one of the buildings he's supposed to be selling. He's known about it for months, but with the economy the way it is, that building isn't being sold or rented anytime soon.

"Anyhoo, he said on the phone to one of the uniforms that he'd rather have someone who seemed decent in there, rather than leaving it empty and waiting for less desirable people to move in, who he'd then have to get evicted. Our friendly realtor had met Frank a couple of times on the street and was impressed by him, so when he saw him, or at least someone who looked very much like him, going into the building, he kinda kept forgetting to do his official monthly checks on the place."

As he finished, Todd pulled the car into the parking lot of an old donut shop, beside another small sedan. Danny looked at the place, and said, "You're right, that does sound crazy. And this is the place?"

Took shook his head, "Nah, it's just down the street. But our man over there said the parking lot of the building we need is full of glass and stuff, so it would be safer on the wheels to park here and walk down. This is just another building he's trying to offload."

They both got out of the car and walked over to the realtor. He was a thin, nervous looking guy in his thirties, and the first thing he said was, "You aren't gonna tell my boss I was letting someone stay in one of the buildings, are you? I would lose my job. I was just trying to do a guy a favor."

Todd shook his head, "If he's not our man, we won't say a word. If it is him, then you'll be a hero for finding him, so all will be good."

"And if it's not, and your boss starts anything, let us know and we'll have a quiet word with him," added Danny. "Can we get to this place now? I have a friend who would be very happy to see Frank again."

The trio headed down the street and stopped at the edge of the parking lot of the building they were looking for. They could see the glass and other debris spread across the lot, from the sidewalk right up to the building. Danny asked the realtor, whose name turned out to be Harry, "Are you supposed to keep this lot in order? Keep it a little more presentable?"

Harry shrugged, "Well, yeah, but like I said, who wants places like this right now? If by some miracle someone did show an interest I would've come down and got the place cleaned up."

Todd said to Harry, "It might be a good idea if you stayed back here and waited for us to check it out. You got the key?"

Harry handed over two keys, "This one is for the Yale, the other is for the padlock. There is no alarm, and no electric either."

"Thanks. Now wait here. We'll be back in a sec."

As they carefully crossed the lot, stepping round the piles of glass and trash, Todd asked, "How do you want to play this one?"

Danny replied, "Apparently he is easily spooked, especially by official looking people, so if it is Frank in there, then he'll run. You cover the back while I go in the front?"

"Sounds like a plan," Todd said as he handed over the keys. "Give me a couple to get into position. Oh," he added with a grin, "don't forget that the key marked 'Yale' is for the Yale lock. If I hadn't been told that I'd never have figured it out."

Danny grinned as he took the keys, then concentrated on getting close to the door without disturbing the mess that surrounded it. It had an almost planned look to him, as though someone had tried to make it hard to get to the door. As he waited for Todd to get into position, he wondered what the faint, cloying smell was in the air. It seemed somehow familiar.

Mentally shrugging his shoulders, Danny carefully fitted the key into the padlock, quietly opening and removing it. Next came the Yale, whose mechanism was working beautifully, and Danny slowly pushed the door open. There was a little resistance to start with, then the door opened easily, though very noisily. The noise was obviously coming from what had been a stack of cans that had been placed behind the door as a crude alarm system, but which were now bouncing and rolling across the floor.

Realizing that caution would no longer serve, Danny thrust the door wide open, leaped over the cans that were still rolling everywhere, bounced off the wall and ran into the large open room that made up most of the first floor. He pulled up as his nose more clearly registered the smell that had teased it outside, but now filled his nostrils with a nauseating stench that he sadly recognized.

With the smell of death in his lungs, Danny played his flashlight round the large, dusty room until it came across the expected body. The handful of rats on the corpse paused in their feasting and stared at him.

Danny shook his head and walked outside, calling to Todd, "Hey, King, come round here. It doesn't look like he'll be running anywhere."

#

Todd stood guard over the body, keeping the larger vermin away and cursing the flies, while Danny called it in. "We don't have a positive ID. This body isn't exactly in great condition. Looks like there has been a rodent buffet, and the body had taken a lot of injuries before death, I think. There's only one person who I think could say for sure if it is him, and once he's at the morgue she can take a look.

"Try and keep a lid on this until I can call her and break the news myself. Send a crime scene unit down with a butt-ton of portable lights. Hell, you know the drill. Let the Chief know, and tell him we will confirm identity as soon as we can. We cool? Okay, catch you later."

Danny closed his phone as he made his way towards the distant realtor. Harry asked, "Did you find anyone? Is it him?"

Danny shrugged, "We found someone alright, but we're not sure who it is. They can't really tell us who they are and help us with an ID, because they appear to have died a few days ago. Now, we'll have to take some statements later, so stick round. Please don't call anyone. If this news breaks before we want it to, you could be in a world of trouble."

Harry nodded his understanding, then asked, "Is it okay if I wait in my car? I feel a little uncomfortable just standing here."

"No problem. I'll send someone up to take the statement in a while." Danny then turned to head back to the warehouse, intent on doing a little poking round to hopefully give the crime scene technicians a head start.

#

As the morning progressed, more pieces of the puzzle slowly fell into place. The victim's entry points to the building, and paranoid defensive precautions were found, and the office he apparently lived in was thoroughly searched. After a barrage of pictures were taken, the corpse was removed to the Medical Examiners office.

Now the crime scene was being analyzed inch by inch, as the detectives and Crime Scene Investigators looked for clues to both the killer's identity and the victim's. This was a long, painstaking process, but one that had to be done by the book, especially as they could not confirm how the killer managed to get in and out of the building.

The sheer volume of blood splattered round caused everyone problems, as there could be important clues under it, and it made walking and avoiding the mess an obstacle course. Luckily, some slightly raised platforms placed by the crime scene investigators, leading across the room helped there, but moving safely across them presented its own challenges to some people.

Danny briefly considered looking round upstairs, but decided against it because of the volume of trash on the stairs. He would leave it to the crime scene techs to work their way upstairs, because they would be far less likely to destroy clues than his blundering approach would. With little more that he could achieve here, Danny decided to chase up the ME.

#

The morgue was located in the basement of the main city hospital, conveniently located Downtown. Danny rode the elevator into the depths of the old building, and arrived in what could be termed the lobby. The doors to the right led to the Stacks, where decades of mouldering patient records were slowly turning to dust, while those to the left went to storage facilities for some of the hospital supplies. These both contributed to the dry, dusty atmosphere down there, but the most pervasive smell was the industrial strength antiseptic coming from the doors straight ahead.

As Danny pushed one of the doors open, the smell blossomed into an all out assault on his nasal passageways, and a gust of cold air spilled out. One of the hospitals interns was doing their spell of duty as a medical assistant while the regular one was off sick, so Danny did not recognize him. The intern recognized him as a police officer, however, and said, "Doctor Maddox has finished the preliminaries, and said you could go right it."

"Can't wait," replied Danny, going through the doors to the main part of the morgue. He had never felt comfortable seeing bodies cut up like slabs of meat at a butchers, but was professional enough to hide it.

The bright overhead lights reflected off the white tiles and stainless steel that adorned the room, and the pale form that Danny assumed was Frank laying on one of the steel tables in the center of the room.

Now that the body had been undressed and cleaned up, many of the wounds were much clearer, though no less horrific. Seeing the ruin that was the face, Danny doubted that Sweet-lips would be able to make any kind of ID. Doctor Maddox looked up from his notes when Danny came in, and said, "Lately you seem to be giving me some much abused bodies. At least this one had part of his head, unlike the last one you served up. And so much blood loss here, too. Do we have a vampire on the loose in the city?"

Danny shrugged, "I don't make the bodies, I'm just lucky enough to find them. I don't think any blood was drained, given how the murder scene was decorated, and I haven't heard of secret, mythical beasts operating round here, but you give me solid evidence of one, I'll do my best to find it. Now, do you know how and when he died? And is there any chance of an ID?"

Maddox looked at his paperwork, "Well, based on temperature, decomposition rates and parasite infestations, he's been dead about a week, most likely six days but could be as little as five. My SWAG is he probably died late Wednesday night, which would fit with your missing guy."

"Is a Scientific Wild Ass Guess more accurate than a mere WAG?"

"Well, it does involve a degree of experience and education, so it is somewhat more accurate. There are a few more tests to run to narrow things down further, but the temperature inside that building over the past week is a tad of an unknown which throws all our calculations.

"As to how he died, that would be exsanguination, which doesn't surprise me given the descriptions of the crime scene. He bled out through two wounds, one across the throat with a sharp knife that severed all the veins and arteries. The second wound is in his lower back, also a very sharp blade, but much larger, a heavy hunting knife by the look of the wound, which cut him open very messily, and incidentally severed his spine.

"Remember, these are preliminary findings, and the full autopsy will give firmer conclusions and more details. In addition to those wounds, there is heavy damage to the jaw. As you can see, there is not a tooth in his head, and judging by the number of broken stumps and fractures to the jaw I'd say they were hammered or wrenched out. Most, if not all, were removed post mortum, which was some consolation to the victim.

"Rodents have had a field day with the body, with much of the soft outer tissue, and even some parts of the internal organs, chewed and even totally removed. I'll have more solid details later, but I expected you would want something to work with right away. Blood work and such is in the works, but I doubt it will make much of a difference. This man was murdered, by a very strong right-hander."

Danny nodded, "Thanks, Doc. I don't envy you your job. I take it those evidence bags have his clothes in them?"

"They sure do. No personal effects were found on him, and because of the tooth issue and rodent damage to the fingers, we have no chance of an ID from medical or government records. A friend or relative may be able to identify him, though."

"I'd hoped for that. Could you get me a photo of just the top half of his face? I don't want his friend to see the carnage in his mouth."

Maddox pulled a picture from his paperwork, "I had already guessed you would be needing something like that. I'll get the official report to you as soon as I can."

"I'll be looking forward to it," said Danny as he picked up the evidence bags after signing the release paperwork. He then tucked the picture inside his jacket, thanked the Medical Examiner again, and headed back to the Police Station.

#

After dropping off the evidence bags containing the blood soaked clothes with the laboratory technicians, Danny went back to his car, then drove to where Sweet-lips lived. He parked across the street, confident that any traffic cops would recognize an unmarked police sedan, and leave it unmolested even if it was parked in a somewhat illegal place.

Pulling out his cellphone, he checked both ways before crossing the street, and hoped that Sweet-lips would answer his call. She picked up almost immediately, "Danny, you found him? Where is he? Is he okay?"

"Hold on, Karin, we found someone, but they are pretty beat up, so we can't get a positive ID. If I showed you a photo of his face, do you think you'll be able to recognize him?"

"Of course. Where are you?"

Danny smiled as he answered, "Standing outside your door waiting to be let in, whenever you get a moment."

"Hold on, I'll be right down." Sweet-lips dropped the phone, ran out of her apartment and down the stairs to the front door. She fumbled briefly with the lock in her haste, but quickly had the door open, saying, "Where is the picture?"

Danny took her arm, conscious of how scantily clad she was, and led her inside, "Let's go up to your rooms and I'll show you then."

Together they went up the dingy stairs and into the tiny apartment. As Sweet-lips closed the door, she said, "Don't mind the mess, I never have been one for housekeeping. And I hope you'll ignore the drug paraphernalia beside you too."

Danny shrugged, "You've been too useful to me to bust on you a minor possession charge." He reached into his inside jacket pocket and pulled out the picture. He formally asked, "Do you recognize this man?" as he passed the picture over to her.

Sweet-lips took it with trembling hands, looked at it briefly, then let it fall to the ground as her hands flew to her mouth, "It's Frank. What happened to him? Why doesn't the picture show his mouth and nose? Is he dead? Why are you only showing me the top part of his face?"

Danny put his arms round her, saying, "You really don't want to know the answer to that right now. Someone killed him, and his body is pretty messed up. You wouldn't like me to give you the details. It's starting to look like he was killed the night he left here. Do you know anyone who had a problem with him?"

Sweet-lips stifled a sob, trying to hold it together so she could answer Danny's questions, "He seemed to get on fine with everyone. I can't think of a single person who had a bad word to say about him. But I do remember him saying he thought someone had been following him, but he was always so paranoid that I didn't think much of it. I just don't know who could have done anything bad to him."

Shaking her head, she collapsed onto the bed, nearly pulling Danny down with her. She spent several minutes crying uncontrollably, while Danny tried his best to comfort her. Finally the tears dried up, and Sweet-lips sat up, wiping her eyes with a t-shirt that was laying on the bed. She tried to smile bravely, "Sorry about that. What now?"

Danny sighed, "The usual routine. We'll process the crime scene, see what clues we can get, same from the body. Most killers leave some evidence behind, we just have to find it. We'll interview people in the area, and along Lincoln Avenue too. Check camera footage if we can find any. Like I said, all the usual things, and then if we haven't cracked it by then we'll just have to hope for a break. We've got a good record of catching murderers, and I know we can get the media involved in the investigation easily."

Sweet-lips asked, "How did you find him?"

"It was your work with the media that found him, actually. A realtor remembered seeing Frank in and round the building where we found him, so it shows what good a public appeal can achieve. I'll be making sure the Chief realizes that, and maybe that will recover my ratings with him somewhat. Now, is there anything I can do to help you?"

Sweet-lips thought for a moment, "If I can't see Frank's body, could I at least see where he died?"

Danny frowned, "Not right now, it's an active crime scene. Also, it's a quite a mess, and I don't want you to have that image stuck in your mind. Maybe when it's cleaned up, and the techs are all done, I'll take you down there, but not right now."

Sweet-lips sighed, "Okay then, I trust you on this. I don't need anything or anyone right now. I have all the support I need over there," pointing to her drugs and related equipment.

"Okay," replied Danny, "but don't overdo it. Someone will be back in a more official capacity to take a statement later on. Now I think I should brief the Chief."

With a wan smile, Sweet-lips said, "Nice rhyme. I hope you haven't been waiting for the opportunity to use it. Anyway, you go catch the scumbag who did this to my friend."

Danny rose and went to the door, "Yes, Ma'am. We're already on the case."

#

Danny called ahead from the car, getting through to the Chief's secretary, and ended up having to demand access to the Chief. He knew that whatever else was on his schedule, the Chief would want to know the latest details on this case. Danny was proved right by the warm reception he received from the Chief when he arrived.

Now, seated across from the Chief in his opulent office, he filled him in on everything they knew so far. "And now we're just waiting for the forensics and autopsy. Hopefully by then we'll have more than enough clues to figure out who did this."

The Chief nodded, "It is good that we found him so quickly, looks good on the department, even if it was a citizen who gave us the lead. Your informant was right, and we did the right thing it seems. Now we just have to find the murderer and quickly bring them to justice. Asking the media for help before has made this a high profile case, and we can't afford another high profile unsolved like Father Williams. Everything you need, throw it at this case. Overtime is approved and damn the cost and the budget. Get to it, Detective."

#

The killer routinely monitored the police radio transmissions. As well as having scanners at home, he had a radio in his work vehicle that was exactly the same as the one in Claytown City's patrol cars. He heard about the possible locating of the missing person, and the discovery of the charnel house that was the crime scene and last resting place of the bum.

As updates were posted throughout the day, including confirmation of the victims identity (although not his full ID), and the large scale operations being planned to catch the perpetrator, the killer just smiled, while the Beast purred in the background.

The killer said, "I wonder if they'll start linking their unsolved cases together yet?"

The Beast replied, "No, I do not think they have caught on to us yet. We are just a statistical blip right now. But that will change somewhat tomorrow, I feel."

The killer grinned, filled with anticipatory joy, "Oh, yes, tomorrow will make them wake up and smell the coffee. They may not get the full message, but they'll see some of the words for sure."

#

While the killer ran through his fantasies and plans, Sweet-lips floated in a drug induced haze, and the Chief wandered through his worries about possible negative media stories. Danny, on the other hand, was working hard on the case. Piece by piece parts of the investigation puzzle came in, and he put the pieces together.

One of the pieces was communicated to him by Todd

King, who called to say, "We've got a twist here. The CSI boys have just shown me that they found two different types of shoe prints in the blood. Looks like we could be looking for two perps here."

"Interesting," said Danny, "or one perp and a witness, either there at the time or came in afterward. Remember Tricky Mickey? We really need some kind of camera footage from any businesses round there."

You could almost hear Todd shrug through the phone, "We're asking, but a lot of them loop tapes, or overwrite footage. It's been nearly a week, after all, and most places would only keep a couple of tapes for the system."

"Yeah, I know. And there aren't many businesses open in that area right now. Man, life would be so much easier for us if we could mount our own cameras round the city."

Todd laughed, "I'll let you put that to the Civil Liberties groups, shall I?"

"Pah, if they aren't guilty of anything, why would they care? What about Frank's civil liberties, or Father Williams'?"

"Preaching to the choir, Danny Boy, preaching to the choir. Hey, I better go check how they're doing upstairs. Might be something unusual up there. I doubt it, but we can but hope."

Danny replied, "Okay, my Liege. Catch you later." As he put down the phone, Danny thought, "Two people? A killing team?", and wondered how that would fit in the puzzle. If only he could find a corner or an edge, it would make life so much easier.

#

The killer was trying to unobtrusively watch the Watson house from a few blocks away. He had timed his arrival to the normal time that Detective Watson would return home, but he suspected that having to deal with the killers latest victim would hold him up some.

Nevertheless, the killer wanted to see how the rest of the household reacted to such changes to their usual routine, and he was pleasantly surprised that everything seemed to carry on as normal. At the expected time he saw Karen Watson come out for her daily jog, and he smiled as he put the car in gear and prepared to follow her to the park. He planned to find a good spot to watch her and check which route she took today. If all the data fell into place neatly, tomorrow would be a very different jog for Karen.

#

BLOG: Based on data from my local police district, coupled with some additional personal knowledge, I have applied the geographic and other profiling techniques to a series of murders in my city. I have come to the following conclusion: There is a high probability, nay, more a certainty, that there is a serial killer operating in the immediate area, and it appears the police are unaware. Who would have thought it?

Chapter 16

Danny finally made it home hours after he would have preferred, his head still filled with the whirling details of the Frank case. He found that his wife Helen had left his meal in the refrigerator, and he heated it up, ate it while still puzzling over the case, and then staggered to bed. It seemed to him that his head had barely touched his pillow when his alarm started it's insidious beeping.

Groaning, he turned it off before it disturbed Helen, and staggered to the kitchen. Luckily, even half asleep, he could automatically fill and prepare the coffee pot, and he even thought to add extra grounds to the mix to give the brew some extra kick.

Ten minutes soaking under a steaming hot shower, followed by thirty seconds on cold, woke him up enough to face the day. With the extra caffeine in his coffee, he decided he should be able to stay awake until midday at least, and maybe even get some constructive work done too.

He left the house while everyone else was still sleeping, and drove through the deserted streets to the police headquarters. When he got there, he found on his desk the reports that had filtered in overnight. Sighing, he sat down to work his way through them, and prepared the orders to track down the two perps suspected of killing Frank.

People steadily trickled in as the sun rose higher, and Todd finally came in a little after his usual time, grinning bashfully, "Sorry, I slept through my alarm. If it hadn't been for the wife I'd still be sleeping."

"No problem," replied Danny, "I know how you feel. I plan on an early night today, no matter what. I'm even glad to see the coffee is running in this place, and you know how much I *love* the coffee here. It looks like we got a few surveillance tapes from businesses near the warehouse, so make yourself at home and start watching, while I get on with collating the reports."

After sitting slumped in front of the computer screen for a couple of hours, Todd looked up suddenly, "I might have something here, but I'm not totally sure. Could you take a look and give me a second opinion?"

Danny wheeled himself over to Todd's desk, and asked, "Watcha got?"

"Well, we know Frank left Karin Temple's place just after seven. We've got some footage of him going through Downtown round then, so I started looking at the footage from these new tapes after that time. With me so far?"

Danny nodded, "Still here. Go on."

"We've only managed to get footage from five cameras, and it only covers the approaches from the north, east and west. No eyes directly on our building, or coming from the south. So there are a lot of holes in this coverage, but who knows what we'll be lucky enough to find on what we have.

"Anyway, about eight o'clock I finally picked up Frank coming in from the east. No-one was following that I could see. There weren't many people on the streets, and most were heading out of the area. I've picked up two people who headed the right way, but I only could see one coming back. Anyhoo, I've got stills on all this. But I also saw some other people heading away from the area close to the murder time. This guy here sparked my interest."

Danny leaned close to the screen and saw a person of average build, wearing dark shoes, pants and hoodie. There also appeared to be a book-bag slung over his shoulder. "Okay, so what's your interest in this one?"

Todd shrugged, "Call it gut instinct. You can't see any identifiable features, but it just looks like he is being ninja, trying to fade into the dark."

"Come on, lots of people dress like that."

"I know, but the timing is so good, and my gut just says this is our man. So I check back through the footage before seven, to see if he'd come through earlier, and maybe been waiting a while. Well, I found this guy rolling through in the early afternoon."

Danny looked at the screen closely again. This new person fit the description of the first suspect, but the style of clothes was subtly different. "Close, but not the same guy."

Detective King smiled, "That's what I thought at first, until I ran the two clips side by side." He clicked with his mouse, and two video sequences looped beside each other.

Danny watched for a few moments, then exclaimed, "What the? They walk the same way, move the same way. Controlled, but almost predatory. But why change clothes into an almost identical outfit in the middle of the night?"

He turned to Todd, and they said in unison, "Because his other clothes were covered in blood."

Danny smiled, shaking his head slightly in amazement, "It makes sense. Get the boys on the ground asking about him. If it is one of our suspects, that boy came prepared, like he knew he'd end up a mess. But you know we can't assume it is him, and we'll need to get all the other people checked out too. Good work."

As he wheeled himself back to his desk to continue with his work, he muttered to himself, "You know, there is something familiar about that walk."

#

The owner of that walk was trying to concentrate on work, but the killer was filling up with anticipation that he could barely suppress. He was starting to find that there was a difference between killing as part of a cathartic release of repressed rage and violence, and killing for the pure orgasmic pleasure of it.

Since his surrender to emotion when he killed Frank, and his new pact with the Beast, he knew he was changing, had already changed. Intellectually he recognized that he was evolving as a killer, a process he had suspected from the start might happen. Before he had been worried about that potential change in him, just as he had worried about the state of his mental health, but now he was not worried at all.

Well, if he was being totally honest, a small part of him was concerned, but the other ninety nine percent was eager for the bloodletting to begin. "Let them try and find me. Even with all those cops running round downtown, and everywhere else, asking the same old questions, they won't find me."

The Beast growled in the background, "We are too good for them to catch. And if by some miracle anyone gets too close for comfort, we can always get out of Dodge, or remove the threat. Messily."

#

After making sure Detective King was ready to distribute the potential suspect and witness details to those who needed it, Danny thought it would be wise to update the Chief. He took a couple of still shots from the camera feeds with him, along with the large binder that comprised the Murder Book.

He carefully popped his head into the quiet anteroom, and asked the receptionist, "Hey, Gill, is he available? There are a couple of new things I wanted to show him."

Gill Miller looked up from her typing, and pursed her lips disapprovingly, "For you it seems I'm supposed to make time and shuffle his overloaded calendar just so he's available at your beck and call. But this time, luckily for all his important meetings that I may have been forced to shuffle, he is currently in and available to any visitors. I'll let him know you're here."

She waved him towards the comfortable seats placed round a low table, then picked up her phone, "Chief, I have Detective Watson here hoping you have time to see him. Yes, Sir, I'll send him in."

Danny had not even had time to sit before Gill hung up the phone, and she looked at him with a slightly sour expression, "Go on in. I'm sure you know the way."

Danny was amused by her put upon and standoffish attitude, and tipping an imaginary hat, he said,

"Thank you, ma'am. A pleasure doing business with you." He smiled as he heard her mutter, "Well!" as he walked into the Chief's inner sanctum.

The heavy door closed softly behind him, and Danny waded through the deep pile carpet on his way to his usual chair in front of the desk. The Chief stood and extended his hand, "Ah, Detective Watson. You bring good news, I trust."

Shaking the proffered hand before they both sat down, Danny replied, "Well, I have news certainly. A possible suspect," and passed over the two pictures of the black clad man.

The Chief looked at them, "Surely you mean two suspects, neither of which is particularly identifiable?"

"We do believe there were two people at the scene, but we believe these pictures show the same man, at different times of the day of the murder. Between shots he has changed his clothes. He was identified by his walk, which is rather characteristic, and strangely familiar."

The Chief smiled and shook his head, "So to find this suspect we need to watch every male in the city walk, is that it?"

"Well, Sir, it may not be much of a lead, but it is more than we had before. We know that this suspect is male, as you said, about five foot ten, maybe six foot max, slightly above average build. That at least knocks out sixty to seventy percent of the suspect pool. Admittedly him dressing in black with that large hood makes him difficult to identify, especially as so many young men, and women come to that, dress like it.

"But we have a description, and that walk, which

will...." Danny paused, waiting for the nagging intuition to break free, "Got it. I knew I'd seen that walk before. And the description is a good match too, even if it is vague."

The Chief rested his chin on his cupped hand, "Detective, would you care to elaborate, or at least make some sense?"

Danny looked up, a look of slight surprise on his face, "Sorry, Sir. I just had a thought strike me. I think this is the same person that killed Father Williams."

The Chief sat upright, and barked, "What? Are you sure?"

"I'm not one hundred percent positive, but a quick comparison with the footage in the Williams' file would prove it. But that then raises a whole new barrel of questions, because those two victims didn't exactly move in the same business or social circles."

The Chief replied, "I suppose it could be a simple connection, such a Frank seeing something on the night of the first murder?"

Danny nodded, "It could be. We'll need to start asking some different questions. But it makes it doubly likely that this is our man, because what are the odds of him innocently being in the area of two homicides?"

"Not likely," said the Chief. "Good work, Danny. I think we should get these pictures out to the media stat."

Danny nodded and rose to leave, "I'll double check the video first, then get the message out to the contacts. When I have more news, I'll be back."

#

Confirmation did not take long, and the description was transmitted to all officers, and spread to the media as well. With that task done, Danny decided to call his informant, "Hey, Sweet-lips, it's Danny. How are you doing?"

She snorted, "About as well as you'd expect after losing a friend. If I didn't need the money I wouldn't even be thinking about working tonight. All I want to do is get wasted, or just curl up in a corner and cry."

"I can maybe help you out a little there. I am allowed to pay informants, as you know, so I'll take a look at the fund. You've helped out enough to deserve something extra. I noticed you didn't have a TV in your place, so I expect you haven't heard the new development."

"You've found the murdering scumbag?" Sweet-lips interrupted.

"Sorry, no, not yet. But we know that this isn't the first time the scumbag in question has broken the law in a big way. We believe it's the same guy that killed Father Williams."

"What? Are you sure?"

Danny smiled to himself, "That's exactly what my Chief said. You don't have his office bugged do you? Anyway, I'm ninety nine percent sure, which is good enough for me. So this should make it easier to find the perp, especially if we can figure out why he killed Frank. One theory is he saw something to do with the Father Williams case, and was killed so he couldn't talk."

"Oh, no, that can't be the case. If he knew anything, he would've told me. I remember specifically asking his to do that when we first talked about poor Father Williams. He said the first he knew was when he saw all the black and whites outside the church."

Danny deflated a little, "That blows that theory then. Unless he saw or heard something later, but that would have to be after he left your place. No, that wouldn't work. Dammit. Did they know each other?"

Although it couldn't be seen down the phone, Sweet-lips shook her head, "No, I don't think they even met. For one thing, Father Williams' outreach programs were more aimed at helping us hookers, and Frank's uniform paranoia even included priests and delivery drivers."

"Scratch theory Number Two. Well, I suppose that has helped by eliminating those lines of inquiry. Now I just have to think of where to go from here. Oh, can you let the 'ladies of the night' know that Detective Chavez will be down later tonight to talk to them? A few of them have been less than helpful to us lately, and you could get them to cooperate."

Sweet-lips chuckled, despite her dark mood, "We're not vampires, we are prostitutes. It's not blood that we suck either. I don't need to explain the difference, do I?"

"Er, no. I don't need you to draw a picture, thanks. Now, will you be okay cash-wise until I can get out to you tomorrow?"

Sweet-lips smiled, "Yeah, I'm good for now. Thank you for all your help and support."

"No problem. I'll catch up with you tomorrow, okay?"

"Okay, until tomorrow, then."

As he hung up, Danny called across to Todd, "I think it's no dice on them knowing each other, or Frank being a witness to the Father Williams killing. It has to be something personal that triggered the homicides."

Todd had an incredulous look on his face, "Personal? How? The dude only had one friend that we know of, and he was totally paranoid about most people. Nice and polite, but still pretty much a paranoid nut job. The only way it could be personal is if he hacked off a stranger somehow, who decided to kill him for it. That doesn't make any sense to me."

Danny shrugged, "Neither does the fact our suspected killer stabbed Frank and sliced his throat, but used a shotgun on Father Williams. If I had access to a gun and I wanted to waste someone, it would be an easier option than using a knife. The two sets of footprints doesn't make much sense either, especially when we can't find this partner slash witness on any cameras. A lot of things don't make sense, but it is what the evidence suggests, and we have to find out how it does make sense and hangs together in reality, and get a killer or two off the streets."

Todd held up his hands in surrender, "Okay, I get it. I guess I should start cross-referencing the two murder books then, look for similarities between the two cases?"

Danny shook his head, "Nah, that's for me to try first. You can get out on the street and do some follow ups with the beggars. They've got to have seen something, even if they don't realize it. Also check the businesses along Lincoln to see if we can 'borrow' their security footage if they have any that shows the street, for as far back as they have it.

"By the way, we can't discount the possibility that it is just a coincidence that Father Williams murderer was walking those streets at that time. It really could be a statistical fluke, so we have to find that second person, or some witnesses. Get men walking to the south of the crime scene. Feet on the ground, asking questions. Maybe someone, somewhere, saw something."

Raven had just walked in, ready to start her late shift, and caught the end of this speech. She said, "Have we really got the manpower for this?"

Danny replied, "We just have to do what we can with what we've got. The taxpayers can't complain about too many police officers being on the streets. The Chief has authorized overtime, so that will give us more manpower flexibility. Raven, as you're here now, you can go with Todd and canvass the Downtown beggars. When he's finished it should be about the time the working girls start hitting the streets. I hope they cooperate with us this time. Any that don't, let me know and I'll have a little word with them. Okay folks. Catching the killer is the name of the game, let's start playing to win."

Chapter 17

The killer was intrigued when he found out two of his kills had been tentatively linked by video evidence of how he walked. He knew that although the black outfit worked well to conceal his identity, it was distinctive enough by itself to be recognizable. He had just bargained that the look was common enough that, along with altered killing methods, his various crimes would remain unconnected for a little while longer.

He had already made plans to alter his look, but had not expected his gait would be so easy to spot, regardless of clothing. It was time to think of other countermeasures, such as tight bandages on his knees or ankles to alter his gait. He had no plans to get caught, now or in the future. The Beast was happy that he had been freed from his cage in the killer's head, and neither wanted to be on the wrong side of a prison cell door. Both the killer and the Beast set their combined intellects to the challenges of deceiving the police for quite a while longer.

#

Danny spent the afternoon cross-comparing the two murder books and making notes. These notes were sparse, particularly where they related to similarities between the two murders. Apart from the style of outfit the murderer wore, and the surprise element and overpowering force of the attacks, there were no other similarities. Different weapons, different locations, different types of victim. He supposed they had taken place at roughly the same time of day, being in the slim slice of night before midnight came, and the two victims were male, but apart from these two suppositions, there was nothing.

It just did not make sense to Danny, so used was he to finding obvious common features when there were multiple crimes committed by the same person, but the video evidence was compelling. But even allowing for the video data, there still remained one big question, which, when it was finally answered, would make more sense of the existing data and the cases as a whole. It was a simple question – why these two men?

They did not know each other, and there seemed to be no working, social or historic connections between the two of them. The only slim connection was they both knew several prostitutes and had wanted to help them. If those were the criteria, it would make for a very strange case, and be easy to prove the theory next time the murderer struck.

Danny stopped himself at that thought. Kill again? He hoped there would be no more, he knew his team was struggling as it was. But if they did not know the reason for the two homicides, maybe their best chance was if the murderer did kill again.

Shaking his head to remove that unwanted train of thought, he replaced the murder books and locked things away, grabbing his jacket and keys as he prepared to leave. Maybe, he thought, things would make more sense after a good nights sleep.

#

The killer left work just before Danny, and as he drove past the police headquarters he saw Danny heading to his car. "Hmm, our Detective Watson must be knocking off on time so he'll be able to catch an early night," thought the killer.

The Beast grinned, "I think his beauty sleep plans will be going out of the window tonight."

"Oh, yes," agreed the killer, "and when he finally does get to sleep, I think he'll be having a few nightmares."

He drove home as quickly as he dared, parking illegally on the road outside his apartment and dashed inside. Beside the door was his pre-prepared bag of killing goodies, and, after quickly changing into his usual running outfit, he grabbed the bag and hurried back to his car.

Usually he would jog to and from his kill sites, to keep his car clean of any evidence of killing, but today time was of the essence. He drove to a neighborhood near the Presidential Park, and after finding a quiet spot to leave his car, he rapidly exited and jogged to the park.

He expected that anytime now Karen Watson would be entering the Park too, and he made his was carefully through the wooded areas until he was hidden beside what seemed to be her favorite path. Working swiftly, he opened his backpack and extracted the set of greasy overalls he had found while dumpster diving one day. He put them on over his running gear, along with gloves and a Balaclava helmet.

Grabbing a pre-cut piece of fine piano wire, he briefly left his hiding place to tie one end to the bottom of a tree across the track. He left it laying loosely on the ground and covered it with dirt and loose leaves, then grasped the loose end of the wire and returned to his hiding place to wait.

He could not see the whole path from where he crouched because there were too many leafy trees in the way to give a totally clear view. But from the glimpses he had of the track, he was confident that he would recognize Karen as she ran towards him. A couple of times other runners pounded past him, but completely failed to notice the dark shape hiding in the gloom, or the loose line of wire buried across the path.

Suddenly there was a flash of white from down the path, and through the kaleidoscopic images generated by the intervening trees the killer saw his target: blonde hair in a pony tail, tight white top hugging the boobs on the young slim body, black shorts that did nothing to preserve modesty. He grasped the free end of the wire more firmly, and as the girl ran past he tugged hard.

The girl squealed quickly in surprise as her ankles hit the now taut wire, and she crashed heavily to the ground. The killer was on her in a flash, jumping from his hiding place and straddling the girl's back. In his hands was another, shorter length of wire, with a large nail looped through each end. These he gripped in each hand as the blonde struggled under him, then looped the wire round her neck and pulled hard.

Her cries became muffled and her struggles more frantic as the wire cut into her flesh. He pulled up hard, keeping her body pinned to the ground with his knee, and the wire sliced through skin, blood vessels and flesh, until the girl's neck was nearly severed. Only the spinal column stopped the wire from cutting all the way through, but it was more than enough. Blood was fountaining from the wounds, being pumped in vain by a desperate heart through destroyed arteries, and the Beast roared with pleasure.

The pleasure of the kill also pumped through the killers mind and body, and he released the blood soaked garrote and exultantly punched the air. He sat there for a few moments, enjoying the buzz, while the Beast gorged itself on the copper tasting aroma of blood.

The killer shook his head to clear it a little, and stepped off the slowly cooling corpse to get his backpack. He walked back to the body as he took a DNA swab from one of the pockets outside the bag, and crouched down beside the loosely hanging head. For the first time he could clearly see the face of his victim, and was disappointed when he realized the girl was not Karen Watson. Apparently there were other sluttishly dressed blondes who liked to run along these paths.

The killer shrugged, surprisingly not minding too much that his intended target had somehow escaped him, but he was just as happy with such a perfect kill in all other respects. As he took a blood swab he briefly contemplated hiding the body and waiting to see if Karen did come past, but the large amount of blood soaking into the path discouraged him.

As he packed the now sealed DNA kit away, the killer heard someone running up behind him, either a casual jogger or someone drawn by the noise of the attack. He silently cursed himself for lingering too long, and looked over his shoulder as he drew a bang-stick from the interior of the bag.

Coming up the forest trail was a well built guy, whose apparent fitness would allow him to pass as a heavy-weight boxer or linebacker. The man called out, "Hey, is everything okay? What's going on?" The killer saw a look of danger recognition pass over the joggers face as the stranger noticed something wrong with the scene in front of him, either the blood or maybe the Balaclava. The man did not stop running, but his demeanor changed to a more hostile or protective attitude.

Outwardly, the killer did not do much when he noticed the attitude change, barring a slight adjustment of his legs. While the man closed on him, hidden by his body the killer pulled the cotter pin from the bang-stick. He then tensed his body and waited.

A bang-stick is actually a shark deterrent, made out of a simple metal rod roughly eighteen inches long, with a screw on cylinder at the end. With the safety device, the cotter pin, removed and hanging loose on it's chain, the stick could be knocked hard against the snout of a predatory shark. The resultant underwater explosion from the blank charge, and sound and pressure waves, would discomfort the shark without harming it, and encourage it to find it's next meal elsewhere. But in this case, the shark appeared to be the one holding the bang-stick.

As the jogger got close, mouthing words that the killer did not even hear, the killer moved. He was back in the zone, exultant that he was seconds away from another perfect kill, and took his chance perfectly. As he rose, he rotated, spinning round, up and out with his right hand outstretched. A combination of the stranger's momentum and the unexpected thrust by the killer saw the stranger run straight into the bang-stick.

The tip of the stick hit the man just under the sternum, with the killers angle of attack pointing the stick upwards. A fully loaded shotgun shell, not a blank, in the nose chamber was forced back by the impact, jamming the primer onto the firing pin. With the shell actually in contact with the guy's chest, the resultant sound was no louder than a box hitting the floor. It did not sound like a gunshot at all, because the expanding gases from the charge followed the shot deep into the body, rather than creating sound waves in the air. The brutal power of the shot, magnified by the close range contact, blew the air from the stranger's lungs and replaced it with buckshot. Simultaneously his heart was torn apart and he literally stopped dead, although his shocked brain took a little while to catch up with events.

It seemed the only thing holding the jogger upright was the bang-stick pushing up under his ribcage. When the killer pulled it back, the man slumped at the knees, with cooling gases and blood spraying gently from the entry hole in his chest. He crumpled face down on the ground, and the killer smiled with satisfaction. There was no exit wound because the bone and muscle of the ribcage had contained the force of the shot, at the cost of mutilating many of the would be Samaritan's organs.

Again the killer punched the air and the Beast roared, but only briefly as they knew time was pressing. Even if there was no sound of a shot, more people could still be heading this way because of the girl's cry and the guy's shouting. The killer thrust the bang-stick back into the bag and quickly grabbed another DNA swab and went to work. With that trophy safely stowed away beside the first, the garotte and tripwire soon followed the bang-stick into the recesses of the bag. The killer then grabbed the backpack firmly and ran through the woods.

He crossed several paths and plowed through plenty of undergrowth before he stopped in deep brush over a hundred feet from the scene of the double murder. Calming down his breathing, he stripped off the Balaclava and the overalls, pushing them into the garbage bag he had brought along for that purpose. The shoes and gloves followed, and in a short space of time the killer had become just another runner in the park. He took off through the woods, heading away from the two bodies, towards one of the exits of the Park and his car.

#

Danny was halfway through the meal that Helen had gotten ready for him when he got home, and enjoying the break from the police routines. He was trying to forget about work for the time being, and just focus on being with the woman he loved, and the steak and salad in front of him. It felt good to pretend to be a normal person, at least for a while.

He silently cursed when his phone rang, and audibly groaned when he saw the caller ID. He answered grudgingly, "Hey, Raven, this better be good."

Detective Chavez sounded apologetic, "Sorry, Danny, I would have kept this until tomorrow if it hadn't involved Karen."

"What has she done now? I thought she wasn't going to work the streets tonight."

"What?" replied a puzzled Raven, "Since when has your daughter worked the streets?"

Danny slapped his forehead, "Sorry, with the case we've been working on I automatically thought you were talking about Karin Temple." His sleep deprived brain was now confused about why Raven was on the phone.

His heart suddenly went cold when he realized why Raven could be calling, "What happened to her? Is my baby girl okay? Where is she?"

Raven quickly replied, "Calm down, boss, she is

okay. Just a little shook up. You'll need to get up here, preferably with Helen, to calm Karen down and take her home. You might want to stay here afterward, though, because we've got a couple of bodies in the woods."

Danny spluttered, "What? Two of them. Does it look like the guy we've been looking for?"

"Not many CCTV cameras in the trees, so we can't be sure. MO is different for both victims too. Rather than me try and explain on the phone, get up to the Presidential Park. You'll know where, just look for the flashing lights."

Danny nodded, a gesture unseen over the phone, "Okay, we'll be there in a few."

As he hung up he looked at Helen, "Don't panic, but we have to go out right now. Karen needs us. She is okay, but I think she just found a murder scene."

Helen put her hand to her open mouth, and Danny quickly reached out and took her other hand, "It's all okay. Raven said she was just shaken up. Come on, let's go get our girl."

#

A few minutes later, though to the couple it seemed the drive took forever, the Watson family SUV was following a police cruiser along a usually pedestrian only roadway through the Park, heading towards the cluster of emergency vehicles near the woods.

There were a couple of ambulances parked at the edge of the pack, and sitting on the back step of one was Karen, wrapped in a blanket, being tended by a fireman-paramedic. Danny stopped the car nearby, and they both hurried to the side of their daughter. They could see immediately that there was nothing physically wrong with her, but she was visibly upset.

Gentle questioning from Helen brought out the main reason she was upset, and the answer surprised Danny. Karen had said, "I'm embarrassed. I feel ashamed that I lost my cool when I saw the bodies. There was just so much blood, and the smell! I just ran away crying. A friend saw me and asked what was wrong, thinking that someone had said or done something to me. I should have been cooler about it," she finished.

Danny hugged her tight, and asked, "Why do you think that?"

Karen sniffed, "Because I'm a cops daughter. I should be able to take it."

"Hey, you don't have to think like that. Seeing a corpse is never fun, and honestly I've never really gotten used to it. A body is not something that anyone should see, let alone the body of a murder victim. Some of the ones I've seen lately would turn the stomach of the most hardened people."

She looked up at him, "Really?"

Danny tousled her hair, "Really. You don't seem to have puked, so that's a plus. The guy who found Father Williams tossed his cookies all down the steps of the church. You found help, and got the police involved, which was the best thing to do. Many people would have just completely gone to pieces and would still be gibbering right now. Now, I think it would be best if you went home and let your mom pamper you for a while. Can you do that for me?"

Karen tried to crack a smile, "Sure, I can do that. Girls are always ready to be pampered. What are you going to do?"

Danny smiled in return, albeit grimly, "I'm going to catch the scum who did this."

Chapter 18

As he watched Helen leading Karen back to the car, Danny said over his shoulder, "Okay, so what have we got?"

Raven replied, "I know how you prefer to handle a new scene, so let's just go and look."

She led him through the cordon of officers and yellow tape, saying, "We've closed off the whole of this wooded area. Some techs are trying to follow footprints to and from the crime scene, but it's not easy. People go all over the place here, but we're hoping to find the correct, freshest prints. The crime scene looks undisturbed, and the ME says they've only been dead about an hour tops, probably less than thirty minutes."

Danny looked surprised, "You got all this set up this quickly?"

"We think Karen must have found them bare minutes after the attack, and she described the situation in detail to the dispatcher. We trusted her to be accurate and got everything we had available moving here stat. Hell, even if she had been less accurate in the details, knowing there were two bodies here would have got more than just a cruiser passing by.

"Karen may seem shaken up by this, but you can tell her from me that she handled this perfectly. Her and her friends helped preserve the crime scene before we got here. She knew exactly what we needed. It was only once we took over that she really fell apart, but while she was kinda in charge, she was great. Anyway, here we are."

Danny was initially distracted by the praise of

his daughter, and promised to pass on the compliments. He then concentrated on the matter in hand, and looked at the scene in front of him. He was struck by how familiar the female victim looked, then it hit him, "Raven, is it my imagination or does that victim look a lot like my daughter? She's even wearing the same clothes as Karen."

Raven shrugged, "It is common jogging attire. I expect you're just worrying about the similarities because you are scared for Karen. Hopefully it's just a coincidence, but we've got one of the patrol boys keeping an eye on your house for now."

"Thanks for arranging that. I suppose it likely is just the dad in me freaking. I won't ask how the girl died, it looks like someone nearly chopped her head off."

"The Medical Examiner doesn't think it was a knife. It looked too ragged, but he's very surprised at the depth of the injury. No other serious injuries that he could see, so she had to have bled out from that wound. With that much damage, it would have been quick. He did notice an odd mark on her ankle, but wasn't sure if it was related."

Danny frowned, "So, not a knife. It doesn't sound like our man. How did the guy die?"

Raven winced, "It looked like a single shotgun blast into his chest at pointblank range. The trauma to his organs would've killed him instantly."

"Shotgun? So maybe it is our man? With his mysterious partner?"

Raven replied, "So far we don't think so. We have

a couple of witnesses who saw someone fleeing the scene, and it's only one person that's mentioned. We have a pretty good description too."

"Reliable?"

"It should be. One of the witnesses was Quigley."

Danny looked taken aback, "Come again?"

Raven replied, "You know, Quigley. The patrolman who is working on the Father Williams task force that you're in charge of?"

"Yeah, yeah, I know who Quigley is. What I don't get is what he was doing here. Hold on, he jogs through here a lot, doesn't he?"

Raven nodded, "That's right." She pulled out her notebook, "In his own words, 'There was a male, just under six feet tall, slightly muscled, wearing green overalls and a black Balaclava. The overalls were bloodstained. He ran across the path and deep into the woods. I did not see him come out.'"

Danny shrugged, "Alright then, I assume the description has been circulated?"

Raven nodded, "Of course, and once we had enough men we stopped people going in and out of the park. No-one saw anyone matching that description out in the open, so presumably he's still in these woods somewhere."

Danny sighed, "Or he stripped off the helmet and overalls, and suddenly has become a normal Joe visiting the park. He could have just walked right on out of here before the park was closed off."

"If that's the case, we should find the overalls

somewhere, and that could give us clues that will lead to our man."

"You don't think it could be more than just the one perp?" checked Danny.

Raven shook her head, "If you take a look at the ground you'll see the fresh prints in the blood are only one shoe type and size."

"Curiouser and curiouser. I do not like this sudden urge for our citizens to start killing each other. It adds to my workload for a start," said the ME, Doctor Maddox, who had strolled over to join them.

He looked at the two detectives as they turned towards him and added, "I thought I should let you know about that gunshot wound. I know there has been speculation that it was the same weapon that killed our Father Williams. That one was two simultaneous shots from a double barreled weapon. And before anyone asks, I know this was not a single blast from a double barrel, because at pointblank range you would have bruising effect offset to one side where the other barrel was pushed against the skin. If the weapon had not been sawed off, then you would also get the impression made by the foresight. This blast is definitely a single barrel, and no bruising shows for a foresight. Not sure if that makes your job easier or more difficult, but I wish you luck. As always, there will be more details after the full autopsies, but with a pair of victims you will have twice the wait."

Raven said, "Thanks, Doc."

"No problem," he replied as he walked away.

Behind the two detectives the crime scene

technicians were still photographing and cataloging the scene, and Danny asked, "Do we have identification on either of the victims?"

Jacob Quigley chose this moment to come up, and answered for Detective Chavez, "I know the guy is Liam Hendersen. I've seen him round a lot. The girl, I think, is Vicky Boxford. Not seen her here as much, but I recall interviewing her about Father Williams. She doesn't usually run this late from what I remember, so I was surprised to see her."

"Thanks, Jacob," said Danny. "I know you're off shift at the moment, so you can head home now if you want, or you could pick up some overtime?"

"No thanks, Sir. It would be good to get home, get this bag off my back, and hit the shower."

Raven said, "I've always wondered, why do some joggers have book-bags on them, like you do, Officer Quigley?"

Danny supplied the answer, "It's usually a hangover from military days. You run with weights on your back because one day you may have to, and under fire at that. It also makes running without the extra weight seem like a breeze. Some civilian runners have picked up on the habit, too, but I would say Jacob here remembers his military days."

Jacob nodded, "That I do, but I also remember how good a hot shower feels after a run, so with your permission, I shall see you tomorrow." After waiting a few seconds to see if the detectives had anything else to say, he turned and ran off through the trees, heading in the direction of Downtown.

Danny watched him running off until he vanished in

the green leafiness, then turned to Raven, "You stay here and coordinate this mess, and I'll make a start on the eternal paperwork. We already have overtime approved because of the Frank case, so keep them at it as long as they want to. I'll see if the Chief agrees to mandatory overtime tomorrow, to keep more bodies on the streets longer. We need as many people on this as we can. This makes it four, no five unsolved homicides with at least three different perpetrators. It's gonna be a long week."

#

The killer stopped just outside the police cordon, and looked across the park to the activity in the woods. "A job well done," he said to the Beast.

The Beast nodded, "It could have gone better, but it could have been worse. Two kills in one day was a bonus that has left me glutted, and I feel it more than makes up for the disappointment of not catching Ms. Watson. Maybe some other time."

The killer mentally shrugged, "Yeah, it would have been nice, but I am not feeling picky about who falls to my skills. But if we really want to have her, we'll just have to try again."

"It will not be easy," cautioned the Beast, "especially if they suspect she was the target today."

The killer shrugged again, "Nothing ever is easy. If we need to, we'll find a way. I am sure our Danny Boy got a little nervous when he saw how the corpse was dressed, so that counts for something. If they do decide to guard her, that is less cops on the street, so another bonus. I suppose we better get going, and try to get a little sleep. I have the feeling this will be a long, but interesting and amusing week."

\#

BLOG: My last post had a lot of comments, all with a similar theme. Rather than answer them individually, we will go for this response to all of you:

Yes, I am sure there is a serial killer operating in my city, and anyone who looked at the data should at least be suspicions too - way too many unsolved cases above the average.

No, I have not notified my local police. It is far too entertaining watching the run round, all confused by this strange spike in their crime rate. It seems they do not have a clue, and I don't see any reason to enlighten them.

No, I will not say what city I live in. Please see the previous comment. Why would I want to deprive myself of that amusement? Fun like that can be hard to come by.

After reading this far, many of you will no doubt be confused, and probably concerned. You may even think that I am a liar, or am someone with serious issues. I can assure you I am telling the truth, and yes, I have what some would consider to be issues, but then, who doesn't?

I do have my own special information about the serial killer and his activities, and when the police finally start to put things together will be happy to share some of them with you and them in this public forum.

But for now, I prefer the anonymity and protection of the internet. Apart from the entertainment value, I have little wish for the police in any particular city to start looking for me. I am sure IP address searching will narrow things down, but it would only be with clues from my writing tied to the physical evidence that would help them find me to demand my assistance. If they were smart enough. But I don't think they are smart enough for that.

How am I so confident that there is a serial killer operating in my city? Well, the answer is easy - I know there is a killer because I **AM** the killer. Sweet Dreams!

Chapter 19

Danny was reluctant to drag himself out of bed when his alarm started chirping. Nevertheless he did, and made his way to the kitchen to get the coffee brewing. He was surprised to find Karen sitting at the table, staring into space. He went up to her and gently laid a comforting hand on her shoulder, "Hey, honey, can't you sleep?"

She looked at him and tried to smile, "No, every time I close my eyes, I see the bodies and all that blood. I can't seem to get that smell out of my head either."

Danny leaned down to hug her, "I understand. I would like to say it gets easier as the memories fade, but I know from experience that the bodies you are unlucky enough to see will stay with you forever. For me, I can get some measure of peace by finding the killers and putting them behind bars, but that isn't really an option for you. I do know some people you could talk to. It's part of the department, and they know their stuff, and are highly confidential."

"Thanks, Daddy. If I can't get my head round this by myself, I'll do that."

Rubbing her shoulders, Danny continued, "And no-one would expect you to go to college today. You've had quite a shock, and they will understand."

Karen managed a wan smile, "I wasn't planning on it. I got so little sleep last night it would be pointless."

After thinking for a few seconds, Danny said, "We've got some sleeping pills in the bathroom cabinet. I'll get you some after my shower?"

"I don't really like taking pills, but it does sound like a good idea to me. Even catching a few hours would be nice."

Danny set up the coffee quickly, and headed for the bathroom, saying, "I'll be right back."

He didn't spend long in the shower, partly so he could get Karen the pills so she could head to bed, but mainly because of an unusual thought that struck him. He walked from the bathroom wearing Helen's pink fluffy robe, holding the pill bottle in one hand while using the other to towel his hair dry. He put the bottle on the table, "Here you go, Baby Girl. A couple of these should give you some sack time. By the way, I just thought of something that may help you, and bring you a little peace back into your life."

Opening the bottle, Karen looked up with interest, "What's that?"

"Well, I know I get release by catching the crooks. Remember that program you started with all the crime data. You could work on improving that, and I'll keep getting you the latest data, and it might help us to track down some bad guys."

"It was only something I threw together for a little fun."

"If you got it running smoothly, with a way to keep track of different sorts of information for each case, it would be very useful. Like I said, I'll show it to the Chief. It is possible he would agree to using an expanded version to keep track of all the crime details. We have our own, but it has limitations, and this one you made could be tailored to our specific case needs." He did not know if the last part of his offer was even practical, but he thought the mental challenge would do wonders for his daughter. "What do you say?" he concluded.

She nodded, "Okay, after I wake up I'll take a look at it. Let's hope these will get me to sleep finally," swallowing the tablets and chasing them with a glass of water. "I'll see you later?" she asked in the form of a question.

He hugged her again, "I hope so, baby, but I may have to do a lot of hours today."

She nodded again, "I understand, you catch that punk."

"I plan on it," replied Danny, as Karen headed towards her bedroom. "I plan on it," he repeated to himself more quietly, "You don't do things like that in my city and expect to get away with it."

#

The killer had woken surprisingly early, but was relaxing in bed for now. Although he knew he had to get ready for work, he felt he could enjoy a few moments indulging himself with the memories of the previous night. The Beast was drowsy and content, it's hunger well satisfied by the bloodletting, and it watched with pleasure as the events were remembered.

The killer was surprised at how effective the garrote had been, and relished the feel of the blood running over his hands. As he was still aiming to confuse the police, he knew he could not use the garotte or the bang-stick again, at least until he became public knowledge. The bang-stick, like the shotgun, and he supposed all firearms, was not really a satisfying weapon for him, but they were fast and highly effective, so they had uses in emergencies.

He wondered what primary weapon he should use next. He had a variety of knives, but two had been blooded on Frank. And if he decided on a certain knife, where should he strike for best effect? Or would this be time to switch to a totally different style of weapon? This was an interesting puzzle that would keep his mind busy through the tedium of work.

#

Danny made a brief stop on his way to work to pick up a newspaper, and cursed when he saw the headlines. After parking his car he quickly made his way to the squad room and found it already full of people, despite the early hour. Most were just milling round, talking animatedly, apparently waiting for orders or an announcement to be made.

He walked to his desk in the detectives area, checking it for messages as he shucked his jacket. The few that lay there were of little immediate importance, and could be ignored for a short while. He saw even more officers filing in, some of these from a wide variety of shifts. He smiled grimly to himself, knowing that his brother officers had sensed something big was brewing.

Danny climbed on top of his desk, and caught everyone's attention by clapping loudly, "Okay, listen up everyone. Some of you have good cop instincts for trouble, or happened to see the news since ten last night and know we'd have to react. For those who are still in the dark, take a look at this." He held up his newspaper, showing them the glaring headlines: FOUR MURDERS IN THREE WEEKS. WHAT ARE THE POLICE DOING TO KEEP US SAFE?

"I have an answer for them. Right now overtime is approved for everyone. If we can't knock the Park case on the head by tonight, or one of the other unsolved murders, I'm going to get the Chief's approval for mandatory overtime, twelve hour shifts. I've already got permission from him to throw whatever resources we have to at the Frank case, and he'll back me in this – I'm throwing every available officer onto the streets.

"We will rattle every cage, yank every chain, talk to every snitch, grass and informant we have. I want house to house done round the three crime scenes, and when we're done we're doing it again. And again, and again if we have to. We're going to hammer these three cases until something breaks free. Hopefully it will be one of our cases, and not the City coffers." This last brought a smattering of nervous laughter, releasing some of the tension that had been building.

"I know all of this could play hell with other crimes, I know this will cause us problems in our personal lives, but if we can't protect the people we serve, what use are we? Something strange is going on out there, and we need to knock this bloodletting on the head. I need to see every man and woman giving it everything they have, and then some. I've worked up some starting schedules, and your leaders have them waiting. Any questions?"

Standing unnoticed in the doorway, the Chief spoke into the silence, "Good speech, and I agree with everything that Detective Watson said. The only question that I have is what are you all still doing here?" The mass of officers broke up in a rush, heading to find out their tasks for the day, and Danny climbed down from his desk.

The Chief strode towards him, "I meant it Danny, I am backing you all the way on this. You have not exceeded the authority I gave you, and you are right to hit this hard the way you are planning. I will do what I can to keep the media off out backs, and getting them working on our side, as well as keeping the City Council appeased. You have shown considerable talent and commitment over the past few months, and before that as well, and you deserve some recognition for it.

"Currently you are paid and ranked as a Sergeant. Effective immediately, to be consistent with your current implied authority, you can now consider yourself to be ranked as a Lieutenant. Brevet only, unfortunately. It will have to wait for the paperwork to catch up before it is official and for the pay increase to apply. My door is open to you twenty four seven, and I will make sure Gill is well aware of the situation."

For a moment Danny was speechless, then pulled himself together to answer, "Thank you, Sir. I will do my best to meet your expectations and uphold the traditions."

The Chief patted him on the shoulder, "You do not just meet expectations, you exceed them. Now go catch me a killer or three."

#

That was the overriding plan that Danny had as he spent the morning marshaling his forces. He now became the hub of a major operation, and had to find and dust off old emergency plans, or make new ones up on the spot.

With the Chief running interference on the media, he got the local TV and radio stations to put out information on the Park killings, along with an appeal for any witnesses. Information was also rerun for the Father Williams and Frank cases, and a new combined tip line was set up and publicized.

The Chief stressed to everyone he spoke to that there was no reason to suspect that the four homicides were all related, that there were major differences between the crimes, and that it was efficient resource management to combine parts of the three investigations. When asked about the apparent increase in officers on the street, the Chief replied, "You have a problem with more of us spending more time pounding the shoe leather? I would have thought people would find it reassuring having my officers everywhere they turn."

Despite 'only' being a political appointee, the Chief took his role as the head of the Police Division very seriously, and worked hard to get his officers what they needed. This in turn made the officers more willing to work for him, and for them all to feel like a well meshed team.

The response from the public was an increase in calls and tips, generating a mass of information to be collated and categorized. A rather disgruntled Gill Miller, along with other secretaries from all over the building, was dragooned into this side of the operation. Fortunately for Detective Lieutenant Watson, Gill attacked her task with her usual efficiency, and made sure the other 'helpers' were working at their hardest too.

Claytown was not a large city, so only had a modest police force, but Danny was determined to make the best use of everyone employed by the department. He knew that long term these actions would harm the department, but as a hopefully short term emergency measure it would boost the crime fighting capabilities of them all. "Desperate times require desperate measures," he thought, and switched to the next task on his list.

#

Sweet-lips was still feeling terrible over the loss of Frank, but was determined not to become a basket case over it, as she knew Frank would not have approved. So she tried to keep to her usual routine, which was why just before noon she stepped into her favorite diner for a cup of their strongest coffee.

As she sat at the table nursing the steaming mug, she noticed a newspaper laying on an adjacent table. It suddenly occurred to her that she had not kept up with local or national affairs lately, for years really, mainly because of her preoccupation with crack, and wondered what was happening outside her normal plane of existence.

Curiously, she looked at the front page and was greeted by the same headlines that Danny had displayed to the squad room. Her stomach turned at the thought of even more senseless losses of life, and wondered how it could be stopped. She then started thinking what she could do to help the police in general, and Danny Watson in particular.

As she sat there sipping her coffee and thinking things over, an idea struck her. She smiled at the thought, drained her coffee and stood to leave. She knew how she could help, but first she needed to make herself more presentable and potentially useful. Her first stop would be home, and then she would go from there to the public library to verify some details. Then she would pay Danny a visit.

#

The killer was amused by the increased police

presence on the streets. "They won't be able to keep this up," he said to the Beast, "they just don't have the available manpower or the funds. I give it a week before they are forced to cut back. If they don't, all those long shifts will erode their capabilities through fatigue."

The Beast had been drowsing happily by the still burning bars of his former cage, "Hmm, I can wait a week. I am still so gorged I feel I am going to explode."

The killer nodded, "I can see that. You are looking like a kitten full of milk relaxing by the fire."

The Beast snorted, "Pu-leaze! If you must use an Earthly analogy, I would prefer to be described as a majestic lion snoozing in the midday sun of the African savanna, beside the gently cooling remains of his kill."

"You know, the lion doesn't actually make any kills. It is the lioness that does all the hard work. Reminds me of another team I know of."

The Beast had an evil grin on his face, "I guess that must make you a woman then."

The killer laughed, "Not unless someone did some radical surgery when I wasn't looking!"

The Beast unsheathed its razor-sharp claws, "I got the tools if you got the time?"

"Actually, I think I'll pass."

"Seriously, it is no bother."

"Seriously, I like all my parts in one piece. If I wanted a banana split I'd go to an ice cream parlor. Anyway, these extra cops will make it a little harder to stalk people for a few days."

The Beast shrugged, "So why bother to stalk new targets? There are people closer to home that you could take out, and you already know their routines like clockwork."

The killer thought for a few moments, "Good point. I can think of one irritant that lives real close, and I already know his patterns and everything. As a bonus doing that could screw up any geographical profiling the police might try to do. Good idea."

The Beast preened, "I am not just all good looks and muscle, there is a brain to go with all this beauty and brawn."

"Oh, come on. You need to get out in the real world a little more."

The Beast chuckled, "I have been trying to tell you that for months, and you only just realize it? But not for a couple of days, eh? I am still stuffed from my last outing."

"Well, just let me know when you are hungry, because we both have habits to feed."

Chapter 20

Danny pulled his car into a parking bay outside the hospital. As he headed to the morgue he had the feeling he was spending more time here than at home. Pushing open the double doors he found Doctor Maddox sitting on the desk in the anteroom, holding a pair of folders, kicking his heels against the front of the desk. When he saw Danny come through the door, Maddox held out the folders, "I am not psychic, Security let me know you were coming down, so I thought we would chat in here. I am guessing you are getting tired of looking at dead bodies."

"You can say that again, Doc," replied Danny.

The Medical Examiner held out his hand, "Please, call me Henry. We seem to be seeing so much of each other lately we should be on first name terms. If we see each other any more than we have been, my wife may start to get suspicious."

Danny chuckled as he shook the proffered hand, "I'm Danny. You must be getting fed up with seeing me by now."

Henry Maddox shrugged, "You have been sending me a lot of bodies lately, but at least they are interesting ones. That makes up for having to do the paperwork. Now, I have not got much more than I had last night, but we know that the girl, Vicky Boxford, was laying face down when she was killed. I think I know how she was subdued too. If you look at the pictures of her ankles, you will see shallow cuts and the faint start of some bruising.

"It is my opinion she ran into a tripwire and the killer was fast enough to jump on her back before she could get back up. There is faint bruising consistent with that on her back, and from the depth of the laceration on her neck I would say this guy is very strong. It is not easy to pull a wire, which I suspect was a weapon like a garotte, through the muscles and tendons in the neck, but he managed it quite well. She bled out through that wound, which was the only major wound she sustained, and it would have been very quick."

Danny was flicking through the relevant photographs, then put that folder to one side. He opened the other, "And Liam Hendersen? Any oddities about him? It looked to me like a shotgun at close range, but no-one reported hearing a shot."

"That does not surprise me. Take a look at the picture of the wound."

Danny found the appropriate photograph, and saw an entrance wound roughly three quarters of an inch in diameter, which is about what you would expect to see from a close range shot with a twelve gauge shotgun. There was a black ring about an eighth of an inch wide surrounding this hole. Danny looked up, "What was it? Pointblank with a twelve gauge?"

Henry nodded, "As pointblank as it gets. The barrel had to be touching the skin. Plenty of powder residue round the wound, and I even found scraps from the cartridge inside him. There was a hell of a lot of damage in there. He did not know what hit him. No impression of the foresight, so I am presuming a sawed off. There was little sound for bystanders to hear because all the gases ended up inside the body, rather than ripping quickly through the air. That is about it with Liam. Nothing else came up."

"Okay, thanks, Doc, I mean Henry. These are my copies?" Danny asked as he held up the two folders?

"That they are," replied Doctor Maddox, "I should also tell you that there were no defensive wounds on either body. I do not think they even had time to fight back before they were killed. Oh, and apart from the apparent efficiency of the kills, this does not match with what I saw on the bum or the priest. It looks like we may have two crazies on the loose."

Danny grimaced, "Not for much longer, not if I can help it."

#

At the Federal Bureau of Investigations headquarters in Quantico, Virginia, Special Agent Joe Lander was working his way through his usual list of suspicious web entries, looking for any indication of criminal activity. This list was automatically complied each day by a piece of unusual software at the NSA, and if certain keywords came up on a web page in a manner that matched warning flags within the code, the site was flagged for further review by the appropriate agencies.

Joe had been used to seeing the URL that lead to an intriguing blog appear on his list every few days, and was not surprised to see it come up this morning either. He had left reviewing this site until after lunchtime, expecting it to be the usual slightly flawed psychological insights, but now that he read it he was starting to get very concerned.

By the time he reached the words 'I AM the killer. Sweet Dreams!' he was already working in another window on his computer, tracking down the location of the site hosting server, and preparing to backtrack to the originating IP address. He half expected this blog statement to be some kind of prank, but considered it was better to be safe than sorry. After all, if there really was a serial killer in the United States who was starting to confidently brag about his exploits online, finding his location would be a very useful step in apprehending him.

His instincts were already twanging before the site host location came up, and now they started screaming when he saw the server was a previously flagged one in the Ukraine. Joe expected it would not be easy to get the information he needed from the server owners, as the equipment was used to host brutal porn, torture and snuff movies. This firm worked well to protect the identities of the people who posted the horrific files, and previous attempts by law enforcement agencies in the US and abroad to get answers in a legal manner had been rebuffed or ignored.

So instead, Joe settled down to hack his way in to the server to follow the trail back to the originating computer. While not strictly legal, it was a method that had caught others who posted criminal activities on the web, and if his hacking was noticed Joe was sure the server owners would not want to draw any attention to themselves.

#

Karen Watson was also working at her computer, typing data from the old crime reports into the database she had built. She had woken up at noon, grateful to have gotten six hours of sleep, even if it was a medicated slumber. Now, to keep her mind busy and away from the visions of bloody corpses, she was furiously concentrating on making sure her data entry was accurate. This concentration did successfully push the scene in the woods out of her conscious mind, although she could still feel it nudging away at her subconscious.

Strangely, every now and then the metallic smell of blood and the rank smell of faeces would strike her, which she found highly distracting and nauseating. While she had not expected to ever see a dead body, if she had thought about it she would have never considered the smell. Looking back to yesterday evening she was not surprised by the smell of blood, which made sense given the nature of the murders.

What was really unsettling her was knowing that death could cause the bladder and sphincter to relax, voiding waste from the body as part of the inbuilt flight reflex. Logically it make sense to lighten the load if you are planning to escape, but emotionally it was scarring her to see that level of dignity stripped from the victims. Even a naked victim would have more dignity in her eyes than one that had soiled itself.

Karen remembered an old aphorism that she had found amusing when she had heard it growing up, but now she could see the darker, more cynical side to it - Remember to put clean underwear on in the morning, because if you get knocked down by a bus and people see that you have dirty underwear on, you would die of shame.

She had a strong desire not to be humiliated like that when she died, but working on the crime database project helped push these sickening thoughts away. Shaking her head, and sniffing the scent of the freshly cut flowers beside her, she got back to the routine of reading, typing and double checking her work.

#

Sweet-lips had spent the afternoon using computers too, an unusual activity for her, but she needed to follow her hunches and look up a few facts. She was surprised that the Web did not hold all of the information she needed, despite many peoples thoughts that everything could be found online. Maybe she just was not looking in the right places, so she had instead resorted to looking at some of the more obscure and rarely viewed books in the reference section.

While she was hunched up over one of these tomes, Sweet-lips looked up to see a patrolman walking through the library, simply checking people out. She noticed that it was primarily the males who were under the greatest scrutiny. Any person, male or female, that was wearing dark clothes, particularly hoodies, were asked to provide some identification and were quietly asked what they were doing at certain dates and times.

A part of her smiled as she realized some of what she had found in the old books would help Danny and the other officers find the people committing these heinous crimes, or at least put a crimp in their behavior. She paid for a few copies of some relevant pages to be made, and headed out of the library, on her way to talk to Detective Watson. First though, she needed to head home and pick a couple of things up, and get to the store to buy a couple of large cartons of orange juice.

#

Once again the killer found that his day job helped him in his nefarious activities. He had decided to review his knowledge of Ray Stubbs' apartment building, ready for a future nighttime visit, and almost immediately ran into one of the residents. All it took to assuage her fear of a stranger was one look at his outfit and a jaunty, "Just doing an inspection, Ma'am, nothing to worry about," from the killer.

And true to his word, he actually did do the kind of inspection his work would require, but that was all just a cover to see him to the top floor. If he wanted he could take down Mr Stubbs now, but as the foyer security cameras had recorded his entry and he had been seen by a witness, it was a less than good idea to do that if he wanted to keep his freedom. So he simply finished his inspection, and made sure that the lock on the fire door was jammed open, and went about the rest of his day.

#

It was late in the day and Danny was feeling exhausted, but stayed at his desk hoping that a good break would come in from one of the officers. It seemed to most people that the men and women of the Police Department were trying to interview everyone in the city, but given the lack of clues available to them, that was not far from the truth.

When his phone rang he looked up expectantly, but deflated slightly when he saw it was not an officer on the street, rather it was the reception desk. Still, he mused, it could be a citizen who had come in with some much needed information, so he answered with a positive sounding, "Detective Watson here."

The harassed sounding reply came from one of the secretaries, steamrolled into this new position for today, "I have a Ms. Karin Temple down here asking for you and only you. Did you want me to send her away? She's only a hooker, after all."

Danny replied, "No, because she's the one who got

our butts moving and looking for Frank, the dead homeless veteran, so we shall treat her with a little more courtesy and respect. I'll be down in a minute to talk to her." He hung up, shaking his head at the attitude of the secretary, and went down to see what Sweet-lips wanted.

When he got to the reception area he was surprised at how respectably turned out she was, in a plain black sweater and dark blue jeans. Even her hair had been toned down. "Hey, Ms. Temple, how can we help you today?" he asked, putting on the charm just to show the secretary how it could be done.

As they walked through the security door, Sweet-lips said, "Can we go somewhere a little private? I have something to run past you that you may like."

"You know who one of the mystery killers is?" asked Danny, hopefully.

"No, but I can show you how you could improve your chances of finding them."

"Now that gets my attention," he replied, opening the door to one of the more comfortable interview rooms in the station, "Come in here. I'm all ears."

Sweet-lips looked at the room in surprise, seeing the comfortable chairs scattered round a coffee table, with floral pictures on the walls. The only things that betrayed the fact this was an interview room were the cameras discretely mounted in the corners, and the official issue tape machine by one of the walls. "Nice place. I didn't know people could be interviewed in such splendor. Whenever I got arrested I got dumped in a gray painted cinder block room with uncomfortable steel chairs, not forgetting the optional handcuffs."

Danny shrugged as he sat down, "Sometimes we need to be more gentle in our interview techniques. This is used for abuse victims, kids, people like that who need a subtle helping hand. Now, what did you want to talk to me about?"

Sweet-lips laid a folder on the table, sat back in her chair, and said, "I don't think you'll be able to maintain the extra officers on the streets for much longer. I don't know how you did it, but no matter how good it looks to those worried about the murders, I expect the budget will implode if you keep it up." She paused, taking a long swig from the bottle of orange juice she carried, "Now, I found a legal way to quickly boost the number of officers you have available, and actually save money into the bargain."

Danny looked puzzled, "What? How? And what got you thinking of this?"

She shrugged, "I'm not just a dumb hooker. I wanted to do something to help Frank, and I found the perfect way. I expect you'll have to run this all past the Chief, but I want to be the first citizen to offer their services as an Auxiliary Officer."

Danny grasped the implications of this immediately, seeing it as an elegant solution to the pressing manpower issue, and a way that the common citizen could help out in this crisis. For most Police Departments, a couple of murders would not cause any staffing problems, or even be unusual, but Claytown was only a small city and budget cuts had hurt them over the years. Danny reached out eagerly for the folder, asking, "Are these the details on it?"

Sweet-lips nodded, "Copies of the relevant

Ordinances from the City files, and as far as I can tell they've never been repealed. They may be a little out of date, but the basic principle is still valid today."

Danny flicked through the handful of sheets, quickly reading the details. He then stood up, "Come on, we are going to see the Chief."

#

Without Gill Miller guarding access to the Chief Cerberus style, it was easy for Danny to walk in, knock on the open door and get an instant appointment. With Sweet-lips in tow he made his way to the chairs arranged in front of the huge desk, and said, "Chief, I don't think you've been introduced to this young lady. This is Karin Temple, who has come to me with a striking way we can weather this crisis."

The Chief delicately shook Sweet-lips' hand, and indicated she should take a seat, saying, "Ms. Temple. Delighted to meet you. I am sorry we could not give you better news about your friend, Frank."

Sweet-lips replied, "There was nothing more that anyone could have done. His killer struck before anyone even knew he was missing. Really it is because of Frank that I am here. You know part of my history, how I've been living my life the past few years. All that is going to change because I want to help catch his killer, and to do that I'd even be willing to give up the crack I have craved for years. I'll do it all for the memory of Frank."

The Chief looked slightly puzzled, "Those are great sentiments and laudable goals, but I fail to see how that involves Lieutenant Watson and myself."

Sweet-lips flashed Danny a look on hearing about his promotion for the first time, and Danny said, "It's very recent." He then addressed the Chief, "Sir, it actually is very relevant, and Ms. Temple has done a lot of research and ground work before coming here and volunteering her services. I have reviewed it and looks like a great idea to me, but I feel this decision is above even my new authority.

"To summarize, there is an old Ordinance from when Claytown City was founded that states, 'should an emergency situation arise, if so advised by the ranking police officer, the elected Mayor of Claytown City can order the formation of the Auxiliary Services to assist the police, for the duration of the emergency, or until such time as they are no longer necessary.' That is modernizing the language somewhat, and there are details on pay, equipment and so on, but the upshot is we could enlist citizen volunteers to help us right now, and at a fraction of the cost of paying all this overtime. I know there would be plenty of wrinkles to iron out, but the idea seems sound to me."

The Chief thought for a moment, his chin resting on his steepled hands, then said, "Okay, I can see part of how this could work, but I can also see certain issues coming up, namely suitability of volunteers and criminal records."

He turned to Sweet-lips, "Despite your good sounding intentions, you are still a convicted prostitute and drug user, which is not the kind of person we look for in recruits and allow them to serve in the Police Department."

Sweet-lips nodded, "Yes, Sir, I understand that,

and can see how unconventional it would be. But this is an unconventional situation, and the Ordinance even has something in it to ensure the correct type of person can be enlisted. If two serving police officers can vouch for the recruit, then past crimes and behavior doesn't affect the enlistment. Also, Auxiliary Services Officers are specifically restricted from certain duties, and aren't even allowed to bear any weapons, apart from staves. I guess that a stave would now be the equivalent of a baton or night stick.

"The idea is that they can fill in for minor administration roles, enforce traffic laws and act as an extra pair of eyes on the street, easing the burden on the main police forces. I'd hoped that as I'm already a registered Confidential Informant, that would go a long way towards establishing my suitability and credibility." She attempted to sit at her idea of attention while waiting for the Chief to mull this over.

He turned to Danny, and said, "Right then, I could buy into that part, but I would prefer some boiler plating of the enlistment conditions, to be on the safe side. Only officers ranked Sergeant and above can provide the recommendation. Now, what about uniforms and equipment, and the cost of outfitting and training this force? How large a force are we talking about, anyway?"

Danny replied, "You have to understand that I'm working some of this out on the fly, but then that does seem how my day has been so far. A uniform can be as simple as a marked t-shirt and a cap, and we might get lucky and have that stuff donated by a local business. The size of the force could be as big as we need it, and is really only limited by the number of volunteers we get. If we matched our nominal strength of the Police Department it would still work out cheaper than our overtime bill, and make a lot more people available."

The Chief sat back, his hands resting on the arms of the chair, and while he thought he idly drummed his fingers on the woodwork. After a short time he said, "I guess another way to look at this is the way Sheriffs can swear in deputies to assist them. I even recall some notorious criminals sometimes became deputies so they could bounty hunt each other. Or something like that. I can see no problem with this proposal in the short term. Detective Watson, work out the details while I call the Mayor to get his approval and authorization. Auxiliary Officer Temple? Welcome aboard."

Chapter 21

As they walked back through the hallways, heading towards Danny's desk, he said to Sweet-lips, "The admin pukes will have gone by now, although to be honest they weren't doing admin today anyway, so we can't get you all signed up and badged officially. I'm guessing you'll want to start working immediately though. You must have had something in mind or you wouldn't have gone to all this hassle."

She nodded, "I'm known throughout the city as a street girl, so it would be easy enough for me to talk freely with the girls and the other night people, get more info from them than Detective Chavez or anyone else would."

Danny thought for a moment, a handful of seconds that took him to his desk, and he sat down, "Okay, I can see that working, at least short term, but you do you think they'll react when they find out you're a cop now?"

Sweet-lips shrugged, "Well, I won't exactly be a cop, just an Auxiliary helper, and I'll make sure they know the difference and the reasons why. I know how to talk to them in language they'd respond to, and I'll also be making it clear I don't care about any breaches of the law that don't involve these murders."

"Sounds fair to me, but I reckon after you've worked for me more officially than you've before, even if it is just on this one case, you'll have a hard job going back to being a working girl, and keeping that trust with them."

"I don't want to be a prostitute anymore. I told you, I am giving that up. It was just an easy way to keep me in crack. No crack, no need to be a hooker. And I will stay clean, as long as I don't run out of juice," she added, taking a swig from the bottle she still held.

Danny looked puzzled, "What does OJ have to do with anything?"

"When you are suffering from withdrawal symptoms, drinking orange juice or cola helps to lessen the effects. It's not perfect, and I have to admit I also had a doobie to help chill me, but that is better than crack."

"I'll turn a blind eye to that for now, but if they decide to drug test you in future and you fail, that is your lookout. And if I see you taking any drugs from now on, I can't ignore it, understand?"

Sweet-lips nodded, "I gotcha, clean is the word."

"Good. Now I better start making a few plans to handle some Auxiliary recruits if the Mayor okays your idea. I don't see why not, but even if he doesn't, I'd still find a way to get you on the books, if you can stay clean."

Sweet-lips replied, "I can do that. It's what Frank wanted me to, one of the last things he said to me, so I am going it for him. Did you want me to start tonight?"

"I can't give you any badge or equipment until tomorrow, but I doubt you'd want to be wearing any kind of uniform anyway. So I guess you could start right now. You okay with that?"

Sweet-lips nodded, "The sooner we can get Frank's killer behind bars, the better."

"Okay then, Auxiliary Officer Sweet-lips, get to it."

#

Agent Lander frowned at his computer screen. Whoever posted the blog entries was a tricky one for sure. Any uploads to the server had been routed through at least half a dozen similarly unsavory servers, bouncing across the world from one jurisdiction to another. Many of these had very lax laws that made his job officially harder.

Unofficially, he had an easier time, following the routing back along the chain by using some very special software written by a hacker friend of the Bureau. It was not legal in any sense, but Joe Lander reasoned that breaking these particular laws only hurt criminals and other undesirables, and could save lives. Besides, as long as the exact method he used to get these results was not fully documented, his bosses would be able to turn a blind eye to the process, preferring to concentrate on the results.

And on the subject of eyes, the Special Agent was finding his were becoming heavy after nine hours of staring at a computer, and figured it was time to get home. He needed some sleep or he would start to make mistakes, and that would not help save anybody. Luckily he lived only minutes from the Quantico facility, and gratefully abandoned his desk for his bed.

#

Danny Watson heard back from the Chief that the Mayor had provisionally granted approval for the activation of the Auxiliary Services, with an initial strength limit of twenty four officers. The Mayor had specified that the majority of these

Auxiliary Officers would be used on the tip lines and minor administrative areas, freeing up any regular officers from these roles. Additionally, they were only to be used for other duties with approval of two people above the rank of Lieutenant. That ruling effectively meant that apart from Danny and the Chief, the only other person who could approve a more active role for an Auxiliary would be Peter Sampson, the Lieutenant in charge of the Patrol Officers. Lieutenant Sampson also oversaw the more administrative side of the Police Department, so he would be the one processing most of the paperwork for the new recruits.

Lieutenant Sampson had gone home by this time, so Danny could not talk to him directly, but instead he fired off a series of memos to Peter and his subordinates. These were also carbon-copied to the Chief, and detailed all the measures required to recruit, equip and provide very basic training for the Auxiliary Officers. With this accomplished, after checking that nothing new had come in from the officers on the street, Danny headed home himself to get some well earned rest.

#

Sweet-lips left the Police Department without any uniform, without even a badge, but she did have fire in her heart and was determined to avenge Frank. If that meant working openly for the police, then so be it. She walked down Lincoln Avenue, heading towards her preferred intersection, and pulling out her cellphone she made three calls in quick succession.

Prostitutes do tend to be gregarious, often flocking together in groups for safety reasons, as well as offering a wider selection to the customers. Despite this natural gathering, the

Claytown hookers felt little need to have a dominant hierarchy, as the women could work out issues between themselves, all equals acting together to solve problems. However, there were still times when leadership and direction of some form was required, and the three hookers that Sweet-lips had called were the undisputed leaders that the girls officially did not have.

They all met under the tree beside the church, and Sweet-lips said, "Thanks for coming. I know you all have work to do, but you know I've had something bothering me for a while, and I needed to talk to you girls together."

Heather Nelson, a petite young woman with seductive skin the color of coffee, replied, "This is to do with Frank?"

Sweet-lips nodded, "That's right. But before I carry on I wanted to let you know something. Because of the recent murders, the police will be looking for citizens to become volunteer officers to help them catch the killers. Because Frank was such a good friend to me, I have signed up."

When she saw the looks on the faces of the three working girls, Sweet-lips held up her hands, "Don't worry, all I care about is getting these murdering scum behind bars. I laid down some ground rules about how I would operate, and the police agreed to my terms. Whatever else you all do, I don't care and won't tell about it. I just need your help in this."

Heather, known to many as Nightshade, by unspoken consensus was the spokeswoman for the other two. "We know you have talked to all of us before, and the other girls too. I don't know what else we could add."

"I spoke to everyone individually before. I am hoping a joint brainstorming session will throw something new up."

"Well, okay," replied one of the remaining girls, a heavyset blond called Chelsea, "because it is you asking, we can do that."

"Thank you. Right, now think back to the night Frank disappeared. Do you remember seeing anything strange? Anyone unusual?"

Heather laughed, "Honey, you know we always see unusual people!"

"Okay, I deserved that. Think another way then. Do you remember seeing anyone hanging round the previous days, especially if you haven't seen them since? Or repeat cars at that time? Not customers, obviously, but people who just seemed a little out of place."

Chelsea thought for a moment, "Well, there was that black car driving round, a few days before Frank went missing. It was just going up and down Lincoln, and along the side streets, like the driver was looking for someone. He sure wasn't looking for business, 'cos we wuz all strutting our stuff."

"Hey, I remember that," said Heather, "Not sure if it was black, but it was a dark color for sure. A mid sized sedan of some kind. I didn't catch the make or model, but it was kinda dark even without the light."

Sweet-lips nodded, "I saw it too, but didn't think much of it. But if we all thought it was odd, then chances are it could be something."

Heather looked up, "Wasn't that the night Old

Jimmy said he saw the ghost?"

Sweet-lips gave her a puzzled look, "Ghost? I don't remember hearing anything about that. What's the story?"

Chelsea replied, "A couple of the old boys were talking, an' I was listening in, and I recall Jimmy was one of them an' he was real worked up. He said he was woken up by this figure who he could hardly see, was dressed all in black, and the ghost just looked at him hard and vanished. Someone else said the same thing happened to them, but it weren't no ghost, it was some dude wearing a black hoodie or something."

Heather was thoughtful, "Yeah, that's right. I remember seeing a dude like that the next day too. Just hung round a lot, real close to my place. Like he was watching someone...." Her voice trailed off as she realized something, "Oh, no, that is how they said that murderer was dressed. Damn, he was stalking Frank for sure, and I didn't realize. He could've been checking all of us out for days, but chose poor Frank for some reason. He could come back for any one of us!"

"Calm down, Heather," said Chelsea, "we don't know if he kills women or not. This is the guy who offed Father Williams, and I've heard these whack jobs go after a type, not random folks. They said that nut who killed them runners in the park is a different guy. No-one is after us hookers yet. That's right, Sweet-lips?"

Sweet-lips answered, "Yeah, that is the official line, but honestly they really don't know. These killings have been too clever, and the cops are stumbling round in the dark a lot. That's why I decided to help them. They sure need a lotta help right now."

Heather looked her up and down, "Honey, how did you get them to hire you? Bad habits and a rap sheet usually stop you getting into a pig pen, unless it's on the wrong side of some bars. And, no offense, you're a crack smoking hooker."

Sweet-lips shrugged, "I guess they are that desperate for help they'll take anyone. Kinda like the Sheriffs in the Wild West, so I heard. Is anything is nudging your memories? No? Well, if you girls think of anything else amongst yourselves, you've all got my cell, right?"

The other girls nodded, and Heather said, "We'll check with the others too, see if we can refresh a memory or two."

"Okay, thanks a lot girls. I won't forget it. And I'll make sure the regular cops don't forget your help either. Catch you later, I better go report in."

#

The killer was finally on his way home after a longer work day than usual, and noticed the group of prostitutes further down the road. He said to the Beast, "Reckon they do a group discount when there is that many of them?"

The Beast shrugged, "They probably charge more, but what do I care? I only like them when they are dead and bleeding. Oh, look at that. The rate has just gone down now, one of them is heading this way."

The killer smiled, and jokingly asked, "You wanna play?"

"I would not normally turn down a feeding

opportunity, but it is probably a touch too exposed here. I thought I was the reckless, bloodthirsty one?"

The killer grinned, "Maybe I'm getting a taste for it, kinda enjoying things more. I reckon tomorrow night, if I'm not too tired, we should pay a visit to our old friend, Mr. Stubbs."

"Well, I may be full right now, but I am never going to say no to a chance like that!"

#

Sweet-lips was furious when she left the Police Department. She had spent a truly frustrating fifteen minutes arguing with the woman currently on desk duty. It seems that although everyone in the city knew she worked as a prostitute, this secretary, again covering the front desk, would not believe her when Sweet-lips said she was working for Danny now. It took all Sweet-lips all her powers of persuasion to get the woman to even take a message, and all her resolve not to hit her. She made her way home, wanting so bad to get some crack to take the edge off the world, but instead looked forward to a joint to ease her to sleep.

#

When Danny woke that Friday, after he had got the coffee brewing he stopped to look in on Karen. She had either conquered her demons enough to sleep, or had found the bottle of sleeping pills. Danny went into her room, and crouching beside the bed, gently shook Karen's shoulder. "Hey, girlie, wake up. There is something I wanted to tell you before I go to work."

She sat up, looking momentarily confused, then

smiled sleepily, "Morning, Dad. Those pills really do help you get a good nights sleep. Wow, the problem could be waking up.'

"It doesn't help that it is before six, but I needed to talk to you, and it could be good news. I'm gonna take a shower and meet you in the kitchen for a coffee? Why don't you go ahead and serve yourself, have a chance to wake yourself up before we talk?"

Karen rubbed her eyes, then stretched, "Coffee sounds good. If it's good news as well, don't keep me waiting."

Danny smiled as he stood up, "I'll be as quick as I can."

#

The killer was awake at an early hour too, full of energy, despite the rigors of the past few weeks, lack of sleep and the still dark sky. He was comfortable in the night, because of its ability to hide him, and did not feel that sleepy during the hours of darkness.

Once he had got some tea brewing, he mentally nudged the Beast awake, and fired up his laptop. The Beast said to him, "Hey, what did you do that for? I was only dozing. And what are you doing up this early?"

The killer shrugged, "No idea. I'm just feeling a kinda buzz, you know?"

The Beast looked round the killers buzzing mind, "Well, things do seem a little hyper in here. Are you going to check the blog?"

"Oh yes, got to see what they've said since I was

last on. Hmm, hold on." The killer had worked his way through his elaborate routing to gain administrator access to his blog, and along the way had noticed several cyber tripwires had been sprung, apparently unnoticed or unheeded by whoever was searching. From the pattern of trips he could see that someone was trying to find where he was located. He sighed, "Okay, so maybe bragging online wasn't such a good idea. But it feels so good, thumbing your nose at the whole world. I don't see that the searcher has got down the line yet, and I doubt they'll be able to make the final connection, but we'll see."

The Beast shrugged, "I would have warned you, but I did not think you would have listened. So I did not bother, it seemed like a waste of effort. Not that I would want to stop you, because who cares, we were bound to be noticed eventually. Now, what has been said?"

The killer started scrolling through the dozens of comments, quickly reading them as his anger rose. "Let's see, about half are totally disbelieving, many of them abusive or mocking. Of those that seem to believe me, most want some kind of proof. Oh, and we have a couple of special requests, it seems. I don't think we'll fulfill those wishes, unless we happen to be in the neighborhood. But this is making me mad. They want proof, I'll give them some."

The Beast sat back, enjoying the killer's rage, and watched as the words appeared on the screen.

#

BLOG: It seems there is a high level of suspicion and disbelief at my recent entries, and demands for proof. While I am not going to provide my social security number or ZIP code, I will leave some clues along with some warnings.

I can see that some are trying to hack my trail, and if I find them then they will join the five from this county that I have offered as bloody sacrifice in the past two months, with others slain before that.

Another will join this list today, a man with the initials RS, and he will have his hands removed as a sign and warning to you all that I am serious, deadly serious.

I missed the dicks daughter recently, but took two in her place. If pressed by them, then every member of my local police department, and their families, will become potential targets.

Believe I am here, that I am for real, or my wrath will be taken out on as many victims as I can lay my hands, and it will take a lot of blood to quench my burning rage.

#

The Beast nodded approval, but was wary that his host was heading towards an event horizon that could prove disastrous for them both, and the rate of acceleration was increasing. Inwardly, the Beast shrugged, after all it was only the carnage that it was interested in. This would be sure to get it what it truly desired – blood.

Hiding its fears inside, outwardly the Beast looked eager, running its tongue over its fangs, and asked, "Are we going to hunt? That blog was great, just what was needed, and has me all fired up. When do we hunt?"

The killer logged off his computer and stood up. Hurriedly dressing in his running outfit, he grabbed a newly prepared kill bag. "We hunt now," he replied as they headed out the door.

Chapter 22

Jimmy Butler, also known to many as Old Jimmy, was woken by his bladder. At his age, heading somewhere into his sixties, parts of his body were not as robust as they used to be. He had little choice but to answer the call of nature, so Jimmy crawled out of his old and tattered sleeping bag and made his way to a side window. Whenever he was sleeping in a building, he made sure not to urinate inside, being considerate enough to think that others may want to sleep there. He knew that not everyone was as fastidious as him, or showed the same respect for others, but values like that had been driven into him from childhood.

As he sprayed the bushes growing up past the window, Jimmy looked out onto the deserted square that nearby buildings formed. It was like a central courtyard, made by the various buildings that went round the edges of this city block. A large part of it was graveled, previously used as a rough parking lot by many of the old buildings previous tenants, but now the whole area had an abandoned look and feel to it.

That air of abandonment was why Jimmy chose this place to hole up for a night or two. If people see bums entering empty buildings, they tend to call the police or the owner of the building, but this courtyard surrounded by vacant properties made it easy for him to get a roof over his head without being spotted. Jimmy was wary, and tended to move round a lot, never staying in one place for long, no more than a few days. It made him feel more secure, and cut down on the chances of people complaining about his presence. He had no problems sleeping in doorways or beside dumpsters, but sometimes it was just nice to have a roof over your head for the night.

Finished with his watering of the vegetation, Jimmy decided as he was awake now he might as well get his day started. He headed back to his tatty sleep bag, with the equally battered rucksack that doubled as his pillow. Reaching into one of the side pockets of the bag, he found the small tin that held his stash of tobacco.

He never had to buy tobacco, because he had no qualms about picking up discarded butts to strip them of any remaining tobacco. Any smokes that he made from this stash, using cheap cigarette papers, were never thrown away. Instead they were extinguished carefully and shredded back into the tin. As this had been his practice for many decades, and thanks to the law of averages some of the tobacco had been used and reused for years, some of what he was loading into the flimsy paper could have been used to re-tar roads.

Jimmy was not bothered though, even if it could be a pain to light these cigarettes at times, because thriftiness like this had allowed him to continue his quiet, but frugal, lifestyle for years. He checked that the discarded soda can he had been using as an ashtray was where he expected, then lay down to enjoy his quiet morning smoke.

#

Karen looked up when Danny came into the kitchen, and could not help but smile, "You need some pink fluffy slippers to complete that outfit."

Danny looked down and grinned bashfully, "Yeah, I know. But I don't have my own robe and I don't think you want to be looking at my moobs when I talk to you." He fetched himself a cup of coffee and sat down opposite his daughter.

She asked, "So, what's this good news I've been waiting impatiently for?"

Danny frowned, "Not sure if 'good news' was the right phrase, maybe 'good opportunity' could've been better. If I was to offer you the chance to come work at the Police Department as a kinda data analyst, at least until we clear the town of these damn killers, would you be interested?"

"Heck, yeah! When could I start? What would I have to do?" cried Karen exuberantly, surprising Danny with her complete enthusiasm for the idea.

"Wow, you really are up for this. You'll like the extra good news that comes with this offer, you'll even get paid for it. Not much, but it's better than nothing. Last night the Mayor activated what's known as the Auxiliary Services, which was designed to assist the local police in times of emergencies. With citizens being dropped left and right by these unknown scum, it was felt this qualifies as an emergency.

"I could use someone with brains, and that I trust, to plow through the data we have on all these murders, and find and analyze any links. I've done it myself, but only on paper, and didn't get too far. I know someone with your skills could ferret the answers out. You still up for it?"

Karen nodded, "After what I saw in the Park, all I want is to do anything I can to help put the murderers behind bars." She then shrugged, "I guess I must be your daughter, a mini-cop through and through."

"Well, you've got thirty minutes to get ready before I leave for work. Jump to it, Mini-Officer."

Karen jumped to her feet, threw a messy salute in the direction of her father, as she headed to her bedroom with a cry of, "Aye, aye, sir."

Danny smiled as he went to get ready himself, thinking, "That's my girl."

#

The killer's smokescreen jog did not last long. He just needed to get a dozen blocks North and East to a beautifully secluded area he knew. He had found in the past an entire block that was surrounded by vacant and disused buildings, and he ran into the resulting courtyard so he would be well out of sight from anyone. He already had the bag off his shoulder and was opening it before he had even stopped.

With the Beast urging, "Hurry, hurry," the killer pulled out the gray sweatpants and hoodie, and quickly donned the clothing after shucking the running gear. Next he wrapped a scarf round his lower face, just leaving his eyes peeking over the top, and pulled up his hood. Closing the bag, he swung it over his back again, and jogged out of the courtyard.

#

Old Jimmy sat up with a start. He could hear someone moving outside the abandoned house he was in. When he looked out of the nearby window he was expecting to see the police coming to clear him out, and he took his time, moving slowly and carefully so as not to draw any attention to himself.

He was surprised when he looked out through the bushes that partially screened the opening and saw the figure dressed all in gray, and he was reminded instantly of the ghost he had seen before. Apart from the apparent color difference in the clothes, everything else matched his memories from the last time – height, build, the way the figure moved. Jimmy was frozen with fear, terrified that the Ghost was coming for him, and did not even want to move until long after the gray clad figure had run off.

#

With time so pressing, the killer was not devious in his route to Ray Stubbs' apartment. Indeed, he ran as fast as he could, partly to shave time, and partly to build up the momentum he would need when he reached the fire escape. It was not until he began his killing spree that he realized just how much of a security risk they posed to buildings, especially if you were athletic. In theory the ladders were supposed to be suspended far enough above the ground that they could not be reached from below, but a powerful leap, especially if boosted from a handy object below, could get you on the rungs.

Beside the fire escape outside the apartment building were a pair of conveniently located large planters, an attractive decoration, but also the gateway to his next kill. A quick jump on one, followed by a lunging leap, saw the killer onto the ladder, and his momentum quickly carried him up the rungs and onto the lowest platform. Running lightly on his toes, he ran up the steps all the way to the top floor, and paused briefly to get his breath back, listening to see if his activities had been noticed.

He tried the handle to the security door and was glad to see that no-one had noticed the broken lock, and quietly eased the door open. The killer slipped inside, pulling the door closed behind him, and padded towards the door to Ray's apartment.

The Beast was purring in anticipation as the killer used his putty knife to pop the lock, but this changed to a growl of frustration as the security chain stopped the door short. "Great," the Beast grunted, "now what do we do? Breaking that will make too much noise."

"Chill, I've got it covered. We've been in there before, and that chain wasn't screwed down real good, so..." the killer pulled a flat-headed screwdriver from his bag of tricks, and slid it behind the chain housing. Instead of being flush with the door frame, there was a pronounced gap that betrayed the weakness in its setup. A little pressure was all it took to force the screws out of their holes, and all with causing no more noise than a faint tinkle as the pieces fell on the carpet.

The Beast grinned, "Now we are talking. Come on, let us get some blood flowing!"

The killer carefully stowed the screwdriver and the putty knife, and pulled out a blackjack. "Your wish is my command," he mentally said as they slipped inside.

Closing the door quietly, they looked round the apartment, which was bathed in light from the moon shining through the windows. The place was mostly devoid of furniture and decorations, with the living room containing only a reclining chair opposite an entertainment system. From what they could see of the other rooms, the general decor was spartan to the extreme.

"Still living the simple life," the killer commented.

"Not for long," snickered the Beast.

With so little furniture it was easy to move through the bare apartment, skirting the small lonely table and chair in the dining room on their way to the open bedroom door. The killer looked in and saw Ray Stubbs sleeping in his bed, and quietly crept into the room.

Despite his care, a floorboard creaked loudly, waking Ray, who sat up and said, "Hey, who are you?"

The killer swung the blackjack at Ray's temple, knocking him unconscious in an instant. He then whispered in Ray's ear, "I am your death."

Glancing round the room, the killer saw a pile of dirty clothes in the corner, and grabbed a shirt from the top. He ripped it quickly into strips, and stuffed the remains into Ray's mouth, pulling strips across the makeshift gag and round his head, securing the gag tightly in place. Satisfied with his arrangements to keep Ray quiet should he come round, the killer opened his bag and removed a large meat cleaver, and grinned evilly.

Climbing onto the bed, he knelt with his knees on Ray's shoulders, legs holding the body still, and pulled one of the arms into position against the wall. The killer raised the cleaver above his head and swung hard. It slashed into the waiting wrist, coming up hard against the bone, and Ray murmured slightly, almost unheard because of the gag. Blood was flowing freely from the wound, and the Beast was crooning, "Again, again!"

The blade fell again, and the flesh parted and the bone cracked. The pain caused Ray to twist his head and start to struggle, even though he was still out of it. A third time the cleaver crashed into the wrist, shattering the bone and causing the hand to hang limply by a few tattered shreds of flesh. A final quick slash removed these last strands and the killer caught the hand before it fell.

The intense pain and pulsing blood brought Ray out of his stupor, his eyes opening wide and darting with fear. The killer waved the amputated appendage in front of Ray's terrified eyes, and said, "Can I give you a hand, Ray?"

Ray was screaming and struggling, the noise muffled by the gag and his movements hampered by the killer straddling him. Trying to free himself was impossible, indeed every twist made it feel like his shoulders were being wrenched from their sockets. In desperation, he tried to strike at the shadowy figure pinning him down with his remaining hand.

The Beast roared, "Do the other one!" and the killer snatched the flailing limb and pinned it to the wall. Two solid blows later and Ray was unconscious again, driven back under by the incredible pain, while his remaining wrist was much battered by the cleaver. The bone was barely damaged because of the struggling, but now Ray no longer moved the killer could hack down again and again until the other hand fell.

The blood was pulsing less freely now, as the pressure dropped in Ray's body, but both the killer and the Beast could feel his heart beating wildly, trying to pump the remaining blood round the body. Instead it was spraying it out, all over the wall and bed. The killer doubted Ray would regain consciousness again as the blood loss deprived his brain of oxygen, and stood to survey his handiwork.

In the background he could hear the Beast purring loudly, but the killer was intently focused on the gory scene in front of him. If anyone had seen the beatific smile on his face they would have assume that the killer, to say the least, had some mental issues that needed some attention. After gazing at the blood soaked walls and dribbling stumps that terminated Ray's arms, he sighed and said, "Picture perfect."

He moved to collect a drop of blood for his collection, and was amazed to see Ray had his eyes open, and they were still moving, attempting to focus. The Beast noticed too, and paused in his sounds of feasting delight to say, "We cannot leave a job unfinished like this. He seems determined to hang onto life. I find that a little offensive."

The killer nodded, "I agree. Let's see what we can do about that." He was still holding the cleaver, with blood dripping from the blade, and the killer swung it in a powerful overarm sweep that left the blade embedded in the now split skull. "Much better," he commented as the eyes glazed over.

The Beast nodded, "A much clearer ending. Very artistic too. I think we should leave it like that. Very nice indeed."

The killer surveyed the macabre effect, "Oh yes, that will do nicely. Now let's finish up here and get going. Sadly the day job is calling."

#

Danny was chafing to get moving himself when Karen finally returned to the kitchen. She was wearing tan jeans and a white sweater, and had her hair pulled back into its usual ponytail. "This was the best I could do. I don't really have many 'business' clothes."

Danny said, "It works for me. We haven't decided on how Auxiliaries will be dressed, but I reckon we'll go for a pretty casual look, just to keep costs down. Are you ready to go?"

Karen nodded, then threw a lazy salute, clicking her heels together, "Yes, Sir!"

Danny chuckled, "It needs more practice. Come on, let's get moving and see what the day will bring."

#

The killer was ready to get going now. Despite the gore that splattered the bedroom wall and bed, he had only got a little on his pants and shirt. Well, that was really only a 'little' by his usual standards. Regardless, once he had got to the living room, he stripped down to his underwear and replaced everything with an almost identical outfit. The bloody clothes were stored in the usual garbage bag, and everything was carefully packed away. The only item missing from his initial load-out was the cleaver, and that was being deliberately left behind. Having only handled it with gloves since he last cleaned it, he was not worried about any evidence like fingerprints being on the weapon.

The Beast said, "Come on, if you planning on getting to work, you need to get moving."

"Yeah, I know. I'm ready now. But I much prefer this kinda work to my boring day job."

The killer opened the door slowly, saw the landing was clear, and moved to the fire escape. It did not take long for him to descend and drop to the sidewalk, and the gray clad figure slipped away between the houses, taking another indirect route home. Before he got close the killer knew he would have to change back into his jogging equipment, then dash to his own apartment for a quick shower and yet another change of clothes.

#

Sweet-lips shook her head. She could not remember how she ended up in these musty stone tunnels, or why she was here, but felt the need to get up and outside into the fresh air. It felt like she had been walking through the tunnels for hours and experienced a rush of relief when she saw the flight of stairs up ahead. Sweet-lips carefully climbed them, unsure where the light was coming from, but was glad the dim glow was there. There were several cracked and broken treads that if she had encountered them in the dark she would have been sure to trip on.

At the top of the stairs was a heavy wooden door that she struggled to open, pushing hard against the resistance caused by the bottom of the door dragging against the floor. Sweet-lips blinked in amazement at the room in front of her, which resembled a Victorian ballroom. Unlike the tunnels and the stairs below, it was well lit by the many chandeliers hanging from the arched and gilded ceiling. Supporting this ceiling were ornately painted pillars lining the sides of the room, with scenes of beautiful rolling green countryside, with matching oil paintings lining the walls.

The only thing that spoiled the amazing effect was the line of half a dozen dark robed figures spread in a loose semicircle in front of her. The most striking feature of these figures were their belts, apparently made of chains with human skulls hanging loosely, which was as disconcerting to

Sweet-lips as the way the deep cowls left the strangers faces hidden in deep shadow. One of them stepped forward slightly, and said in an oddly hissing voice, "Lady, we have been waiting for you. It is time."

On cue the strangers simultaneously drew swords from the scabbards hanging from their belts, and advanced a pace towards her. Sweet-lips recoiled instinctively, bumping into the door behind her. This suddenly closed all too easily, not dragging on the floor at all, and clicked shut with a final click. Without taking her eyes off the robed figures, Sweet-lips reached behind to grasp the door handle, which would not budge. She realized she was trapped.

Sweet-lips dropped her hand to her side to get her cellphone from her belt, planning to call for help, but instead found the handle of a sword. Instincts she did not know she had kicked in, and Sweet-lips drew the blade and held it two-handed in front of her, the tip held steady pointing at the throat of the closest stranger. She muttered, "What the hell is going on here?"

Another one of the figures replied in barely recognizable grunting tones, "You have an appointment with your Maker. We are here to ensure you arrive in a timely manner." The six took another cautious step forward together, tightening the half circle round her.

Sweet-lips said, "Oh, forget this," and feinted to her left before slashing her blade to the right with a vicious backhanded blow. The figure on the far right of the line blocked her strike easily, almost contemptuously, but the move allowed her to slip past them and out of the circle. This put her into free space behind the strangers, somewhat negating their numerical advantage.

Although seemingly skilled with a sword, the figure closest to her was slow on its feet, and she darted back in close before dropping and rolling sideways, cutting at the ankles of the two figures before her. The first was too slow to reach, and received her blade slashed across both shins, while the second barely had time to jump awkwardly backwards. Sweet-lips was on her feet in an instant, darting towards the one who jumped, forcing him further off balance with a quick swipe that she hurriedly turned into a rolling back swing aimed at the figure moving towards her from the center. This was easily parried, but again brought her the time she needed to disengage and gain some space.

Sweet-lips turned as if to run, but completed the circle to lunge back in and stab the closest stranger, sinking the tip of her sword into an elbow joint, causing the figure to cry out and drop their own blade. She wrenched her sword free, hearing the bones crack as she twisted, and slowly retreated backwards down the room. The four uninjured strangers carefully followed her. Every time they got too close for comfort, Sweet-lips leaped forward with skills she never knew she had, driving them back briefly, before their determined advance continued when she retreated.

One of the figures appeared to nod inside the darkness of its cowl, and stepped to one side. "Very good, Lady. You are better than we were led to believe." It reached inside its black robes and pulled out a double barreled flintlock pistol, ornately decorated in black and silver. "But you still have an appointment to keep, and our Master does not like to be kept waiting."

The triggers were pulled, both hammers dropped, striking sparks that ignited the powder in the pans. A moment later the two heavy lead balls were blasted towards Sweet-lips, aimed at her chest, and she had nowhere to run.

Chapter 23

Sweet-lips jerked awake with a start, heart racing, and instinctively patted herself down, checking for injuries. She lay back down with a sigh, glad it was just another nightmare, but frustrated that she was getting them. Since she had quit smoking crack, with her last hit on Wednesday night, she was being plagued by a mixture of insomnia and vivid dreams when she finally did get to sleep.

She knew these were just psychological withdrawal symptoms, along with the anxiety she was feeling as well, but that did not make it any easier to deal with. On top of that she regularly had to deal with what is known a 'coke bugs', the feeling of small insects crawling under her skin, which no amount of scratching seemed to help. From her research, Sweet-lips had confidence that by Sunday, having been clear of the drug for three days, the worst of these symptoms would subside. Even with that good news, she knew that some of the symptoms could still nag at her for weeks or even months to come.

Feeling a little guilty about it, she rolled a joint, hoping it would calm her nerves. Sweet-lips had hoped to quit all drugs, even alcohol, but she knew that to help addicts through withdrawal and improve their chances of staying clean, official medical facilities used alternative drugs to ease patients through the worst times. As she could not afford to go into a clinic, and desperately wanted to help catch Frank's murderer right now, Sweet-lips figured the occasional pot smoking seemed the best all round solution.

A few hits later she was feeling a lot calmer, and figured as she was awake she could go into work.

That thought struck Sweet-lips as a little amusing, considering she had not held down a legal job for years, but she kicked the covers away and headed to the shower to freshen up. Besides, she thought as the water flowed over her, she needed to have a word with Danny about a certain unhelpful desk driver.

#

Danny pulled his car into the police house parking lot a little later than he would have liked, but grunted with approval when she saw how many cars were already there. To his surprise, even the Chief's Lexus was parked in its designated bay.

He made his way past the flustered looking secretary who was covering the front desk, indicating that Karen was with him. Heading towards his desk his eyes took in the chaos that was the squad room and the surrounding offices, but unlike his daughter he could see the patterns and good signs in the apparent mess.

Todd was seated at his own desk, already at work and answering questions from the various sergeants who were trying to organize their squads. Danny cocked an eyebrow at him, "Been here long?"

Todd shook his head, "'Bout half an hour, maybe, and before you ask nothing new had come up. We've collected evidence that will solve a dozen crimes when we've got the time to deal with them, assuming the peeps involved don't split. But we can't find anyone connected with these killings, any of them. Whoever these perps are, they are keeping their heads down and keeping quiet."

"Great," grunted Danny, "but at least we don't have any new bodies to add to the collection." He saw the look on Detective King's face and asked,

"Or do we?"

Todd shrugged, "Well, I just heard about a call that came into dispatch. Someone over on Fifth and Queen called saying some red liquid was dripping through the ceiling of their apartment, and there was no response when they knock on the door. There are a couple of patrol guys heading over, and the landlord is on his way too."

Danny groaned, "Anyone told the Chief the good news?"

"Actually, it was me that notified Detective King," replied the Chief from behind him. "I came in early to arrange the television appeal for any Auxiliaries who want to help. The papers and radio are already running the story, so hopefully we will get a few people interested."

"Thanks, Chief," said Danny, "and I've got the second recruit right here," indicating Karen.

"Ah, Miss Watson, welcome aboard. Let me take you to see Lieutenant Sampson so you can deal with the necessary paperwork while your father, sorry, while Lieutenant Watson here catches up."

Danny watched as the Chief steered Karen across the squad room towards the office of Peter Sampson, then said to Todd, "Come on, show me what came in last night."

#

Special Agent Joe Lander was also back at his desk, checking the progress of some of his automated snoopers, and launching his next electronic attack along the trail left by the blogger. He felt that after all the server jumps and misdirects he must finally be near the end of the trail, and while he waited for the results of the latest search, he took a look to see if the Serial Blogger had added any more entries.

A few minutes later he was horror-struck by what he had read, and could not concentrate on any of the other research work he would usual do while his searches ran. Instead he sat watching and waiting for the next link to be discovered. After ten nervous minutes the result came through, and he puzzled, "A school?" He slipped his way into their network to run down traces of the blogger, while furiously typing an email to his supervisor explaining the situation.

A few minutes later his boss replied, "Got your Go Bag? You could go solo on this one. I'll get someone else to cover your other duties. If you need backup when you get there, assuming the locals accept our help, just let me know."

Joe answered, "Always close to hand. I am just double checking the location, the end of the trail smells real. Once confirmed I'll contact their Police Department and let them know the bad news."

Technically Joe had not been truthful with his superior - he had already run some double checks after he could not find a trail beyond the school network. He was on his fourth set of checks, and was convinced this was real.

#

The Chief knocked on the door of the Lieutenant's office, and led Karen inside, motioning her to take a seat. "Lieutenant, this is your first recruit to sign up today as an Auxiliary Services Officer. Ms. Watson, I shall leave you in the Lieutenant's capable hands."

As the Chief turned to leave, both of them heard Lieutenant Sampson mutter under his breath, "Oh, great. The first of the Boy Scouts."

The Chief stiffened, and with his hand still resting on the door handle and his back to the room, said "Karen, my dear, would you be so good as to wait outside for a few moments? I need to have a private chat with the Lieutenant."

"Of course, Sir," she replied, rising and walking back to the squad room. Behind her she heard the door softly close, but found she could still faintly hear the conversation from within.

The Chief barked, "Lieutenant Sampson!"

Peter sat up straight, "Yes, Sir?"

"You were appointed head of the patrol officers by my predecessor, and while I have been Chief of Police I have come to value your organizational and administrative skills, as well as your experience in dealing with the various day to day problems that have come up. However, I have noticed that unusual situations do not sit so well with you, and that you are very resistant to change. Because of this, and other factors, when this recent and highly unusual spate of homicides arose and you seemed unlikely to cope with the new challenges presented, I appointed Detective Watson to lead the investigation, and to marshal all resources as he saw fit.

"In an effort to avoid any urination contests over him appearing to rank below you, but acting as your equal, I promoted him to the same rank that you currently hold. While he has been running these politically charged investigations, I have agreed to every suggestion and backed every decision he has made, which, incidentally, includes the activation of the Auxiliary 'Boy Scouts', as you so nicely put it. The 'Boy Scouts' also have the full approval of the mayor, who agrees with me that this could be a politically skillful move to boost our manpower in the short term, and will enable us to crack these cases open.

"Now, if I ever hear you questioning things I have approved again, I will bust you back to buck patrolman, and you will spend the rest of your days doing the dirtiest jobs I can find for you. Do you understand?"

Peter Sampson's face had gone gray during this tirade, and he quietly answered, "Yes, Sir. Perfectly."

"Good. Now on top of that, I have some good news and some bad news. The good news is you actually did not insult a run of the mill member of the public with your thoughtless comment. The bad news is, you insulted Lieutenant Watson's daughter, which may make things a little awkward for you in future. I trust that you will be on your best behavior from now on?"

"Yes, Sir. Of course, Sir!"

"Excellent. Then I will not take up anymore of your valuable pencil-pushing time," the Chief finished as he opened the door. "Ah, Miss Watson, sorry about the delay. If you take a seat I am sure Lieutenant Sampson will guide you swiftly and painlessly through the formalities. Oh, Lieutenant, I forgot to say I expect one of the businessmen I deal with will be willing to donate a few free shirts for the Auxiliary Service Officers, so we will just need to supply a pair or two of pants for any recruits that need them. As Miss Watson is so well dressed today she can stay as she is for now. Good day to you both."

Peter Sampson was suitability red-faced with frustration and embarrassment, and just quietly said to Karen, "My apologies. I have a few forms that you need to fill out. Would you like to begin?"

Karen gave him a dazzling smile, "Of course, I can't wait."

#

Danny had run through the nightly reports and was puzzling over a cryptic message that had apparently been left by Sweet-lips. He hoped she was coming in early to report, and he was cursing himself for not telling her a time when she should report for duty. But once she got here she would be able to explain the note, and one of the new Auxiliary Service Officer badges would cut down on her problems getting into the building.

He was about to call the front desk to let them know it was okay for Sweet-lips to be buzzed through, when his phone range. As his hand had been just inches away from the receiver, he managed to pick it up before the first ring had finished. "Detective Watson here," he said.

At the other end was Gill Miller, "I have a call here that could go to one of three people, but I think you are the most likely candidate. Oh, by the way, congratulations on your promotion."

"Thanks, Gill. I guess this means we'll be seeing even more of each other."

Danny could almost could almost hear the grimace coming down the phone line, and Gill replied, "I can't wait. Anyway, I have Special Agent Joe

Lander on the line, asking for the senior officer in the homicide department, which I know we don't technically have."

Danny looked surprised, "FBI? I guess I am the man in charge of the death squad here, and doubt he really needs to talk to the Chief, so put him through, please."

"Surely," replied Gill.

When Danny heard the click and change in background noise on the line he said, "Detective Lieutenant Watson speaking, how may I help you?"

In Quantico, Joe was cringing slightly at having to be the bearer of bad tidings, but he swallowed and replied, "Hi, Lieutenant. My name is Special Agent Joe Lander and I work on tracking potential crimes that are committed in the 'real' world, but also show up online. To make it a little easier to explain the reason for my call, could you humor me and go to a web page?"

Danny looked and sounded puzzled, "Sure, okay, I can do that. What is the web addy?"

Joe slowly read out the URL, which Danny dutifully typed in. While it was loading, Danny asked, "So you think a crime has been committed in Claytown City, and you wanted to let me know? You could've just emailed the details over, or is it a Federal issue?"

Joe grimaced again, "It isn't a Federal issue yet, as far as I know, and yes, I could've emailed this but I doubt you would believe it without talking to me as well. And I think time is really of the essence here. Is the page up?"

Danny said, "Yes, it's up. It actually is familiar

to me. My daughter was looking at it as part of her college work, although I don't think she's seen any of the updates posted for a few days."

"If she had, I reckon she would have mentioned it for sure. Could you scroll to the bottom and read the latest post? I was also wondering if you had any unsolved homicides recently?"

As Danny scrolled down he replied, "Yeah, too many for my liking. Weird ones that are pushing us hard. Right, let me quickly read this." There was a pause, then Danny quietly said, "Oh, God. No."

He sat up straight, but was staring into space, "You believe this is real?"

Joe replied, "Well that depends on how well this fits the data from your crime scenes. It looked credible enough for me to look at it, track it down to your city, and get provisional verification from your newspapers and reports submitted to us. That is why I am calling. If it's a crank, you're not likely to have another body on your hands, but if it is real, I'd expect someone to turn up soon. Have you heard anything today?"

Danny thought, "Well, we've got a couple of guys heading to an apartment, there could be something funny going on there." He pulled up some details on the computer, "Let's see, the apartment is leased to a Raymond Stubbs. Oh, crud."

"The initials RS?"

"Can you hold for a moment, Agent?"

"Sure, no problem, I'll be here," replied Joe.

Danny clicked the line to Hold, and called over to Todd, "Are those officers at Fifth and Queen yet?"

"They just arrived. No sign of the landlord though. Probably still in bed."

"I don't care about that. Tell them to kick the door in and take a look. Oh, and tell them to be careful, there may be a perp in there."

Todd caught the urgency in Danny's voice, and contacted the patrol officers, Oso and Greene, to pass on the information. This was acknowledged, and those in the squad room who had heard this exchange waited tensely.

#

Being the more heavily built of the two, Patrolman Greene chose himself as the one who would try and break the door down. Patrolman Oso stationed himself to the right of the door, his service pistol held in front of him in a double handed grip, barrel pointing towards the ceiling, and waited. After the brief run up that the corridor allowed, Greene smashed his boot into the door, just above the lock. While the lock was a good one, the door security was let down by the aging woodwork, and the door flew open. Oso ducked inside, with Greene following once he had regained his poise, and together they checked room by room, shouting "Clear" as each one was determined to be empty of people.

They reached the master bedroom, and while Oso pulled the door fully open, Greene slipped inside before suddenly stopping dead. Oso had been following closely behind and cannoned into Greene's back, but so transfixed was he by the scene in front of him that Greene did not even seem to notice.

Oso took in the view, and whispered, "Matre de

Dios", crossed himself, then pushed past Greene to check the bathroom, which also proved to be empty.

Greene raised his radio to his lips, "Dispatch, we have located Mr. Stubbs."

#

Todd listened to the report from Greene, with the color draining from his face. He acknowledged the report and instructed the patrolmen to secure the crime scene. He turned back to the waiting Watson, "No perp, but Raymond Stubbs is dead."

Danny jumped in, "and he has his hands cut off?"

Todd rocked back in surprise, "How did you know that?"

Danny waved the question off, "I'll explain later. Get a crew headed that way, and I'll be down as soon as I can." Danny took Joe Lander off hold, "Sorry about that. Just getting some confirmation. We just found a body with no hands, with the victims initials being RS. I think this is for real, and you need to tell us what you've found out at your end."

Joe agreed, "For sure. Damn, I'd hoped I was wrong. I can be in Claytown in a couple of hours to show you what I know, and to help you if you need it."

Danny was thoughtful for a moment, "You've already said this isn't a Federal issue, and I'm sure with the information you provide we can handle this without the FBI taking over."

"Oh, no," replied Special Agent Lander, "I have no intention of taking over the case. If you feel your team can handle it, I can just walk away. I am just offering to be there to contribute my advice and experience gleaned from working several cases like this, and any assistance you want. I'll be an adviser, nothing more, and it could give you faster access to databases that you may not usually have. It is an open offer, no pressure or disrespect intended, just a genuine offer of help."

Danny's hackles over another agency interfering in one of his cases slowly went down, "I guess I should apologize. I must be taking this investigation a little personally. We would love a little help, especially if it is specialized like that. Could you email over some of the details you found? It would allow us to match things to our case files while you are in transit."

Joe readily agreed, and emailed his summary files over to Danny, then let him know he would be there as fast as he could. Joe hung up, fired off a quick email to his supervisor to let him know the latest, and grabbed his Go Bag and headed out the door.

#

Danny carefully put the phone down, and walked over to Todd. He knelt down beside him and whispered, "This sounds a little crazy, but I reckon all these homicides are the work of one man, which means we have a serial killer on the loose. You get over to Fifth and Queen, and I'll meet you there after talking to the Chief."

Todd rocked back again with surprise, "You serious?"

"I wish I wasn't, but I am. I'll explain more later, call a few people together and brief them. Keep it under your hat for now." Danny shook his head in dismay at the situation, then rose to find the Chief after discovering that he was not answering his phone.

Danny headed to the Chief's office on the off chance he was there, and peering through the anteroom Danny saw that indeed he was at his desk, and on the phone. That explained why there was no answer, thought Danny, followed by the additional thought that the secretaries needed to be back in their regular roles soon. The Auxiliary Service Officer recruitment would enable Danny to fill the positions they were currently in with Auxiliaries, preferably ones with call center experience.

The Chief saw Danny through the open doorway, and waved him into the office and indicated that he should take a seat and wait. Danny did so, and heard the Chief say, "That sounds great, Tommy. Just run off fifty shirts in a variety of sizes, and get your boy to drop them off. That way we can kill two birds with one stone. Anyway, I have got to run, I need to get to a meeting. Thanks again, Tommy."

The Chief hung up, and Danny said, "I heard you have a meeting to go to, but I'll be quick."

The Chief smiled, "The meeting is with my newest Lieutenant. Do you have good news for me?"

Danny shrugged, "In some ways it could be viewed as good news, but there is a bad flip-side to it. We may have found evidence linking our string of killings together, or it could be a twisted copycat wanting attention. My gut says the links are real, and that means we have a self-confessed serial killer operating in the city."

The Chief rocked back in his seat, "Say that again. A serial killer? I thought the last two at the park were unrelated."

"So did I, but despite the different MO, and different description, we have some evidence to link it all to one person, whose identity is currently unknown. But something tells me that knowing the six killings are related will help us catch this murderer."

The Chief looked puzzled, "Six? I thought we were only looking at four bodies. I expect one is from this Fifth and Queen, or are there two bodies there? If not, where did the other two come from?"

"Remember Mark Harding, from earlier in the year? It seems he may be the first, and I'm on my way to look at the sixth body at Fifth and Queen when I am done here."

Chief frowned, "This is not good. If the press gets hold of this it could look very bad indeed, unless we can give them something positive as well."

"I know, that's why I'm giving you a heads up. You could say no comment, or you could talk to them when we've confirmed the theory and say we have new evidence that will lead us quickly to the perpetrator. You could also say we have an expert come in to assist us, which would be true. It was an FBI agent who found the link, and I've invited him alone to come and give us the benefits of his expertise. With his help, and the extra resources from the Auxiliary program, we should be able to nail this guy quickly."

"You do that, Danny. I want the bodies to stop dropping, and that scumbag off my streets."

Danny rose and saluted, "Yes, Sir."

Chapter 24

As Danny headed out the door of the police station, he ran into Sweet-lips coming in. She asked, "Did you get my message?"

"Come with me, we'll talk on the way." As they went toward his car, Danny continued, "I got a message, but it was pretty garbled. I'm on the way to a new homicide, but I need to hear what you found out too. Time is short, so hop in."

They both got in the car, and as Danny pulled out of his parking space Sweet-lips said, "I knew that fool wouldn't be able to pass on a simple message. She wouldn't even call upstairs to see if I was allowed in."

"That is my bad, I should've given them a heads up. When you get your pass today, that will solves issues like that. Now, what did you find out?"

Sweet-lips recounted her conversation with the hookers, and confirmed some of the details from her own experience, adding that Old Jimmy was not in some of his usual haunts that she checked last night.

Danny said, "This is what I was starting to expect, and I reckon we'll see this stalking behavior in some of the other kills too. Hmm. Are you okay with tracking down Jimmy later? He'll be more likely to talk to you, I reckon."

"Sure, I was going to do that once I'd cleared it with you. What's this about a new killing?"

Danny grunted as he pulled up beside some black and whites on Queen Street, "Come and see for yourself, if you have a strong stomach."

\#

Sweet-lips followed Danny into the building, not because she felt her stomach was all that strong, but because she was curious about how a crime scene looked and was handled. Danny's credentials got them both past the uniforms at the entrance to the apartment building, and into the elevator. It was obvious when they had reached the correct floor because the apartment door opposite the elevator was wide open and inside it was teeming with people.

As they exited the elevator, Danny said, "I doubt you want to see the corpse, so I'll leave you out here in the capable hands of Officer Rose here. Rose, look after Auxiliary Officer Temple for a few minutes. Is Detective King with the deceased?"

Officer Rose saluted, "No problem, Sir. Detective King should be in the bedroom. Just look for the camera flashes."

Danny patted Sweet-lips on the shoulder, then put his game face on. Moving through the small apartment he was surprised at how sparsely decorated it was. Hopefully that would help the crime scene techs, as there would be less for them to go over. Taking a deep breath, he carefully walked into the bedroom, and nodded to Todd King, then looked at the body on the bed. He grimaced at the unreal scene, and said, "Anyone hazard a guess at TOD?"

Todd replied, "You just missed the ME. He sends his compliments on providing another interesting one, and reckons the time of death was about six this morning. We canvassed the building, and no-one heard anything unusual. As you can see, Mr. Stubbs has been gagged, so there were no screams to hear. No obvious clues, not even on the door. It was locked when the patrol boys got here. Initial supposition is that the deceased knew his killer. That's about it for now."

Danny looked at how the corpse was laying in the bed, half covered with the blankets. He said, "If the victim knew his killer, I'd say he knew him very well. Look at how he is almost tucked up in bed. Either the perp stayed the night, or had a key, unless they slipped the lock somehow. If he was that well known to Mr. Stubbs, I am surprised that he was killed, especially in this manner. It just doesn't fit with me."

Todd shrugged, "So we are pretty much nowhere then, just like we are with the other recent cases."

"Remember what I said earlier? We need to get a group together back at headquarters stat. You hand this scene over to one of the patrol sergeants, and I'll call Raven in."

#

Over the years Sweet-lips had found within her many skills that she had developed almost to perfection. Several were not suitable for polite society, or at least in public places, but had come in handy in developing her old 'business' and ensuring repeat customers. However, she had found a talent that had served her well in all her jobs, and she expected to find it useful in her work with the Auxiliaries - She could listen well and encourage people to talk.

Currently she was working on Patrolman Rose and, despite his usually taciturn attitude, she had managed to get him talking a little, and just discovered that he lived within a few blocks of the building they were in. She commented, "I've lived near here for a few years now, and didn't realize there was a cop in the neighborhood."

Behind Rose, Danny came out of the bedroom and pulled out his cellphone, while Rose replied, "I'm not the only one. I know Patrolman Quigley over there lives somewhere downtown, and both Detective King and Lieutenant Sampson live in Maiden Towers, just up the street. Not many people take notice of who lives round them."

Sweet-lips saw Danny heading her way, and said, "I bet you do, though."

Patrolman Rose was nodding his agreement when Danny came up beside them. Sweet-lips said, "What do we do now?"

Danny replied, "We get back to headquarters and a few of us will have a meeting. Something has come up and I need to brief a special team."

Slightly bemused by the coming and going, and the reason she seemed to be included in this 'special team', Sweet-lips trailed behind Danny as he headed to the elevator.

#

The first thing Danny did when they returned to the police headquarters was head to his desk. Partly this was to check for messages, but mainly because he had declared it the rallying point for the detectives coming in. He found his daughter sat in his seat, keenly observing the activities in the room, and said to her, "Hey, Officer Watson, how's it going?"

She smiled and stood up, "Just keeping your chair warm for you, da... Sir. Lieutenant Sampson didn't know what to do with me, so I waited here for you to come back."

"Hmm, I half expected him to throw you on the phones. That is one plan we have for the Auxiliary Officers."

Karen smiled, "Er, I think he is worried he might upset you by putting me in the wrong place. Unofficially, I heard the Chief rip him a new one over his attitude to the Auxiliaries."

Danny sighed, "I suppose I better drop him an email to clarify a few things, but I'm glad I didn't have to track you down and pull you off the phones. I need you for what I'm setting up now. By the way, Karen, meet Karin. You are both Auxiliary Officers and you'll both be on this project. You have some skills that most people don't, and I'd trust you both with my life and my career. Get acquainted while I deal with a few loose ends and get a ball or two rolling."

The two women chatted guardedly for a few minutes, each aware that the other was important to Danny, but not wanting to probe too deeply. Their attempt to find some common ground was interrupted by the arrival of Detective King, who said to Danny, "I've handed the scene over to Sergeant Mendez. She'll make sure all the usual things are done as we would like. Now, what is this meeting about? Are you going to spill the beans on your new theory?"

Danny nodded, "That is exactly what it is about, but before I start I want Raven here too. We're going to take over the small conference room in the corner, so could you wait here for Raven while I take these two over there and get a few things set up?"

"Sure, not a problem. While I'm waiting I could make a start on the latest Murder Book."

"Sounds like a good plan. Speaking of that," said Danny as he unlocked a file cabinet and started removing large binders, "Ladies, if you could grab a few of these and walk this way?"

Sweet-lips picked up half the binders from the desk, and Karen grabbed the rest, following Danny across the room. Karen looked at the spines of the ones in her arms and guessed they contained the details for the other recent unsolved homicides.

When they entered the conference room, Danny dumped his load of files on the central table and flicked the lights on. The others put down their binders beside those, and looked round the room. The conference table was oval, with a chair at each end and two on either side. Along the back wall was a pair of file cabinets and a long, low cabinet made of dark wood that matched the table. The chairs were of higher quality that the ones in the squad room, and the few pictures on the walls and potted plants dotted round made the room seem more relaxed and larger than it actually was.

Danny gave an amused snort as he realized something, "You two having pretty much the same first name will make being informal a little awkward and using your nicknames is pushing informality a little far, so I reckon I'll just have to use your last names. Watson, we'll be getting computers hooked up in here for you and the others to use. I'm going to need info from these files compiled, stored and analyzed. Temple, you any good at data entry?"

Sweet-lips replied, "A little rusty, but I'll soon warm up."

"Good, I'll be needing you to do some of that, but your main task will be hitting the streets and talking to people that we regulars wouldn't be able to get close to."

Danny was interrupted by a discrete cough from the doorway, and Janice Wilson, the resident IT tech, wheeled in a cart of equipment. Working quickly while the others just watched, she unloaded three laptops and connected them to power and network outlets, along with a printer. This she tapped on and said, "This won't be be able to handle heavy printing, but if you need something confidential or in a hurry, this baby'll be just the thing. Apart from him," she added, pointing to Danny, "which one of you is Officer Watson?"

Karen raised her hand, and was told, "Pick a seat and a machine. Here are you login details. I'm sure you know good password drills and are familiar with the Windows platform? Good."

Janice then turned to Sweet-lips, and handed her a slip of paper. "Grab another computer and log in, assuming you are Officer Temple. Cool, any problems, give me a shout."

Janice then went on to unload and connect a scanner to the unused laptop, followed by adding a pair of telephones to go with the conferencing phone already in the room. Pointing to an outlet recessed into the tabletop, she said, "That's for a modem, should your FBI guy need it. The one next to it is another network socket. He should be able to figure it out in two attempts or less. Now, was there anything else?"

The two female officers were a little stunned by Janice's whirlwind movements and personality, but Danny was well used to her by now. He said, "That's all we need right now. I've got your extension if anything else is needed."

"Marvelous," said Janice, as she wheeled the cart out the door, "must dash," were her parting words before she sped away.

Karen asked, "Is she always that hyper?"

Danny nodded, "She sure is. If you need anything, just call her, and she'll have it ready before you can put the phone down." He placed a sheet of paper between the two officers, adding, "This is a list if useful numbers and other info, just in case you need it."

Todd chose that moment to poke his head through the door, "Did anyone here order half a dozen big whiteboards?"

Danny replied, "I guess that would be me."

"Well they've been left out here. Coming through," he added as he dragged a pair to the back of the room, and went back for the others. In the commotion, Detective Chavez came in and quickly introduced herself to the new Auxiliary Officers.

Danny quietly closed the door, then stood at the head of the room where there was already a whiteboard permanently attached to the wall. He took a deep breath, and started, "Now you've all got to know each other a little, it's time to get down to work. I've called you here today because I was informed earlier that we have a special problem in this city, and you all have special skills that will help resolve the problem. We also have an FBI agent, Special Agent Joe Lander, coming down to share the intelligence he has gathered, and to assist us. At this time, this is not, repeat not, an FBI investigation, and Agent Lander will just be an adviser."

Danny pulled some papers from a folder and continued. "You may have noticed a large number of bodies piling up round here. First one to really catch peoples attention was Father Vernon Williams."

He picked up an eight by ten photo of Father Williams, and secured it to the top of the board, noting the date of the murder below. To the right of this he hung another picture, "Then we had two weeks later, homeless Frank. It took us nearly a week to find him, so it seemed almost immediately that we had Vicky Boxford and Liam Hendersen killed in the Presidential Park."

Danny hung the appropriate pictures and noted the dates of death, then added the current date before hanging a fifth photo. "This is Raymond Stubbs, found this morning in circumstances that are highly unusual. But before all this there was also the case of Mark Harding." He added the final photo to the left of the picture of Father Williams, noted the correct date, then said, "I believe that this is all the work of one man. We have a serial killer on the loose."

The three women had looks of disbelief on their faces, while Todd, despite being forewarned, was also looking slightly skeptical. Danny said, "I know, it is a big jump to make, but we already had evidence, albeit technically circumstantial, linking the Williams and Frank cases. The description of that killer actually close to the one we got in the Harding case, and the physical characteristics match with the Park killer. If it hadn't been for the changes in clothes and wildly varying murder weapons, we might have picked up on this sooner. I admit that this is thin evidence, and still somewhat circumstantial, until you factor in evidence brought to my attention by our friendly Fed this morning. Officer Watson, remember one of the blogs you looked at, the guy who was giving all those psych definitions and details of serial killer types? Bring up the page and take a look at the last entry. All of you should take a look."

Danny waited patiently while the page loaded and they all crowded round the screen to read it. There was a chorus of expletives, and the color drained from Karen's face. She looked at her father and said, "Assuming 'dick' is an abbreviation for detective, I was the real target in the Park."

Danny nodded, "That's what I suspected. Technically that means you and I are too close to the investigation to be impartial, but then so would Officer Temple because of her friendship with Frank. But I don't care about that, because we need the best people we can find on this case, and they are all in this room. Now, does anyone doubt that this is all one case?"

Raven said, "Suppose this blog is a hoax, or some kinda copycat or glory-hound?"

Danny replied, "It's possible, but I think we can easily prove or disprove that theory by the end of the day. But regardless, looking at the crime scene today there was just something that rang true, that had a sense of familiarity about it."

Todd snorted, "Yeah, it was like a scene from a horror movie. But unlike a movie villain, this punk doesn't leave us any clues we can use."

Karen piped up, "Maybe not on the face of it, but there are clues we can use." She stood up and went to the whiteboard. "Victimology may not tell us as much as it could because of the variety in the victims, different socioeconomic backgrounds, age, class, race and so on, but this variety does tell us that the killer isn't stuck on a particular 'type' of victim. That means there's either a personal motive that links them all somehow, or in the worst case it's just people picked at random."

She looked round at the surprised faces of the others, barring Danny's proud smile, "What? I'm doing Psychology at school, and I've been looking into the psychology of serial killers, mostly thanks to that blog over there. I found it interesting."

Sweet-lips shrugged and said, "I don't think it's totally random. The street girls saw someone fitting the description of this guy patrolling the Downtown area, like they were searching for someone, before Frank went missing. I personally don't remember seeing them there after that, and I was out for days looking for Frank."

Raven said, "Assuming it was all the work of one person, which I don't completely buy myself, what else do the victims tell us?"

Danny picked up a dry-erase marker and stood by the board. "Well, let's see what we've got? Go to the files and give me info that could be useful."

The others grabbed a file apiece, while Danny took the two Park victims. He jotted the time of death on the board, along with the murder weapons. From memory he added the same info for the other victims, and their addresses. When she noticed the information on the board, Karen said, "None of the deaths have been during 'office' hours, so the perp probably has a day job. Do you mind if I plot some data on a map?"

Danny nodded, "Go for it. There should be a large

one in the drawer over there."

While his daughter fetched that and pinned it to another whiteboard, Danny added the location details for the deaths, then noted down on a separate board the witness descriptions of the murderer after Todd started reading his file out. The others followed suit, and Danny quickly put together an 'average' description of the killer. His work was interrupted by Karen, who said, "All of these deaths are in the Downtown area, or really close by. The addresses of most of the victims are too. I excluded the Park deaths from that statement, and put my house on the list instead, working on the assumption that I was the intended target. This gives us this, what, er, twenty block radius as our killer's comfort zone. That means he either lives or works in this area, or maybe even both."

Danny said, "That's good, very good. Cuts down on where we need to look. Are there any other commonalities anyone can see? Weapons are a broad mix, so I don't think we'll see anything there. He even mixes edged weapons with guns."

Todd shrugged, "The only thing that stands out for me is every crime scene I've been to has been an unholy bloodbath. This boy sure likes to make a mess."

Karen jumped in, "Maybe that is his signature?"

Raven beat Sweet-lips to the punch, and asked, "What do you mean by a signature?"

Karen replied, "Almost every serial killer does something that's unique to them, be it killing a 'type' of person, like prostitutes, taking specific items from the crime scene, leaving something behind, using a particular weapon or method of killing. It can even be combinations, or something else, as long as it's present with every victim or crime scene. Whatever it is, it's something that only they do, so when you see it at a crime scene it's almost as though they had signed their name for you."

Todd said, "It's not as though we run into slaughterhouse crime scenes every day, so that makes sense. And we haven't advertised how bloody the crime scenes are, so I guess that makes it unlikely Mr. Stubbs was a copycat."

Sweet-lips shuddered, "It's still possible though. Chopping hands off is bound to cause a lot of blood."

Danny nodded, "True, but most mutilations take place after death, from what I've read, which would be less bloody, and the deceased was still alive when his hands were hacked off. You could tell by the blood sprays on the wall. The heart was still pumping blood."

Raven said, "Nice. Glad I've missed some of those scenes. I can't see anything else from the files. Every idea I had has already been said."

Danny answered, "Well, we've made a good start. Far better than I'd expected. Raven, I'd like you to stay here and help Watson and Temple to pull out more data from the files that we can compare and analyze in a program that Watson put together." He tossed a memory stick to his daughter and added, "I made a copy. Just load it on one of the laptops. Even the tiniest piece of information could give us a break, so don't leave anything out. Officer Temple, before you get started on that, I'll need you to go see Lieutenant Sampson and do the paperwork needed to get you officially on board. He'll also get you an

ID badge. Once you have that, see if you can find Old Jimmy.

"Todd, you get back to this mornings scene, and see if anything else has come up, or supports or disproves out theories. I've got to coordinate things with the patrol officers and get Auxiliaries where they need to go. Suppose I'd better update the Chief, too. I'll be in and out, but available on my cell. I'll make sure I am back here when the Fed turns up. Temple, come with me and I'll show you to Lieutenant Sampson's den."

Chapter 25

The killer was taking his morning break from work, sat on a disused stoop drinking his coffee. He and the Beast were amused by all the police activity round the apartment building on the corner of Fifth and Queen. "I wonder how they'd react if I walked up there and said, 'Hey, it was me. I did it'?"

The Beast replied, "I doubt they would believe you at first. Actually, I doubt they would even be able to find any evidence to link you to any of the crime scenes, apart from your souvenirs. Oh, and the bag of bloodied clothes from this morning. Even then, given the caliber of these monkeys, I think you would still be able to talk your way out of it."

The killer nodded, sipping more wake-up juice. "But I don't think I'll test that theory. I really do need to get rid of those clothes though. I have a feeling our Dick Watson would be delighted to find them, if it ever crossed his mind to search my apartment. I'll have to think of a nice way to tease him online later."

He stood up, draining the last dregs of his coffee, "Ah, well, break time over. Back to the day job."

#

Sweet-lips was surprised at how quickly the meeting with Lieutenant Sampson went, although it was clear from his tone and some of his comments that he was very unhappy about a hooker becoming a cop, even a temporary one.

Once she had seated herself across from him, Peter

Sampson said, "I have taken the liberty of filling out parts of the paperwork in advance. After all, it was easy to get many of the pertinent details from your, ah-um, other files that we have on you. I did have a few points to clear up though."

He looked up, and Sweet-lips nodded that he should continue. "Well, firstly, how do you want your name to be recorded? Many people would expect you to use Sweet-lips instead of Karin, as that's how you are better known, especially in some circles."

Sweet-lips pursed her lips at his tone, but calmly replied, "Legally, my name is Karin Temple, so surely that should be used? It would look more professional, I feel. That said, if you have a spot for nicknames or aliases, then Sweet-lips could be recorded there, just so the records are complete and accurate."

"Okay, that's that quandary covered. We have your address, phone number, date of birth, next of kin, vital statistics already. No changes since you last 'official' visit?"

"No, everything is still the same. Danny has kept it updated with any changes, as after all, I am a registered CI."

Peter nodded, "Right, now what about previous work history? How would you want your prior job to be listed? Prostitute is what springs to mind."

Sweet-lips shook her head, "How about not? Put down Confidential Informant. After all, it was an important part of my work."

He sighed, then made the notation on the electronic file, "I guess that covers it. I'll just print this off for you to sign."

A few moments later, Sweet-lips was scanning the form. "Yes, everything looks good, except for the picture."

"Oh, I am sorry. I figured as we had several pictures of you on file, it would save time to use one of them."

"Don't you think it would look odd to have my arrest mug shot on my Auxiliary file and ID card? Hmm?"

"If you insist, we can have another picture taken. Follow me."

Less than five minutes after that, Sweet-lips was issued with her ID card and uniform shirt. She tucked both into her purse and headed out to find Old Jimmy.

#

Special Agent Joe Lander was wondering if he should have taken the plane instead of the car, as he saw traffic slowing down ahead of him on the Interstate. In theory the journey would be quicker by road, but if he kept running into holdups like this, it would take him forever.

A thought struck him and he grinned, easing over to the shoulder. The way ahead looked clear, and he activated the light bar fitted to the dash of his government issue Grand Marquis, as well as the siren. Quickly he zoomed past the hold up, for which he could see no logical reason, then pulled into clear air.

Still grinning, he put his foot to the floor and thought, "Here's how you travel Federal express."

#

When he saw Sweet-lips leave, Danny walked through the open door of Peter Sampson's office and closed it. Sitting down, he said, "So, Lieutenant, how many Auxiliaries have we been able to find?"

Peter sniffed with disdain and opened a manila folder. "We have had a few volunteers, but not many. The Chief advised me he automatically would accept any family members of serving officers, so they were easy to include. That counted for half a dozen, who are working the tip lines instead of the secretaries, who were happy to get back to their regular work. Apart from that, not a great deal of response from our public spirit citizens. That said, we did have a few of the dregs volunteer, no doubt looking for easy beer money, but I didn't want to bother you or the Chief over lowlifes like them, so I just sent them away."

Danny frowned, "You sent them away? What were their names?"

Peter pulled out his trash can and rummaged through until he found a pair of crumpled sticky notes. These he passed over to Danny, who looked at them with interest before saying, "Lenny Sideways and Pete Sanchez. They have good eyes on the street. I would snap them up as Auxiliaries, but I doubt they'd want to man the phones, and they'd prefer cash payments too. Heather Nelson? Wow, she's one of the top dogs among the street girls. If she worked for us, she'd get info from every hooker in town. And you, in your eternal wisdom, just sent them away?"

"Well, it is bad enough that we already have one convicted prostitute as an Auxiliary, and I didn't see why we should compromise our force by including more criminals."

Danny sat back, shaking his head. "More pearls of wisdom from the pen pusher. Have you ever heard of Confidential Informants? They usually are, how did you put it, dregs and convicts that we pay for intel on the street. They are very handy, and sometimes incredibly useful at getting information we need to solve cases. The, er, criminal that is on strength already was one of the best CI's that I've ever had. Now I'll grant you that they may not all qualify instantly to have their past sins forgiven and be signed up and given badges, but people with eyes, ears and comfort zones like those shouldn't have been turned away. Not without checking with someone who has a brain first. I am now going to have to waste time and resources tracking them down, and hope that even after your foolishness, they still will want to help us."

Through all this, Danny had kept his voice level and at a normal volume, but the pent-up anger and sarcasm could still be felt. He continued, "I never took much notice of how you ran the uniformed officers, but I'm amazed you ever made it to the rank of Sergeant, let alone Lieutenant and command of this unit. Must have taken a lot of brown-nosing. I'm also amazed that with you and your lack of streetwise talents in charge, the city hasn't been overrun with crime. I can only assume you have some decent men under you, who in spite of your failings are able to run things on the ground well. I can foresee a few problems between us in this working relationship, so I have a proposal to make.

"As your talents are limited to all things relating to paperwork, I suggest you stick to that. Make all the rotas you want and file to your hearts content, and leave the politics, decision making and actual police work to the Chief and myself. It has occurred to me that if you'd been a better commander, we may have already caught this serial killer."

Seeing the look of surprise at the mention of a serial killer, Danny said, "Yes, a serial killer appears to be responsible for our recent glut of bodies. Now, I'm not saying I'm without fault in all of this, notably in not recognizing your shameful incompetence and bad attitude sooner, but if you just stick to your world of paper and leave me to the the rest of the real work, I'm sure we'll get on fine."

Lieutenant Sampson was now red with anger and embarrassment, and spat out, "How dare you? I could have you on a charge of insubordination!"

Danny shook his head as he stood up, smiling wryly. "No, you won't, and for a few good reasons. One, I'm the same rank as you, so it was merely insulting rather than insubordinate. Two, you know the Chief would agree with me. Three, deep down, even you know I'm right. And finally, you don't have the balls," Danny said as he closed the door on his way out.

Chapter 26

Sweet-lips, now also known as Auxiliary Officer Temple, left the main police building and headed towards Lincoln Avenue to start her search for Old Jimmy. This turned out to be way easier than she expected, for as she reached the corner of Lincoln she heard a voice call softly from behind her, "Hey, gurlie, are ya Sweet-lips?"

She turned and saw an elderly black guy crouched behind a dumpster she had just passed, and she walked back towards him slowly. She nodded, "Yeah, that's me. Would you by any chance be Jimmy Butler?"

He gave her a toothless grin and nodded in turn, "Fur ma sins, dats me. Ah heard ya wuz lookin' fo me. A couple da gurls tol' me right dis morning, an day also sid ya wuz like a cop now. Is dat true? Ya gun over ta da dark side?"

Sweet-lips crouched down beside him, "Kinda. Just so's I can help them catch the dirt-bag who killed Frank. He was a good friend to me and I just feel I owe it to him." She held up her freshly minted Auxiliary Officer ID card for Jimmy to see.

"Dat's good. Frank wuz a gud guy. It kinda tuns out ah need ta talk to da po-lice too, right about now. Not summin' ah do usually, but ah saw dat Ghost agin, an ah'm gittin' scared. Dat's why ah'm hidin' here, hopin' ah'd see ya or one o' da nicer pigs. I need ta til ya'll whut ah saw, an' den ah'm gonna go hide. Ah reckon if ah see dat Ghost agin, it'll be da last time fur me, if ya know whut ah mean."

Sweet-lips nodded, "I know what you're getting at. But you could help us catch him by telling us what you've seen."

So Old Jimmy did that, telling her firsthand what she had heard from the street girls, and adding what had happened that morning. When he had finished, Jimmy added, "An ah'll til ya one more ding. Dat Ghost ain't no brudder."

Sweet-lips rocked back, "You saw his skin? He's white?"

Jimmy shook his head, "Nah, ah dint see no skin, but he dint move like a brudder. Remine me ov dem prize fighters too, like he wuz on guard an reddy to fight. Ah'd bet dat Ghost is a white boy."

Her brow wrinkled, "You sure?"

He smiled back at her, "Ya've worked da street, ya know how ya git ta read pipple, right? Well, gurl, ah bin on da street long 'fore ya wuz born. Ah know how ta read pipple real gud."

"It's okay, Jimmy, I believe you. Just had to check. Where you gonna be?"

Jimmy chuckled, "Don mean no disrispeck, but ah ain't tillin' no-one where ah'm goin'. Ah gut a bad feelin' 'bout dis Ghost, so ah'm gonna hide where no-one ken find me. When ah see him caught, Ah'll get in touch, deal?"

Sweet-lips shook his surprisingly clean hand, "Deal. And good luck."

She rose to leave and quickly read a text from Danny before turning back, "Say, you know where Lenny Sideways or Pete Sanchez are?"

#

The killer was heading back to the building he worked from to get his afternoon assignments, when he noticed a couple in earnest conversation at one of the intersections of Lincoln Avenue. One he recognized as a bum that he had see round the city, and the other was the hooker that was now part of that weird Auxiliary Service outfit. He was wondering what her street name was while he waited for the lights to change. Sweetheart, something like that anyway.

The Beast stirred, and said, "It is Sweet-lips. I heard she was one of Lieutenant Watson's informants."

The killer nodded, "Yeah, that's it. Wouldn't it be great to take her out right now? It would get to Danny, I reckon."

The Beast smiled, "You are getting awfully keen to kill again. Starting to enjoy yourself a bit too much?"

The killer smiled in return, although his teeth were far less threatening than the Beasts, "Oh yes, I'm starting to really get it now. I don't know why I resisted for so long. I'm already starting to feel that itch, too."

"So soon? And I thought I was the one eager for slaughter. If you keep this up you might run the risk of exposing us."

The killer snorted, "Strange how out roles are reversing. You're now turning into the voice of caution while I'm becoming more reckless."

The Beast shrugged, "This partnership is too much fun to break up. If things get too hot I recommend we move on, find another city. I know you are prepared for that, and then we could start our spree anew somewhere else, where we are not expected."

The lights changed to green and the killer pulled away, "That sounds like a good idea. But let's see what else we can do before we have to go."

The Beast smiled widely, baring its terrible fangs, "I have no problem with that. No problem at all."

#

It was clear to Danny that Sweet-lips had been able to find everyone she had looked for, given that he had had to oversee a very subdued Lieutenant Sampson signing up two new Confidential Informants and one special Auxiliary. This last, Heather Nelson, also known as Nightshade, he was escorting to the front desk after briefing her on her duties. As they reached the lobby, Sweet-lips was just entering, and holding the door open for a man in his late twenties, who was wearing a suit and tie that just screamed 'Fed'.

Danny left Sweet-lips and Heather to talk, and stepped up to the new arrival, asking, "Are you Agent Lander?"

Joe shook Danny's hand, replying, "That would be me. Did the dress code give it away?"

Danny laughed, "You could say that. I'm Detective Lieutenant Watson, but you can call me Danny. I'm glad you got here so quickly. I fear we have a lot of work to do and not much time to play with. Come with me, I'll introduce you to the team I've set up. Oh, first, Karin, this is Special Agent Lander. Agent, this is Auxiliary Officer Karin Temple."

As the two shook hands, Joe said, "Both of you can call me Joe. What is an Auxiliary Officer? I've never heard the rank before."

As they headed towards the conference room, Danny said, "Auxiliaries are volunteers, normal people who are giving up some of their time to help us catch the perp responsible for these killings."

By this time they had reached the conference room, and as Todd made sure the door was closed, Danny made the introductions. Joe worked quickly to get his laptop up and running, all the while shooting appreciative glances towards the work already done on the whiteboards. He ran a quick check on the search routine that had been tracking the blogger's trail, then stood to get a closer look at the information on the whiteboards.

He turned to the room, "Sorry, just familiarizing myself with what you have so far. It all looks very good, I'm impressed. I take it you've all seen the blog that jumped me to my conclusion?"

There was a chorus of agreement from the Claytown City officers, and Joe continued, "So you can see what snagged my interest. Before I carry on, just wanted to clarify a couple of things. The FBI is not taking on this case unless it can be proved Federal law requires it. I am here purely as an adviser, and to give y'all a hand. Lieutenant Watson is still fully in charge, and my continued presence is contingent on his blessing. The second point is I'm an analyst, not a profiler. Although I do have experience with this type of case, my skill set's more devoted to data analysis and geeky things.

"You may be wondering what flagged Claytown City to me as the possible area for the claimed crimes. This blog has been monitored for some time now, partly because of the content, but mainly because of its Internet location. The data is stored on a very disreputable server overseas, and the post from this morning, and the previous couple, sent me searching for the physical location of the blogger. To cut a long story short, I tracked his electronic trail back to the Claytown High School and College network. So your map showing showing his comfort zone could be further refined to indicate those buildings within WiFi range of that network." Joe picked up a marker and drew a rough circle round the school campus. "It is highly likely our man lives in this area."

Karen Watson asked, "How do you know he's not using one of the school computers? And couldn't he just upload from his parked car near the campus, far from his home?"

Joe nodded, "Good questions. For the first, I've had a tracer running in the school network, and beyond the data I'd expect on the server, the rest of the network is clear. Therefore I concluded the Serial Blogger has to be remotely accessing the network. Given the times of the uploads, it just seemed more likely that he would live close by, especially as the school is pretty much in the center of his comfort zone."

"Hold up," said Raven, "You just said Serial Blogger. What's that about?"

"Sorry, that's how I labeled this person when I first started reviewing his posts. Technically he should be referred to as the 'unknown subject', or Unsub."

Danny was looking at the map thoughtfully, "Well if this 'home' theory pans out, we've got it narrowed down to one and half, two thousand people tops. Let's get together the criminal records of everyone in that area, work out some kind of profile, and see who fits the bill."

#

The Chief was trying to work his way through some of the paperwork that tended to accumulate on his desk, when the phone rang for the nth time. He sighed, thinking that despite her sometimes abrasive manner and controlling nature, at least there were benefits in having Gill Miller field and filter his calls. This call was coming in on a line that only a select few had the number for, which should at least make it important, so he sighed again and reluctantly answered, "Chief of Police."

A bombastic voice bellowed back at him, "Ah, just the man I was looking for. Medusa not guarding your portals today?"

The Chief recognized the booming tones of Bill White, editor of the local newspaper, Claytown News, and replied, "Hey, Bill. Gill is busy harassing some new employees, so the way to my desk is clear today. How can I help out local news-king?"

Bill chuckled, "Oh, just a little thing. We've been working on a story about all these killings, a follow up to the one we headlined with a few days ago, and I wanted your official line on the situation before we went to press. Not disclosing any sources, but the paper is going to let the public know there's a serial killer on the loose, with Ray Stubbs being his fifth victim. A little bird also told us there's Federal involvement now. Would you care to comment?"

The Chief groaned inwardly, "When are you going to press on this? Officially we have no confirmation that the killings are all related, but we could make a further statement this afternoon. One thing I can tell you for sure is the FBI are not running these cases, Lieutenant Watson is in charge."

"Another statement would be great, hopefully with a little more meat in it. We're running a special and want to start printing by five o'clock, so if you've something extra to say, we can get it in there. Now, off the record, what do you say about this theory?"

"Off the record, not to used for news, not even an anonymous source?"

Bill said, "Sure thing, Chief, you can trust me on this. I just wanted your personal take on this, you know, for old times sake."

The Chief smiled at the thought of trusting the press, but answered, "Very much off the record, we are investigating the possibility that there have been six, not five, related killings. I will not say more than that."

"Hmm," mused Bill. "Not five, but six. You must mean Mark Harding. Okay, well thanks for your time, looking forward to the official statement later. Hope it's closer to the unofficial one. Call me by four?"

"Sounds like a plan. I will talk to you later."

As the Chief hung up, he pushed back his chair, and went to find Danny to get an update of his own.

#

The Chief made his way downstairs to the conference room and found Danny, his daughter and a guy who had to be the FBI agent huddled round a whiteboard at the end of the room. Sweet-lips and Raven were looking through files and entering information into a computer. Raven noticed the Chief and made to stand, saying, "Sir?", but the Chief waved her down. He said, "Do not mind me, carry on," as he strode down the room and stopped to listen to the other three, who were still working away, oblivious to anything else.

He looked at the notes on the board curiously, seeing the scattered cryptic notations:

        Downtown Comfort Zone
            Organized
              Blitz
      Frenzy/Rage - Personal?

The Chief stopped reading and started listening when Karen said, "We know this guy is smart, based on the planning and lack of evidence left behind, so any ideas on his job?"

The FBI man said, "It sure won't be menial, unless he's being really tricksy. I'm betting some kind of skilled position, but he won't be upper management because his personality or demeanor just isn't right. He'll resent that, which will feed the frustration he feels."

Danny shrugged, "That sounds likely, but this will need more info than we have right now. You know, given the access to the school computer, he could work there." Danny suddenly saw the Chief out of the corner of his eye, turned and said, "Sorry, Chief, didn't hear you come in. We were just working on a profile for the Unsub. May I introduce Special Agent Joe Lander, the Federal agent who agreed to help us. Joe, this's our Chief of Police."

They shook hands, and the Chief said to Joe, "Glad to have you on board." He then addressed Danny, "I have had the press on the phone. They heard about our Special Agent here, and they are hanging onto the serial killer angle for a news special. Do we have anything to tell them and the public?"

Danny nodded, "We will have soon. We're getting a handle on this guy. If we get lucky we'll nail him before the papers go to press tomorrow."

"We don't have until tomorrow. The Claytown News is running a special edition in a couple of hours, plus there will be the other media tonight. I need to give something to the public by four o'clock at the latest."

Joe said, "We can do that. We can give them the general characteristics of the Unsub, and his comfort zone, along with advice and precautions to take. We know the urgency. If you look at the time line over there, his cooling off period is reducing at an alarming rate. If he follows that trend, he'll try to kill again tomorrow night, maybe even tonight in the early morning. We're concerned he's close to a psychotic break, which would be the start of a general rampage. We're working as fast as we can, and we'll pin this down soon."

The Chief was concerned himself by the prospect of a crazed killer fully let loose on his city, and it showed on his face. Karen Watson saw this, and assured him, "We may not be experts, but we know enough to find him, and we'll get him off the streets for you."

The Chief nodded, and asked Danny, "You will get me the information before three thirty?"

This left the Chief reassured, and he headed back

to his office to hit the paperwork again. The trio continued working where they had left off, with Karen saying, "Any student would have access to the network, even remotely. I do and I don't even go to that campus. If he doesn't work there, he could've studied in the city within the last, what, eight years, to get the login details he'd need. Joe, you couldn't come up with a user-name?"

Joe shook his head, "He's logging into the network itself as 'Guest', but slipping onto the remote access with another login. The systems they have there don't track that very well, so I've put a tracer in to catch that for us."

Karen looked at him coolly, "Did you talk to the college about that? Otherwise it's not strictly legal."

Danny nodded, "That is true, but time is against us. We'll get retroactive permission once we've nailed him."

Joe grinned, "That's what I figured. Sorry, shoulda mentioned it before."

Danny said quietly, "Not a problem. I don't care how we get this guy. If what his blog said is true, he was after my daughter. That makes it personal"

Raising his voice somewhat he said, "Speaking of targets, have we found any links between the victims yet? Include Officer Watson in that category too, just in case she really was the intended one in the Park."

Sweet-lips looked up, "Sorry, we can't find anything to link them all, or even get sufficient partial links. Sure, there are a few commonalities, but nothing that's shared by the majority. We've even gone as far as family members habits too, right down to what grocery stores they used. Nothing."

Joe grimaced, "That makes it seem random, like the Beltway Snipers. If we can't find that link, it will be harder to catch him."

Karen shook her head, "I don't buy into the random theory. The murders themselves are too brutal and full of rage, it just shouts 'personal' to me. That said, maybe we won't find the links until after we get him and more pieces fall into place."

Danny shrugged, "Regardless, at this time victimology won't help us. Let's concentrate on the other things we do know or can extrapolate. Come on, in twenty minutes I'm gonna give this profile to the Chief. Let's get it done and get it good."

#

When the killer heard from a newshound after lunch about the serial killer angle the Claytown News was following in its special, he was both intrigued and amused. He had discounted as frivolous the idea of a Federal involvement, but that changed later in the day when he managed to get independent verification of that tidbit.

The Beast tried to calm his fears, "So what if there is a Fed here? If it was a whole team, them we might worry, but one man? Unless he is a super hero he will not be able to get these flatfeet heading on the right track towards us."

The killer nodded reluctantly, "Yeah, I know. And we've that advantage that keeps us one step ahead of them. I've just got this nagging feeling that something has happened to tip the scales in their favor."

The Beast smiled, "Maybe so. But the escape plan was set before we even started. When we know they are getting too close, we will be out of here. And maybe we could throw some confusion their way by taking out this Federal agent, or someone else close to the investigation."

The killer nodded decisively, "You're right. We still have time to play with. I wonder who we can play with next?"

The Beast spread its arms wide, flashing its claws, "As they say, the world is our oyster, and we do not even need a knife to open it."

#

Raven had been running database searches based on the known criminals living near Claytown City High School and College. With this short list in hand she narrowed it down to white males in an age range of twenty five to thirty, using the characteristics of the profile. She had already run this against criminals that worked in the area and come up dry, so she smiled when she saw just three names, and quickly checked them all against the school records.

She muttered, "Hey, hey, hey," when the name Gary Richardson matched with the school files for one of the Information Technology courses.

Beside her, Sweet-lips looked up from her monotonous data entry, and asked, "What is it?"

Raven replied, "I've just found someone who fits the profile," and she started pulling up more information on Mr. Richardson.

Suddenly she thumped the table, "But he was in County Jail for six weeks, only got out last Wednesday. That puts him in the clear."

Danny had overheard the exchange and hurried over. He reached past Raven to look at the other two candidates that failed to meet the college criteria. "Hmm, I don't think this one's our guy either. Child molesters don't usually escalate to killing a variety of adults. And this last, let's see, insurance fraud. Not likely either. We'll have to check them out further though, just to be sure."

Karen asked, "What if it's someone without a record? Can we get a list of those in the area?"

Raven replied, "We can get some of them, but our databases tend to concentrate on criminals and associates."

Joe smiled, "I know somewhere with more comprehensive databases." He spun his laptop round, "The FBI keeps a closer track on everyone, just in case, and we pull from a variety of sources. I'll just email one of my colleagues to get a list together. It shouldn't take them too long. I'll also get them to pull the whole city, just to cover all bases."

Danny nodded, "That's good, but as we're running out of time, I think I should call the Chief, give him the profile and ask for permission to implement Plan B. It may not be popular, but I don't see we have much choice."

#

The Chief was on his phone, talking to one of the leading public figures in the city, calming her fears about the killings, when he saw Danny's line flashing. "Marissa, I have got to take this call. Trust me, you have nothing to worry about. We have the situation in hand. I will call you later." He cut the connection and picked up the incoming call, "Lieutenant, what do you have for me?"

Danny replied, "If you check your email, you'll find the full profile we've put together, and the one we'll release to the press and the troops."

The Chief clicked round for a few moments, then asked, "Why the differences?"

"Some of the elements of the profile are a little too vague, and could confuse people more than they help. It also contains a false element that should enrage the Unsub when he hears it, unsettling him and hopefully breaking his concentration and pattern. As we get more info, and suspects to match it against, we'll be able to refine the profile further. I figured we could email it to the news boys after we give it to the troops, which is going to happen shortly."

The Chief nodded, "Okay, sounds like a plan. Do you object if Bill White listens in to the briefing, give him a heads up before the other news crowd?"

"If you think so, but you may want to reconsider based on something I'll ask in a moment. We're planning to contact the Unsub via his blog, which could shake him up and cause him to make a mistake, especially when coupled with what we call Plan B. Altogether we aim to break his patterns and force him to react to us, rather than us having to react to his moves. It should also buy us a little more time to catch him too."

"And what is this Plan B?"

The Chief listened intently, with a surprised look on his face, as Danny explained Plan B and the reasons behind it. The Chief asked, "I understand the logic behind this idea, but are you sure it is necessary?"

Danny was firm in his answer, "Yes, Sir, I believe it is. It plays against the tactics we've seen from the unsub, and should save lives."

"Hmm, okay. Some would question the legality of enforcing it though."

"That's why we're making it voluntary, asking for people to do it, not telling them. I think they'll play ball given the level of fear in the city."

The Chief thought for a moment, running the idea through his head, then shrugged, "I see no drawbacks, but I will have to run it past the Mayor. He needs to know about this and have a chance to comment before we make any announcements."

"Agreed," replied Danny, "Let me know when he gives the green light. The sooner the better, so we can get the word out to everyone."

"I'll call him now," said the Chief, disconnecting Danny and keying a number from memory. After a couple of rings it was picked up, and the Chief said, "Mr. Mayor, there is something we need to discuss."

#

When Danny put the phone down he heard Agent Lander calling him to see something on the computer he and Karen were using. Danny replied, "What you got, Joe?"

"Take a look at what this girl put together. We wanted to post something from the law enforcement authorities to shake this guy up, and Karen here has something that I think is perfect."

Danny leaned over his daughter's should, and started reading:

'Message from Claytown City Police Department. We understand that you are a troubled individual and we take pity on you. We urge you to give yourself up so that we can make sure you get the medical attention you so desperately require from a mental health facility, as is evidenced by the displays of your inhuman urges. Give up on your pathetic attempts to get attention, and come to us to get help instead.'

Danny nodded thoughtfully, "Interesting. Going the pity route could be a trigger to force a mistake. He's seemed pretty confident and arrogant, and being kindly referred to as pathetic would hurt. Nice. Send it out, and hopefully we'll catch his location when he replies."

#

The stresses of working a full time job and trying to cope with his murderous lifestyle was starting to tell on the killer. He figured this was part of the reason his cool down period was shrinking to fast. Other top contenders for this cooling off time getting lower was first the inevitable diminishing cathartic effect with each kill – in other words, they were not quite as satisfying as they used to be, but conversely he was also starting to enjoy himself more and did not want to wait so long for some action. These two reasons were conflicting, but he reflected that with the Beast in his head there had been conflicts for a while.

The Beast chuckled at that thought, and said, "We were only in conflict while you were denying your urges. Now I feel we are thinking and working in harmony a lot more."

The killer had to agree, "That's true. We're now one hell of a team. I just wish I didn't have to put up with this work junk as well."

The Beast shrugged, "It has been useful in some ways, but I think we will be moving on soon anyway, so then we can concentrate on being an even more efficient killing team."

The killer grinned, "That sounds good. I just want to tidy up here first, then go out with a bang. But first," he grimaced, "let's get this shift over with."

Chapter 27

Over two thirds of the Claytown City Police Department officers were assembled in the squad room, which was standing room only. The only ones absent were those coming up to the end of their shifts, and they would be briefed on their return to the police headquarters. The officers in the room would be patrolling the streets through the evening and night, and were idly speculating what the meeting was going to be about.

All discussions came to an end as the Chief made his way through the packed ranks. He knocked briefly on the door to the conference room, before opening it and sticking his head in. "We have got the all clear for Plan B, and everyone is waiting out here. I will get Bill on speaker, then we can start."

As the Chief went to Todd's desk and dialed Bill White's number, Danny, flanked by Karen Watson and Joe Lander, stepped in front of the massed ranks of police officers. At the nod from the Chief, Danny cleared his throat and began, "There's been a lot of speculation about the recent killings in our city, including some comments in the press that we can't solve this because the police round here couldn't find their own asses using both hands."

There was a ripple of laughter from the officers in the crowd, along with some grumbles, and Danny continued, "We have discovered a link between all these cases, thanks to some assistance from the G-Man here, and we believe that the last six unsolved homicides committed in Claytown are all the work of one man. Unfortunately we don't know the exact identity of this person, but thanks to rigorous analysis of the crimes we've been able to draw up a profile of the type of perp who's responsible.

"We're looking for a white male in their mid twenties to early thirties, who lives or works in the Downtown area. They are highly intelligent, most likely a white collar worker, but they feel frustrated in their job because they are unable to advance and progress in their chosen profession, primarily for disciplinary reasons, or simply the wrong thing said at the wrong time. He has an explosive temper that he often struggles to keep in check. The perp may have attended or worked at the Claytown City High School and College campus within the past ten years. And finally, he is physically fit, but not overly muscular or stocky, and round five foot eleven, give or take an inch."

Joe spoke up then, "We know this is pretty broad ranging, but it does narrow the suspect pool down considerably. If you see someone that matches this description, call it in. There's a good chance that someone will recognize this description as someone they know, especially if they've been acting more erratically of late, particularly before and after the dates of the murders. This killer's time line seems to be escalating, and although he only killed this morning, we expect him to try and strike again tomorrow night, or even tonight."

Danny continued, "Because our perp has killed mostly at night, and always outside of office hours, we'll be asking the public to assist us by either traveling in groups, avoiding side streets and alleys, or by respecting a voluntary curfew between the hours of six tonight and six tomorrow morning. This is a voluntary curfew, and we're not enforcing it legally, but any single person seen on the streets will be approached by officers to ascertain their reason for being out during the curfew. We know that's a lot to take in, so we've prepared summaries for you all, and the media will broadcast the details to the public as well. Any questions?"

Lieutenant Peter Sampson was standing in the doorway of his office, and asked, "Are you sure our perp fits this description?"

Danny replied, "One hundred percent sure, no. But the techniques used to get this profile are proven, and even if it's only eighty or ninety percent accurate, it will in all likelihood match our man. And as we haven't got close by any other route, this is our best bet right now."

Lou Patterson, a retired patrolman who volunteered as an Auxiliary Officer, raised his hand. Danny nodded to him, "Go ahead, Lou."

"What's to stop this guy from running to the hills when he sees this profile?"

Danny shrugged, "Honestly, nothing apart from himself. But from what we've seen he is arrogant, thinks we're all useless, and he'll likely stay just to prove his own superiority."

Patrolman Denzil Greene piped up, "Hey, that reporter who says we couldn't find our asses has just become a suspect."

To the background laughter from the room, Danny called out, "Sorry, he doesn't fit the profile well enough, but good thinking. We need to suspect everyone who comes anywhere near the profile. Then we can start eliminating them until we find our man. Anything else?"

While Danny answered the various questions, the Chief beckoned Agent Lander over to him. He said,

"So, do you think this will work?"

Joe nodded, "It's the best bet we've got. The profile may be a little rough round the edges, but with the lack of evidence or other viable suspects, this is the best way to go."

The Chief nodded, "I hope it works."

Joe replied confidently, "It will."

A few minutes later the questions had dried up, and the Chief ended the meeting. "You know what to look for, now go catch the scumbag."

#

Sweet-lips leaned back in her chair, trying to ease the crick in her back. She was not used to sitting at a desk for so long, and she was glad she was finished keying all that information into the database created by Karen Watson. Sweet-lips looked over at the door as Danny, Joe and Karen came back into the conference room, caught by surprise. She had been so wrapped up in her work that she had not even noticed them leave. "Where you all been?" she asked.

Danny replied as he slumped into one of the chairs, "We were giving the profile to the guys going on shift, and then again to the ones coming back in. The details have also gone out to the media, and we had to talk to a few reporters to clear some things up."

Sweet-lips nodded, "Oh, okay." She paused, then said, "Danny, I'm saying this as a friend, not as an officer. You look like crap."

Danny snorted, "Thanks, you really know how to give a compliment."

Karen pitched in, "Dad, she's right. You've been putting in crazy hours trying to solve these murders. Right now we are playing a waiting game, seeing if the officers can find him, or see what his reaction is. I doubt there'll be any action before midnight. So why don't we go home and get some rest? You'll feel better for it."

Raven added her two cents, "I know I'll feel better after some sleep. Going through the citywide records and finding nothing fried my brain."

Joe added, "They're right. While we're waiting it makes sense to get some rest. You three head out, in fact everyone should get some shuteye. If anything happens, the beat boys will call us."

He herded the Detectives and Auxiliaries out of the conference room, then locked the door with a key Danny provided. The Chief was still in the squad room, just finishing up a call, and asked, "What is happening? We have a lead?"

Danny shook his head, "Not yet. They've convinced me it would be worth getting some sleep while we wait for developments. Maybe you should do the same, Chief."

"I will stay here for another hour or so, dealing with the media response and those prominent city members who have concerns they want to voice. You all head out, I have got the fort for now."

#

To say the least, when the killer heard the details of the profile, he was very concerned. He knew that he fit the profile almost perfectly, and wondered how long he had left as a free man, and whether he should start running.

The Beast interrupted these somewhat morbid thoughts by pointing out the obvious fact – if the police knew the killer was the man they were looking for, he would already be behind bars.

This thought did console the killer a little, but he was still very aware of the feeling that time was running out. These worries, coupled with the already massive stresses he was under, left him feeling exhausted. Somehow he made it home from work safely, thankful that he only had a handful of blocks to travel, and without even bothering to undress he collapsed on the bed. As he fell rapidly asleep his last conscious thought was he desperately needed this rest to be able to think clearly and plan his next move.

#

Unbeknownst to each other, the killer and Danny were doing exactly the same thing. Despite his own worries, Danny quickly fell into a deep sleep, as did many other members of the special team. Special Agent Lander spent a few hours monitoring the blog and checking his electronic traps, while Sweet-lips enjoyed a relaxing doobie to keep the worst of the coke withdrawal problems away. Karen Watson also needed some medication to help her sleep, but preferred over the counter sleep drugs as opposed to illegal ones.

Meanwhile, Claytown City had its quietest evening since the Prohibition Era, with many people obeying the curfew through fear. Even the majority of the hookers and drug dealers stayed home, although those people who signed up to catch the killer were out patrolling the streets. In squad cars or on foot, in pairs or singly, Police and Auxiliary Officers, along with vehicles manned by volunteers from the Fire Department, ceaselessly swept the Downtown area. Some people, like the prostitutes and bums that lived in the area, just kept a watchful eye out, ready to call in the blue cavalry if they saw something.

There were a couple of false alarms, one of which involved a squad car failing to recognize one of the Auxiliary Officers as they walked up and down Lincoln Avenue. But on the whole, the city was quiet, although the tension in its inhabitants kept many awake past midnight.

#

The killer woke with a start just after one in the morning. He was used to having vivid, almost real, dreams, and recently he had even started to enjoy the occasionally blood soaked nature of some of them. This last dream was also realistic, but the content horrified him. He could not shake the image of himself in a prison cell, being eaten alive by the Beast.

The Beast moved to calm him, "You know I would not do that. It was just a dream, a nightmare. We are a partnership, and even better, we are not going to jail."

The killer wiped his forehead, which was slick with perspiration, and sighed, "Yeah, I know. That profile just has me spooked."

"Do not worry yourself. We can still keep tabs on the cop's progress, and we will know exactly when we have to leave."

The killer nodded, "You're right. I don't know why I get so worried sometimes, especially when I see them floundering about trying to find me, and I'm right under their noses. It occurred to me that we can't use the CCHS network anymore to post through. That Fed tech is bound to have backtracked to there and they'll be watching. Still, nothing is stopping me from viewing our blog, so shall we?"

The Beast grinned, "Oh, yes. I look forward to what our supporters and detractors have posted since this morning. Well, technically, yesterday morning. Let the show begin."

While his computer was powering up, the killer splashed some cold water on his face to rinse off the night sweats and wake himself up a little. He suddenly realized that he was ravenously hungry, and thinking back over the previous day he found he had hardly eaten. Too much going on in my mind and round me to even think about food, he thought, grabbing a box of toaster pastries. One was devoured cold in a couple of bites while he clicked his way to the blog.

Another disappeared as he scrolled through the comments, although the last bite was sprayed across the room when he reached the post from the police. "What? They pity me? I pity them for being such helpless prey. And there's no way in hell I'm gonna just give myself up. Hell, and I was even thinking about leaving when I woke up. What say we go find ourselves some bacon and watch them squeal, just to show them what I think of their message? See if we can really get their attention?"

The Beast extended its claws, and replied, "Yes, that is a plan I like. If they think pity and medication will solve this problem, we will just have to show them the error of their ways."

Still fuming, the killer pulled on a baseball cap and dark colored jacket, shouldered his killing bag, and stepped into the quiet night with more murder in his heart.

Chapter 28

Heather Nelson, known more commonly by her 'regular' job identity, Nightshade, had been patrolling up and down Grover Avenue in her Auxiliary Services uniform since the sun went down. Lieutenant Sampson had been unhappy with her insistence that a woman could patrol alone, and had scheduled several patrol cars to sweep Grover Avenue as part of their regular patrols.

Heather was not worried though. After all, she had survived on the streets as a prostitute for many years and her occasionally demonstrated skills with a pistol she carried in her purse had earned her the 'Deadly' prefix to her street name. Not that a convicted felon was permitted to own a gun, but Nightshade had always been picky about which laws she obeyed.

As she headed North on the right hand side of Grover, moving away from Lincoln Avenue, she marveled at how quiet the streets were with only police cars on the road, and no noisy pedestrians. Night time was usually far quieter than day, as she knew from years of experience standing on street corners, but this silence was surreal, like she had stepped into another world.

She was drawing level the library across the street and was inspecting the bushes for any unusual movement when something caught her eye just round the corner of the building, near the front doors. She put her hand in her purse and gripped her pistol, and quietly stole across the street.

Rather than her usual mini-skirt and heels, she was more sensibly dressed wearing jeans and tennis shoes to go with her Auxiliary Officer shirt, so stealth was now an option. She moved towards the main doors, gun extended and pointing at the dark clad figure crouching by the door, and called out, "Hey, what are you doing?"

The figure looked up and she saw the face under the baseball cap was partially obscured by a scarf and her tension ratcheted up several notches. The figure pulled down the scarf and grinned at her, and her tension eased as she saw a familiar face she had trusted for years, and the figure said, "Hey, Nightshade, didn't expect to see you here."

#

The killer saw the worried expression lift from the hooker's face, and now the Beast grinned too when they saw the pistol being lowered.

Heather replied to his greeting, "I didn't expect to see you either. I thought you only worked days. If you are looking for a freebee, I'm technically off duty from my usual job, and right now I'm," she snorted," helping the police with their inquiries."

The killer laughed at that weak joke, but commented, "That's a good one. Very ironic."

She shrugged modestly, "I'm not just a pretty face. What are you doing here?"

He held up his tablet, "Would you believe trying to get online, but the library wireless network must get shutdown at night."

The Auxiliary Officer looked confused, "You don't have internet at home?"

The killer shrugged, "It's a long story. I just need to post a comment on a web page, that's all."

Nightshade looked thoughtful, then said, "I've got web access on my phone. Wanna borrow it for a few?"

The killer smiled broadly, reaching out his right hand for the phone, "That would be swell, thanks."

She looked down and reached into her purse, and did not even see the killer's left fist swinging towards her temple. It connected with a solid thud, and as Nightshade slumped to the ground the Beast crowed with delight. The killer pull a scalpel from his bag and stepped forward, "Shall we see how long she lasts with her major arteries cut open?"

#

Joe Lander was abruptly awakened by the strident alarm coming from his laptop. This particular tone meant that at least one of the tripwires he had laid across the Serial Blogger's download route had been triggered. He rolled out of the motel bed towards his computer, deactivating the alarm and checking the security log to see which traps had been affected.

He was a little surprised to only see one, on the hosting server, and immediately started a trace to find what route was being used to upload things now. Next he pulled up the blog and started reading the latest entry.

#

BLOG: I don't need your pity, but you do need to learn to fear me. How many will be taken before I get the respect I deserve? One more for sure, despite your attempt at a curfew. I hope you find my latest attempt to grab your attention a little less pathetic, while I feed my urges.

Remember, to deny our urges is to deny that which makes us human.

Nightshade can be deadly for some, but not for me. Sadly for someone, the reverse does not look to be the case.

#

The final part of this blog entry had Joe confused, as did a link that looked like it lead to a video, a new thing on this blog. Confident that his military grade anti-virus software would protect him if the link was malicious, he clicked on it.

After a few moments of buffering, it was clear that this was a live streaming feed, and Joe was shocked at what he saw on the screen - a black woman propped against a brick wall, blood staining and spreading from wounds in her armpits and groin, as well as her wrists and neck, pooling on the ground round her. Her eyelids fluttered softly, then her eyes opened.

#

When Heather came to she found it so hard to open her eyes she almost did not bother. Her eyelids felt like they were made of lead, but she persevered. She also felt a terrible pounding in her head and shooting pains all over her body. With difficulty she focused on the figure crouched in front of her, propping what looked like her own phone against the wall.

With the heaviness growing in her limbs and eyelids as fast as weakness started to overwhelm her, she struggled to finally ask, "Why?" in a barely audible whisper."

The man she had trusted for so long looked at her and shrugged, "It's what I have become, and what I enjoy, and you were available. It's nothing personal, but with this silly curfew there were fewer targets round, and you just walked into my sights. And now, my dear Nightshade, I must be going. It has truly been a pleasure."

He rose and pulled the scarf back over his face, bowed mockingly, and slipped out of her line of vision. Heather tried to move her head to follow him, but the effort was too much for her. She felt her eyes closing, and she slowly slipped into darkness for the last time.

#

Special Agent Lander watched in horror as he saw the woman's eyes close, and reached for the motel phone. He had deliberately left his cell phone free for a future call, and called Danny. He waited tensely for the call to be picked up, his eyes watching the apparently lifeless victim, and also keeping an eye on his trace routine.

A groggy sounding Danny picked up, and said, "Yeah, Lieutenant Watson here. Who is this?'

"Danny, it's Joe Lander. He's just killed again, and the sick puppy has posted live video of the victim on his blog."

Joe could almost hear Danny's eyes snap wide open, and the sleepiness had left his voice when he replied, "Can you see where? Or recognize the victim?"

"I don't know where it is, but it looks like a black woman I saw when I first got to your place. Hold on, I may have something else."

The trace routine had found the source of the video feed, and Joe was surprised to see it was a direct upload from a cellphone. He said to Danny, "I've got details on the feed, it's coming from a cell phone. I'm going to get Quantico to run a trace on it to find the owner and the current location of the device."

"I'll stay on the line, but I'll also be calling this in. Let me know as soon as you get that location."

"It will only take them a couple of minutes," said Joe as he grabbed his cell and picked one of the numbers from the contacts list, "Hey, Marcie, it's Joe Lander. I need an urgent trace on a number."

#

While Danny had been talking to Joe, he had been walking from his bedroom to the kitchen. He kept his cell pinned to one ear while putting the house phone to his other one. The call was answered by the duty sergeant, "Sergeant Magruder, how can I help?"

"Donny? It's Danny Watson. I'm calling an Emergency. Alert all officers on duty, and call in everyone else. I mean everyone, no excuses. I'll deal with the detectives and the Auxiliaries on my team. I suspect we have an officer down, Heather Nelson. Get the closest unit to check on her. I'll stay on the line."

In one ear he heard the acknowledgment from Sergeant Donny Magruder, and his stream of orders to the officers within earshot, and in the other he heard Joe say, "Thanks, Marcie, I've got that. Danny? You still there?"

Danny was heading out of the kitchen again, thankful that the house phone was cordless, and he replied, "Whatcha got, Joe?"

"The phone is registered to Heather Nelson, current location is the north side of the Main Library, near the entrance I think."

Danny nodded, "Got it. Can you get over there? There'll be a black and white heading that way too. I'm heading into base to organize things there."

Joe answered, "On my way," and disconnected.

By now Danny was knocking on his daughter's bedroom door, while talking to Sergeant Magruder, "Donny, I'm ninety-nine percent sure that Auxiliary Officer Nelson is down, just outside the Main Library doors. Get a medic out there now, and wake up the crime scene boys, if you haven't already. I want that area swept so clean you could eat off the sidewalk. You can get me on my cell, but I'm on my way in."

Hanging up, he reached down to shake Karen awake, "Hey, baby girl, we gotta head back. You've got five minutes before I leave without you."

Karen rubbed her eyes and stared at her fathers retreating back. He was dialing numbers on both phones he was holding, while he headed for his own bedroom. As she hurriedly got ready she heard him say, "Raven, get your ass into the station, Todd, get to the Main Library. Officer down, repeat, officer down."

Hearing those words snapped Karen fully awake, and she redoubled her efforts to get dressed and ready to go.

Chapter 29

The killer managed to get back to his apartment apparently unseen, using dark and deserted back alleys, and timing his dashes across main streets in between sweeps by police cars. Had anyone been watching his progress, they would feel it was uncanny the way the killer seemed to know exactly where the squad cars and foot patrols were, but so skillful were his movements that no-one on earth saw him.

Just as he had been ignoring the wailing sirens on the street, when he entered his apartment he took no notice of his ringing phone. Instead he was listening to the contented purring coming from the Beast, and replaying the slow death of Heather the Hooker in his mind.

His clothes were slightly bloodied, and he stripped out of them and dropped them into a trash bag, before heading to the shower. His face was filled with pleasure as he recalled the night's events, and then his previous kills. The Beast broke into his thoughts, saying, "Now you are the perfect killer. Smart, prepared, efficient, and you take pleasure in your work. I salute you."

As he dried himself, the killer said, "Thank you. It's a shame that just as I'm getting into this the heat is getting too much round here."

The Beast replied, "We may be finished here, but there are other places, countless other victims, a lifetime of potential killing pleasure."

The killer grinned, "I'm looking forward to it."

As he dressed in the crowded bedroom, he also double checked his escape kit. Satisfied that everything was ready to roll, he idly picked up his phone and listened to the three messages. Shrugging his shoulders, he said to the Beast, "Let's make an early start on the day job, and scope out the blue team to see how close they are to finding me."

#

When Auxiliary Officer Sweet-lips made her way through the squad room, heading towards the conference room, she could see Danny on his phone. He noticed her and waved, smiling grimly, and carried on with his conversation, "Todd, I'm sending every man and his dog to help you sweep the area. I want everyone within a ten block radius interviewed, and footage from every business you can find. Joe's already trying to get the library tapes. His Fed badge will make them shake a leg. I hope like hell we finally get a break. This guy is making fools out of us."

Sweet-lips sat next to Karen Watson, who was working at one of the computers in the conference room, and said, "What you doing?"

Karen shrugged, "Just trying different variations of the profile against that database the FBI sent over. I've been doing it against the criminal database that we got here too, nothing new. It's like this guy isn't in the list. He should stand out, but we aren't even getting close matches."

Sweet-lips said, "Maybe there is something wrong with the profile?"

"I agree. That is why I am doing smaller filters, seeing what happens. So far, nothing."

"You what?" they both heard Danny shout. "There was a camera right there and you can't see any identifiable features? Not even a glimpse of his face? Great. Well, thanks for taking such a quick look. You better get back here, Joe."

Danny turned to them, "He must have known the camera was there, knew exactly where it was." He shook his head, "What are we missing here? I'm starting to think Old Jimmy was right to call this guy a Ghost. We keep coming up with nothing, just chase his shadow and catch no breaks. It's like he knows exactly what to do to stay ahead, has inside knowledge somehow. If he hadn't posted that stuff on his blog, chances are we'd still be wondering what was happening."

Sweet-lips suddenly sat upright, "We can't find him in our databases, but have we looked at all of the possible databases? We've excluded criminals, we've excluded civilians, but have we looked at us?"

Danny looked worried, "A cop? I really hope not. It would explain how they were always one step ahead. But surely they'd be included in the file the Feds sent over?"

Karen Watson said, "Snap! They are, but were filtered out! It was just people with criminal records hidden, the Feds must have assumed we'd already checked our own staff, and filtered them out too. It's still a long shot, but I'm going to check staff against the profile. It's the only people we haven't looked at."

#

"Uh-oh," said the Beast, "That does not sound good."

The killer had been hanging out near the open door of the conference room, listening to the conversations inside. He had hoped to get an opportunity to sneak in and take a closer look at what the 'special team' had put together on him.

The Beast interrupted his thoughts, "This is an opportunity to do something else, like get out of here before they finally put two and two together. Come on, left foot, right foot, it is called walking."

The killer carefully eased away from the conference room, trying to keep out of the line of sight of the occupants, and quickly made his way through the bustling squad room. Once he got outside the building his quick walk turned into his characteristic run as he sprinted for his car. Slamming the car into drive, he sped away from the police headquarters and headed for his apartment.

#

Karen Watson's hands were flickering across the computer keyboard and mouse, applying filters one by one to the people working for Claytown City Police Department. She said to Detective Chavez, "Raven, get ready to pull up personnel files if we find any close matches."

Raven acknowledged this, while Karen added the basic criteria to the list, "Okay, male, ethnicity white, age twenty five to thirty five, just covering a good range there. Right, twenty three names, time to narrow it down. Height range from five foot eight to six two, now we're down to twenty people. Match schools, well that's most of them, so scratch that. Disciplinary issues, nice, takes us down to five."

She reeled off the five names to Raven, adding, "They all live in Downtown, too."

Danny said, "Lieutenant Sampson doesn't match the 'physically fit' category, so don't worry about checking his file for now. Worth keeping an eye on in future though." This brought a few tense chuckles from the others in the room.

Raven said, "Two of these studied at CCHS twelve years ago, too far back in my opinion."

"I agree," said Danny, "so we are down to two."

Raven continued, "Peter Morris. I think that being homosexual puts a spanner in the works there, and he's also a desk officer only after being shot in the leg a couple of years back. He can't run much, and he looks pretty weedy. One left, not sure if getting a match is really a good thing."

She frowned as she read the final record, "Oh, no, this looks like a perfect match. Discharged from Army for violent behavior, worked at the college campus for two years as security guard, disciplinary issues out of his butt since he worked for us. Hell, he even drives a dark blue Taurus. Danny, it's got to be Jacob Quigley!"

#

The killer, who was indeed Patrolman Jacob Quigley, parked his Taurus illegally outside his apartment and ran inside. He did not bother to close the apartment door as he went in, and only paused twice on his way to the bedroom. The first was to power up his computer, and the second was to grab his collection of blood drop trophies.

He flung open his bedroom door and smiled as he saw his escape route sitting waiting for him – a jet black Kawasaki Ninja ZX9R motorcycle, equipped with panniers. These contained an assortment of clothing, a new prepaid cellphone, a variety of alternative identification documents, and over ten thousand dollars in cash - everything he needed to start over somewhere else. The bike was not registered to him, and carried plates from a different State, which would hopefully slow down any license tracking a stray cop might do.

Ironically the motorcycle had originally belonged to one of his victims, Ray Stubbs, which the killer had stolen eight months previously as part of a secret vendetta against a childhood enemy. One quick respray later, a change of plates and scrubbed VIN, the killer had a perfect escape vehicle if he ever needed it.

Now it was, so the killer wheeled the machine into the living room, then stopped beside the computer. He smiled as he hooked up a set of cables and with a few clicks of the mouse his final surprise was ready. Pulling the helmet firmly over his head, he wheeled the bike into the street and fired up the engine. After making sure the apartment door was closed, he mounted the Ninja and rode away.

#

Danny hushed the rising babble from the special team, indicating the open door leading to the squad room. He went to the far end of the room and pulled out his cellphone. "Donny, it's Danny again. You've got a good view of the squad area, right?"

A puzzled Sergeant Magruder replied, "Sure I do. It's not far from your desk, so you should know. Why you asking such an odd question?"

"Have you seen Officer Quigley today?"

"Sure, he came in about fifteen minutes ago, was over by your conference room door for a while, then left just as if all the hounds of hell were after him."

Danny said to the others, "He must have heard us. He's bolted, come on."

He grabbed his keys, closed his phone and hurried from the conference room. He stopped beside the Duty Sergeant's desk, and said, "Donny, put out an APB on Quigley. He is to be considered armed and dangerous, and should be approached with caution."

Donny Magruder looked amazed, and said, "Are you serious?"

Sweet-lips picked up the desk calendar, and said, "Let's see, is it April First? No, it's not," and dropped the calendar back on the cluttered desk. "Yes, he's serious. Quigley is now the prime suspect in the serial killer investigation. Get to it!"

As Sergeant Magruder hurried to obey, Danny and Sweet-lips follow the others to the waiting car.

#

With Sweet-lips and Karen crammed in the back of the nondescript sedan, Danny riding shotgun, and Raven driving like she was on the Monster Mile, they sped the few blocks to Quigley's apartment. As they got closer, Danny turned to the two Auxiliary Officers, and said, "You two stay outside. You aren't even armed. Raven, I'll lead, you follow."

Raven swung round the corner, braking hard to avoid the blue Taurus parked by the building entrance. She said, "Looks like he's still here," as they got out of their car.

Danny said, "Let's hope he sees sense when we go in. He's got nowhere to go."

Raven pulled the lobby door open, and Danny ducked inside. Immediately he was faced with the closed door to Jacob's apartment, and standing to one side he banged on the door, "Jacob, it's Danny Watson. We need to talk to you."

There was silence from inside, as Raven took up position on the other side of the doorway. Danny banged on the door again, "Quigley, come on out. If you don't, we'll just come in and get you."

There was another screech of tires from outside as a black and white pulled up, disgorging Patrolmen Greene and Cortez. As they came into the lobby, Danny said, "Take the door down."

The heavily built Cortez dropped his shoulder and charged the door, which sprang open with a crash. Danny was first in, gun swinging to cover the living room and adjacent kitchen. Greene and Cortez moved to check the bathroom and bedroom, shouting "Clear" almost simultaneously. Raven stepped into the room, holstering her pistol as she said, "Unless he's hiding under the sink, it looks like the bird had flown."

"Yeah, but we may have a bigger problem. Guys, get out of here now," said Danny, dropping to his knees to look under the computer table. Raven looked at what was written on the screen.

#

BLOG: My time in Claytown is done. It has been amusing watching you miss what was right under your nose. Maybe what is under my computer will finally get your attention. Some doors are not meant to be opened.

Ticktock....

Beside the final word was a timer counting down, with only fifteen seconds left. Danny stood up, "Everyone out. There's a bomb under there. Out! Now!"

Chapter 30

Karen and Sweet-lips heard the sudden shouts from inside the apartment, and expected this to be the end of the chase, with the suspect apprehended.

What they did not expect was the explosion that tore through the downstairs of the building, showering glass and debris across the street, knocking them to the ground.

Ears ringing from the blast, they stared in confusion at the blazing ruin in front of them, unable to comprehend the scene.

#

As the killer rode his bike swiftly out of city, he had a radio tuned to the police band. He had heard the call for officers to get to his apartment, and the APB with his description and car details. With his head start and change of vehicle, he was not worried.

Now he heard over the radio the explosion from his booby trap, followed shortly after by the sound waves that had traveled from the blast and caught up with him. He grinned, and said to the Beast, "Checkmate, I believe. Now to find new killing grounds."

The Beast nodded, "We got out just in time. But before we leave," and it inclined its head towards the pedestrian it had sighted further up the street.

The killer smiled, "Ah, yes, indeed," and throttled back slightly, moving his hand down to the makeshift scabbard attached to the side of the bike. As he closed on the luckless pedestrian he drew the blade, a machete so large it could almost be called a falchion, and swung hard towards the neck of his final victim in Claytown.

He felt the shock of the impact travel up his arm, almost causing him to drop the blade, and in the mirrors the killer saw the corpse fall to the ground, blood gushing from the almost severed neck.

The Beast roared approval as the killer sheathed the blade, planning to collect some blood from it later, and the killer roared along, crying out, "And one for luck!" The motorcycle sped away from Claytown City, carrying the two in their search for new hunting grounds.

The End?

Acknowledgments

My first thanks must go to you, the reader - thank you for buying and reading this book. I hope you enjoyed reading it as much as I enjoyed writing it. Of course, while I would still scribble my stories down even if people did not buy them, people like you allow me to write, live inside and eat more than just Ramen Noodles, something for which I am grateful.

Many books and television shows have inspired this novel, with the biggest shout out going to Criminal Minds, followed by the writing of Karen Slaughter and Micheal Connelly. There were many other inspirations and research sources, but those are the top three.

Robin was the usual suspect in the role of proof reader, correcting some of my personal language oddities. Sarah Rose, my daughter, did the awesome artwork for the cover. And last, but by no means least, the patience and support of my loving wife. Words cannot describe how much of a help she is to me.

While many people contributed either personally, or through being authors of my research, all mistakes are of course mine. Hopefully you did not find too many, as I have striven to keep this as accurate as possible (barring the occasional use of artistic license).

About the Author

Born in Basingstoke, Britain in 1978, he emigrated to the USA in 2007 to be with his American wife and to raise a family. Majoring in College in History and Computing, he worked in various parts of the computer industry (programming was fun, tech support, not so much), although all his spare time was spent reading and researching a wide variety of subjects that interested him. This reading inspired him to write, and he hopes his writing inspired you.

Facebook :
http://www.facebook.com/SerialBlogger

Facebook :
http://www.facebook.com/BobScottAuthor

And finally........

If you enjoyed reading this book, check out Prison Scorpion, the authors debut novel about a break out from a maximum security prison.

Facebook :
http://www.facebook.com/PrisonScorpion

Made in the USA
Charleston, SC
18 February 2015